Our wish for you this Christmas?

**Feel the warmth…
Experience the magic…
And celebrate the enduring legacy of**

BETTY NEELS

Two stories about the spirit of Christmas

Christmas Wishes

In this season of love, all they have to say is yes…

Romance readers around the world were sad to note the passing of Betty Neels in June 2001. Her career spanned thirty years, and she continued to write into her ninetieth year. To her millions of fans, Betty epitomized the romance writer, and yet she began writing almost by accident. She had retired from nursing, yet her inquiring mind still sought stimulation. Her new career was born when she heard a lady in her local library bemoaning the lack of good romance novels. Betty's first book, *Sister Peters in Amsterdam,* was published in 1969, and she eventually completed 134 books. Her novels offer a reassuring warmth that was very much a part of her own personality. She was a wonderful writer, and she will be greatly missed. Her spirit will live on in all her stories, including those yet to be published.

BETTY NEELS

Christmas Wishes

TORONTO • NEW YORK • LONDON
AMSTERDAM • PARIS • SYDNEY • HAMBURG
STOCKHOLM • ATHENS • TOKYO • MILAN • MADRID
PRAGUE • WARSAW • BUDAPEST • AUCKLAND

ISBN 0-373-83567-1

CHRISTMAS WISHES

Copyright © 2003 by Harlequin Books S.A.

The publisher acknowledges the copyright holder
of the individual works as follows:

THE PROPOSAL
Copyright © 1993 by Betty Neels

A CHRISTMAS WISH
Copyright © 1994 by Betty Neels

This edition published by arrangement with Harlequin Books S.A.

® and TM are trademarks of the publisher. Trademarks indicated with
® are registered in the United States Patent and Trademark Office, the
Canadian Trade Marks Office and in other countries.

Visit us at www.eHarlequin.com

Printed in U.S.A.

CONTENTS

THE PROPOSAL

CHAPTER ONE

THE HAZY early morning sun of September had very little warmth as yet, but it turned the trees and shrubs of the park to a tawny gold, encouraging the birds to sing too, so that even in the heart of London there was an illusion of the countryside.

The Green Park was almost empty so early in the day; indeed the only person visible was a girl, walking a Yorkshire terrier on a long lead. She was a tall girl with a tawny mane of hair and vivid blue eyes set in a pretty face, rather shabbily dressed; although her clothes were well cut they were not in the height of fashion.

She glanced at her watch; she had walked rather further than usual so Lady Mortimor, although she wouldn't be out of bed herself, would be sure to enquire of her maid if the early morning walk with Bobo had taken the exact time allowed for it. She could have walked for hours… She was on the point of turning on her heel when something large, heavy and furry cannoned into her from the back and she sat down suddenly and in a most unladylike fashion in a tangle of large dog, a hysterical Bobo and Bobo's lead. The dog put an enormous paw on her chest and grinned happily down at her before licking her cheek gently and then turning his attention to Bobo; possibly out of friendliness he kept his paw on her chest, which made getting to her feet a bit of a problem.

A problem solved by the arrival of the dog's owner—it had to be its owner, she decided…only a giant could control a beast of such size and this man, from her horizontal position, justified the thought; he was indeed large, dressed in trousers and a pullover and, even from upside-down, handsome. What was more, he was smiling…

He heaved her to her feet with one hand and began to dust her down. 'I do apologise,' he told her in a deep, rather slow voice. 'Brontes has a liking for very small dogs…'

The voice had been grave, but the smile tugging at the corners of his thin mouth annoyed her. 'If you aren't able to control your dog you should keep him on a lead,' she told him tartly, and then in sudden fright, 'Where's Bobo? If he's lost, I'll never—'

'Keep calm,' begged the man in a soothing voice which set her teeth on edge, and whistled. His dog bounded out from the bushes near by and his master said, 'Fetch,' without raising his voice and the animal bounded off again to reappear again very shortly with Bobo's lead between his teeth and Bobo trotting obediently at the other end of it.

'Good dog,' said the man quietly. 'Well, we must be on our way. You are quite sure you are not hurt?' He added kindly, 'It is often hard to tell when one is angry as well.'

'I am not angry, nor am I hurt. It was lucky for you that I wasn't an elderly dowager with a Peke.'

'Extremely lucky. Miss…?' He smiled again, studying her still cross face from under heavy lids. 'Renier Pitt-Colwyn.' He offered a hand and engulfed hers in a firm grasp.

'Francesca Haley. I—I have to go.' Curiosity got the better of good sense. 'Your dog—that's a strange name?'

'He has one eye.…'

'Oh, one of the Cyclopes. Goodbye.'

'Goodbye, Miss Haley.' He stood watching her walking away towards the Piccadilly entrance to the park. She didn't look back, and presently she broke into an easy run and, when Bobo's little legs could no longer keep up, scooped him into her arms and ran harder as far as the gate. Here she put him down and walked briskly across the road into Berkeley Street, turned into one of the elegant, narrow side-streets and went down the area steps of one of the fine houses. One of Lady Mortimor's strict rules was that she and Bobo should use the tradesmen's entrance when going for their thrice-daily outings. The magnificent entrance hall was not to be sullied by dirty paws, or for that matter Francesca's dirty shoes.

The door opened onto a dark passage with white-washed walls and a worn lino on the floor; it smelled of damp, raincoats, dog and a trace of cooked food, and after the freshness of the early morning air in the park it caused Francesca's nose to wrinkle. She opened one of the doors in the passage, hung up the lead, dried Bobo's paws and went through to the kitchen.

Lady Mortimor's breakfast tray was being prepared and her maid, Ethel, was standing by the table, squeezing orange juice. She was an angular woman with eyes set too close together in a mean face, and she glanced at the clock as Francesca went in, Bobo under one arm. Francesca, with a few minutes to spare, wished her good morning, adding cheerfully, 'Let Lady Mortimor know that Bobo has had a good run, will you, Ethel? I'm going over for my breakfast; I'll be back as usual.' She put the little dog down and the woman nodded surlily. Bobo always went to his mistress's room with her breakfast tray and that meant that Francesca had almost an hour to herself before she would begin her duties as secretary-companion to that lady. A title which hardly fitted the manifold odd jobs which filled her day.

She went back out of the side-door and round to the back of the house, past the elegant little garden to the gate which led to the mews behind the terrace of houses. Over the garage she had her rooms, rather grandly called by Lady Mortimor a flat, where she and her young sister lived. The flat was the reason for her taking the job in the first place, and she was intent on keeping it, for it made a home for the pair of them and, although Lady Mortimor made it an excuse for paying her a very small salary, at least they had a roof over their heads.

Lucy was up and dressed and getting their breakfast. She was very like her sister, although her hair was carroty instead of tawny and her nose turned up. Later on, in a few years' time, she would be as pretty as Francesca, although at fourteen she anguished over her appearance, her ambition being to grow up as quickly as possible, marry a very rich man and live in great

comfort with Francesca sharing her home. An arrangement, Francesca had pointed out, which might not suit
her husband. 'I hate you working for that horrid old
woman,' Lucy had said fiercely.

'Well, love,' Francesca had been matter-of-fact
about it, 'it's a job and we have a home of sorts and
you're being educated. Only a few more years and you
will have finished school and embarked on a career
which will astonish the world and I shall retire.'

Now she took off her cardigan and set about laying
the table in the small sitting-room with its minute alcove which housed the cooking stove and the sink.

'I had an adventure,' she said to her sister, and over
the boiled eggs told her about it.

'What kind of a dog?' Lucy wanted to know.

'Well, hard to tell—he looked like a very large St
Bernard from the front, but he sort of tapered off to-
wards the tail, and that was long enough for two dogs.
He was very obedient.'

'Was the man nice to him?' asked Lucy anxiously,
having a soft spot for animals; indeed, at that very
moment there was a stray mother cat and kittens living
clandestinely in a big box under the table.

'Yes—he didn't shout and the dog looked happy. It
had one eye—I didn't have time to ask why. It had a
funny name, too—Brontes—that's—'

'I know—one of the Cyclopes. Could you meet the
man again and ask?'

Francesca thought about it. 'Well, no, not really...'

'Was he a nice man?'

'I suppose so.' She frowned. 'He thought it was
funny, me falling over.'

'I expect it was,' said Lucy. 'I'd better go or I'll miss the bus.'

After Lucy had gone she cleared away the breakfast things, tidied the room and their bedroom, and made sure that she herself was tidy too, and then she went back to the house. She was expected to lunch off a tray at midday and she seldom got back until six o'clock each evening; she arranged food for the cat, made sure that the kittens were alive and well, and locked the door.

Her employer was still in bed, sitting up against lacy pillows, reading her letters. In her youth Lady Mortimor had been a handsome woman; now in her fifties, she spent a good part of her days struggling to retain her looks. A face-lift had helped; so had the expert services of one of the best hairdressers in London and the daily massage sessions and the strict diet, but they couldn't erase the lines of discontent and petulance.

Francesca said good morning and stood listening to the woman's high-pitched voice complaining of lack of sleep, the incompetence of servants and the tiresome bills which had come in the post. When she had finished Francesca said, as she nearly always did, 'Shall I attend to the bills first, Lady Mortimor, and write the cheques and leave them for you to sign? Are there any invitations you wish me to reply to?'

Lady Mortimor tossed the pile of letters at her. 'Oh, take the lot and endeavour to deal with them—is there anything that I should know about this morning?'

'The household wages,' began Francesca, and flushed at Lady Mortimor's snide,

'Oh, to be sure you won't forget those...'

'Dr Kennedy is coming to see you at eleven o'clock. Will you see him in the morning-room?'

'Yes, I suppose so; he really must do something about my palpitations—what else?'

'A fitting for two evening gowns at Estelle, lunch with Mrs Felliton.'

'While I am lunching you can get my social diary up to date, do the flowers for the dining-room, and go along to the dry-cleaners for my suit. There will be some letters to type before you go, so don't idle away your time. Now send Ethel to me, have the cheques and wages book ready for me by half-past ten in the morning-room.' As Francesca went to the door she added, 'And don't forget little Bobo...'

'Thank you or please would be nice to hear from time to time,' muttered Francesca as she went to get the wages book, a weekly task which at least gave her the satisfaction of paying herself as well as the rest of the staff. She entered the amounts, got out the cash box from the wall safe and put it ready for Lady Mortimor, who liked to play Lady Bountiful on Fridays and pay everyone in cash. The bills took longer; she hadn't quite finished them when Maisie, the housemaid, brought her a cup of coffee. She got on well with the staff—with the exception of Ethel, of course; once they saw that she had no intention of encroaching on their ground, and was a lady to boot, with a quiet voice and manner, they accepted her for what she was.

Lady Mortimor came presently, signed the cheques, handed out the wages with the graciousness of royalty bestowing a favour and, fortified with a tray of coffee, received Dr Kennedy, which left Francesca free to tidy the muddled desk she had left behind her and take Bobo for his midday walk, a brisk twenty minutes or so before she went back to eat her lunch off a tray in the now deserted morning-room. Since the lady of the house was absent, Cook sent up what Maisie described as a nice little bit of hake with parsley sauce, and a good, wholesome baked custard to follow.

Francesca ate the lot, drank the strong tea which went with it and got ready to go to the cleaners. It wasn't far; Lady Mortimor patronised a small shop in Old Bond Street and the walk was a pleasant one. The day had turned out fine as the early morning had indicated it might and she allowed her thoughts to roam, remembering wistfully the pleasant house in Hampstead Village where they had lived when her parents had been alive. That had been four years ago now; she winced at the memory of discovering that the house had been mortgaged and the debts so large that they had swallowed up almost all the money there was. The only consolation had been the trust set aside for Lucy's education so that she had been able to stay on as a day pupil at the same well-known school.

There had been other jobs of course, after learning typing and shorthand at night-school while they lived precariously with her mother's elderly housekeeper, but she had known that she would have to find a home of their own as quickly as possible. Two years ago she had answered Lady Mortimor's advertisement and since it offered a roof over their heads and there was no objection to Lucy, provided she never entered the house, she had accepted it, aware that her wages were rather less than Maisie's and knowing that she could never ask for a rise: Lady Mortimor would point out her free rooms and all the advantages of working in a well-run household and the pleasant work.

All of which sounded all right but in practice added up to ten hours a day of taking orders with Sundays free. Well, she was going to stay until Lucy had finished school—another four years. I'll be almost thirty, thought Francesca gloomily, hurrying back with the suit; there were still the flowers to arrange and the diary to bring up to date, not to mention the letters and a last walk for Bobo.

It was pouring with rain the next morning, but that didn't stop Bobo, in a scarlet plastic coat, and Francesca, in a well-worn Burberry, now in its tenth year, going for their morning walk. With a scarf tied over her head, she left Lucy getting dressed, and led the reluctant little dog across Piccadilly and into the Green Park. Being Saturday morning, there were very few people about, only milkmen and postmen and some over-enthusiastic joggers. She always went the same way for if by any evil chance Bobo should run away and get lost, he had more chance of staying around a part of the park with which he was familiar. The park was even emptier than the streets and, even if Francesca had allowed herself to hope that she might meet the man and his great dog, common sense told her that no one in their right mind would do more than give a dog a quick walk through neighbouring streets.

They were halfway across the park, on the point of turning back, when she heard the beast's joyful barking and a moment later he came bounding up. She had prudently planted her feet firmly this time but he stopped beside her, wagging his long tail and gently nuzzling Bobo before butting her sleeve with his wet head, his one eye gleaming with friendliness.

His master's good-morning was genial. 'Oh, hello,' said Francesca. 'I didn't expect you to be here—the weather's so awful.'

A remark she instantly wished unsaid; it sounded as though she had hoped to meet him. She went pink and looked away from him and didn't see his smile.

'Ah—but we are devoted dog owners, are we not?' he asked easily. 'And this is a good place for them to run freely.'

'I don't own Bobo,' said Francesca, at pains not to mislead him. 'He belongs to Lady Mortimor; I'm her companion.'

He said, half laughing, 'You don't look in the least like a companion; are they not ladies who find library books and knitting and read aloud? Surely a dying race.'

If he only knew, she thought, but all she said cheerfully was, 'Oh, it's not as bad as all that, and I like walking here with Bobo. I must go.'

She smiled at him from her pretty, sopping-wet face. 'Goodbye, Mr Pitt-Colwyn.'

'*Tot ziens,* Miss Francesca Haley.'

She bent to pat Brontes. 'I wonder why he has only one eye?' she said to herself more than to him, and then walked briskly away, with Bobo walking backwards in an effort to return to his friend. Hurrying now, because she would be late back, she wondered what he had said instead of goodbye—something foreign and, now she came to think of it, he had a funny

name too; it had sounded like Rainer, but she wasn't
sure any more.

It took her quite a while to dry Bobo when they got
back, and Ethel, on the point of carrying Lady Mortimor's tray upstairs, looked at the kitchen clock in
triumph.

Francesca saw the look. 'Tell Lady Mortimor that
I'm late back, by all means,' she said in a cool voice.
'You can tell her too that we stayed out for exactly
the right time but, unless she wishes Bobo to spoil
everything in her bedroom, he needs to be thoroughly
dried. It is raining hard.'

Ethel sent her a look of dislike and Cook, watching
from her stove, said comfortably, 'There's a nice hot
cup of tea for you, Miss Haley; you drink it up before
you go to your breakfast. I'm sure none of us wants
to go out in such weather.'

Ethel flounced away, Bobo at her heels, and Francesca drank her tea while Cook repeated all the more
lurid news from the more sensational Press. 'Don't
you take any notice of that Ethel, likes upsetting people, she does.'

Francesca finished her tea. 'Well, she doesn't need
to think she'll bother me, Cook, and thanks for the tea,
it was lovely.'

Lucy would be home at midday since it was Saturday, and they made the shopping list together since
she was the one who had to do it.

'Did you see him again?' asked Lucy.

'Who?' Francesca was counting out the housekeeping money. 'The man and his great dog? Yes, but just
to say good morning.' She glanced up at her sister.

'Do you suppose I should go another way round the park? I mean, it might look as though I was wanting to meet him.'

'Well don't you?'

'He laughs at me—oh, not out loud, but behind his face.'

'I shall come with you tomorrow and see him for myself.'

On Sundays Francesca took Bobo for his morning run before being allowed the rest of the day free. 'He's not likely to be there so early on a Sunday…'

'All the same, I'll come. What shall we do tomorrow? Could we go to Regent Street and look at the shops? And have something at McDonald's?'

'All right, love. You need a winter coat…'

'So do you. Perhaps we'll find a diamond ring or a string of pearls and get a reward.'

Francesca laughed. 'The moon could turn to cheese. My coat is good for another winter—I've stopped growing but you haven't. We'll have a good look around and when I've saved enough we'll buy you a coat.'

Lady Mortimor had friends to lunch which meant that Francesca had to do the flowers again and then hover discreetly in case her employer needed anything.

'You may pour the drinks,' said Lady Mortimor graciously, when the guests had settled themselves in the drawing-room, and then in a sharp aside, 'And make sure that everyone gets what she wants.'

So Francesca went to and fro with sherry and gin and tonic and, for two of the ladies, whisky. Cool and polite, aware of being watched by critical eyes, and disliking Lady Mortimor very much for making her do something which Crow the butler should be doing. Her employer had insisted that when she had guests for lunch it should be Francesca who saw to the drinks; it was one of the spiteful gestures she made from time to time in order, Francesca guessed, to keep her in her place. Fortunately Crow was nice about it; he had a poor opinion of his mistress, the widow of a wholesale textile manufacturer who had given away enough money to be knighted, and he knew a lady born and bred when he saw Francesca, as he informed Cook.

When the guests had gone, Lady Mortimor went out herself. 'Be sure and have those letters ready for me— I shall be back in time to dress,' she told Francesca. 'And be sure and make a note in the diary—Dr Kennedy is bringing a specialist to see me on Tuesday morning at ten o'clock. You will stay with me of course—I shall probably feel poorly.'

Francesca thought that would be very likely. Eating too much rich food and drinking a little too much as well… She hoped the specialist would prescribe a strict diet, although on second thoughts that might not do—Lady Mortimor's uncertain temper might become even more uncertain.

Sundays were wonderful days; once Bobo had been taken for his walk she was free, and even the walk was fun for Lucy went with her and they could talk. The little dog handed over to a grumpy Ethel, they had their breakfast and went out, to spend the rest of the morning and a good deal of the afternoon looking at the shops, choosing what they would buy if they had the money, eating sparingly at McDonald's and walking back in the late afternoon to tea in the little sitting-room and an evening by the gas fire with the cat and kittens in their box between them.

Monday always came too soon and this time there was no Brontes to be seen, although the morning was fine. Francesca went back to the house to find Lady Mortimor in a bad temper so that by the end of the day she wanted above all things to rush out of the house and never go back again. Her ears rang with her employer's orders for the next day. She was to be earlier than usual—if Lady Mortimor was to be ready to be seen by the specialist then she would need to get up earlier than usual, which meant that the entire household would have to get up earlier too. Francesca, getting sleepily from her bed, wished the man to Jericho.

Lady Mortimor set the scene with all the expertise of a stage manager; she had been dressed in a velvet housecoat over gossamer undies, Ethel had arranged her hair in artless curls and tied a ribbon in them, and she had made up carefully with a pale foundation. She had decided against being examined in her bedroom; the *chaise-longue* in the dressing-room adjoining would be both appropriate and convenient. By half-past nine she was lying, swathed in shawls, in an attitude of resigned long-suffering.

There was no question of morning coffee, of course, and that meant that Francesca didn't get any either. She was kept busy fetching the aids Lady Mortimor considered vital to an invalid's comfort: eau-de-Cologne, smelling salts, a glass of water…

'Mind you pay attention,' said that lady. 'I shall

need assistance from time to time and probably the specialist will require things held or fetched.'

Francesca occupied herself wondering what these things might be. Lady Mortimor kept talking about a specialist, but a specialist in what? She ventured to ask and had her head bitten off with, 'A heart consultant of course, who else? The best there is—I've never been one to grudge the best in illness...'

Francesca remembered Maisie and her scalded hand a few months previously. Lady Mortimor had dismissed the affair with a wave of the hand and told her to go to Out-patients during the hour she had off each afternoon. Her tongue, itching to give voice to her strong feelings, had to be held firmly between her teeth.

Ten o'clock came, with no sign of Dr Kennedy and his renowned colleague, and Lady Mortimor, rearranging herself once again, gave vent to a vexed tirade. 'And you, you stupid girl, might have had the sense to check with the consulting-rooms to make sure that this man has the time right. Really, you are completely useless...'

Francesca didn't say a word; she had lost her breath for the moment, for the door had opened and Dr Kennedy followed by Mr Pitt-Colwyn were standing there. They would have heard Lady Mortimor, she thought miserably, and would have labelled her as a useless female at everyone's beck and call.

'Well, can't you say something?' asked Lady Mortimor and at the same time became aware of the two men coming towards her, so that her cross face became all charm and smiles and her sharp voice softened to a gentle, 'Dr Kennedy, how good of you to come. Francesca, my dear, do go and see if Crow is bringing the coffee—'

'No coffee, thank you,' said Dr Kennedy. 'Here is Professor Pitt-Colwyn, Lady Mortimor. You insisted on the best heart specialist, and I have brought him to see you.'

Lady Mortimor put out a languid hand. 'Professor— how very kind of you to spare the time to see me. I'm sure you must be a very busy man.'

He hadn't looked at Francesca; now he said with grave courtesy, 'Yes, I am a busy man, Lady Morti- mor.' He pulled up a chair and sat down. 'If you will tell me what is the trouble?'

'Oh, dear, it is so hard to begin—I have suffered poor health every day since my dear husband died. It is hard to be left alone at my age—with so much life ahead of me.' She waved a weak hand. 'I suffer from palpitations, Professor, really alarmingly so; I am con- vinced that I have a weak heart. Dr Kennedy assures me that I am mistaken, but you know what family doctors are, only too anxious to reassure one if one is suffering from some serious condition…'

Professor Pitt-Colwyn hadn't spoken, there was no expression upon his handsome face and Francesca, watching from her discreet corner, thought that he had no intention of speaking, not at the moment at any rate. He allowed his patient to ramble on in a faint voice, still saying nothing when she paused to say in a quite different tone, 'Get me some water, Francesca, can't you see that I am feeling faint? And hurry up, girl.'

The glass of water was within inches of her hand. Francesca handed it, quelling a powerful desire to pour its contents all over Lady Mortimor's massive bosom.

She went back to her corner from where she admired the professor's beautiful tailored dark grey suit. He had a nice head too, excellent hair—she considered the sprinkling of grey in it was distinguished—and he had nice hands. She became lost in her thoughts until her employer's voice, raised in barely suppressed temper, brought her back to her surroundings.

'My smelling salts—I pay you to look after me, not stand there daydreaming—' She remembered suddenly that she had an audience and added in a quite different voice, 'Do forgive me—I become so upset when I have one of these turns, I hardly know what I'm saying.'

Neither man answered. Francesca administered the smelling salts and the professor got to his feet. 'I will take a look at your chest, Lady Mortimor,' and he stood aside while Francesca removed the shawls and the housecoat and laid a small rug discreetly over the patient's person.

The professor had drawn up a chair, adjusted his stethoscope and begun his examination. He was very thorough and when he had done what was necessary he took her blood-pressure, sat with Lady Mortimor's hand in his, his fingers on her pulse.

Finally he asked, 'What is your weight?'

Lady Mortimor's pale make-up turned pink. 'Well, really I'm not sure…' She looked at Francesca, who said nothing, although she could have pointed out that within the last few months a great many garments had been let out at the seams...

'You are overweight,' said the professor in measured tones, 'and that is the sole cause of your palpitations. You should lose at least two stone within the next six months, take plenty of exercise—regular walking is to be recommended—and small light meals and only moderate drinking. You will feel and look a different woman within that time, Lady Mortimor.'

'But my heart—'

'It is as sound as a bell; I can assure you that there is nothing wrong with you other than being overweight.'

He got up and shook her hand. 'If I may have a word with Dr Kennedy—perhaps this young lady can show us somewhere we can be private.'

'You are hiding something from me,' declared Lady Mortimor. 'I am convinced that you are not telling me the whole truth.'

His eyes were cold. 'I am not in the habit of lying, Lady Mortimor; I merely wish to discuss your diet with Dr Kennedy.'

Francesca had the door open and he went past her, followed by Dr Kennedy. 'The morning-room,' she told them. 'There won't be anyone there at this time in the morning.'

She led the way and ushered them inside. 'Would you like coffee?'

The professor glanced at his companion and politely declined, with a courteous uninterest which made her wonder if she had dreamed their meetings in the park. There was no reason why he shouldn't have made some acknowledgement of them—not in front of Lady Mortimor, of course. Perhaps now he had seen her here he had no further interest; he was, she gathered, an important man in his own sphere.

She went back to Lady Mortimor and endured that lady's peevish ill humour for the rest of the day. The next day would be even worse, for by then Dr Kennedy would have worked out a diet.

Of course, she told Lucy when at last she was free to go to her rooms.

'I say, what fun—was he pompous?'

'No, not in the least; you couldn't tell what he was thinking.'

'Oh, well, doctors are always poker-faced. He might have said hello.'

Francesca said crossly, 'Why should he? We haven't anything in common.' She added a little sadly, 'Only I thought he was rather nice.'

Lucy hugged her. 'Never mind, Fran, I'll find you a rich millionaire who'll adore you forever and you'll marry him and live happily ever after.'

Francesca laughed. 'Oh, what rubbish. Let's get the washing-up done.'

As she set out with Bobo the next morning, she wished that she could have taken a different route and gone at a different time, but Lady Mortimor, easygoing when it came to her own activities and indifferent as to whether they disrupted her household, prided herself on discipline among her staff; she explained this to her circle of friends as caring for their welfare, but what it actually meant was that they lived by a strict timetable and since, with the exception of

Francesca, she paid them well and Cook saw to it that the food in the kitchen was good and plentiful, they abided by it. It was irksome to Francesca and she was aware that Lady Mortimor knew that; she also knew that she and Lucy needed a home and that not many people were prepared to offer one.

So Francesca wasn't surprised to see Brontes bounding to meet her, followed in a leisurely manner by his master. She was prepared for it, of course; as he drew level she wished him a cold good-morning and went on walking, towing Bobo and rather hampered by Brontes bouncing to and fro, intent on being friendly.

Professor Pitt-Colywn kept pace with her. 'Before you go off in high dudgeon, be good enough to listen to me.' He sounded courteous; he also sounded as though he was in the habit of being listened to if he wished.

'Why?' asked Francesca.

'Don't be silly. You're bristling with indignation because I ignored you yesterday. Understandable, but typical of the female mind. No logic. Supposing I had come into the room exclaiming, "Ah, Miss Francesca Haley, how delightful to meet you again"—and it was delightful, of course—how would your employer have reacted?' He glanced at her thoughtful face. 'Yes, exactly, I have no need to dot the *I*s or cross the *T*s. Now that that slight misunderstanding is cleared up, tell me why you work for such a tiresome woman.'

She stood still the better to look at him. 'It is really none of your business...'

He brushed that aside. 'That is definitely something

I will decide for myself.' He smiled down at her. 'I'm a complete stranger to you; you can say anything you like to me and I'll forget it at once if you wish me to—'

'Oh, the Hippocratic oath.'

His rather stern mouth twitched. 'And that too. You're not happy there, are you?'

She shook her head. 'No, and it's very kind of you to—to bother, but there is really nothing to be done about it.'

'No, there isn't if you refuse to tell me what is wrong.' He glanced at his watch. 'How long do you have before you have to report back?'

'Fifteen minutes.'

'A lot can be said in that time. Brontes and I will walk back with you as far as Piccadilly.'

'Oh, will you?'

'Did I not say so?' He turned her round smartly, and whistled to Brontes. 'Now consider me your favourite uncle,' he invited.

CHAPTER TWO

AFTERWARDS Francesca wondered what had possessed her. She had told Professor Pitt-Colwyn everything. She hadn't meant to, but once she got started she had seemed unable to stop. She blushed with shame just remembering it; he must have thought her a complete fool, sorry for herself, moaning on and on about her life. That this was a gross exaggeration had nothing to do with it; she would never be able to look him in the face again. The awful thing was that she would have to unless he had the decency to walk his dog in another part of the park.

She was barely in the park before he joined her.

'A splendid morning,' he said cheerfully. 'I enjoy the autumn, don't you?' He took Bobo's lead from her and unclipped it. 'Let the poor, pampered beast run free. Brontes will look after him; he has a strong paternal instinct.'

It was difficult to be stand-offish with him. 'He's a nice dog, only he's—he's rather a mixture, isn't he?'

'Oh, decidedly so. Heaven knows where he got that tail.'

For something to say, for she was feeling suddenly shy, 'He must have been a delightful puppy.'

'I found him in a small town in Greece. Someone

had poked out his eye and beaten him almost to death—he was about eight weeks old.'

'Oh, the poor little beast—how old is he now?'

'Eight months old and still growing. He's a splendid fellow and strangely enough, considering his origin, very obedient.'

'I must get back.' She looked around for Bobo, who was nowhere in sight, but in answer to her companion's whistle Brontes came trotting up with Bobo scampering beside him. The professor fastened his lead and handed it to her. His goodbye was casually kind; never once, she reflected as she walked back to the house, had he uttered a word about her beastly job. She had been a great fool to blurt out all her worries and grumbles to a complete stranger who had no interest in her anyway. She wished most heartily that there was some way in which she could avoid meeting him ever again.

She thought up several schemes during the course of the day, none of which held water, and which caused her to get absent-minded so that Lady Mortimor had the pleasure of finding fault with her, insisting that she re-type several letters because the commas were in the wrong place. It was after seven o'clock by the time Francesca got back to her room over the garage and found Lucy at her homework.

'You've had a beastly day.' Lucy slammed her books shut and got out a cloth and cutlery. 'I put some potatoes in the oven to bake; they'll be ready by now. We can open a tin of beans, too. The kettle's boiling; I'll make a cup of tea.'

'Lovely, darling, I've had a tiresome day. How's school? Did you get an A for your essay?'

'Yes. Did you see him this morning?'

'Yes, just for a moment...'

'Didn't you talk at all?'

'Only about his dog.' Francesca poured them each a cup of tea and then sat down to drink it. 'I wish I'd never told him—'

'Oh, pooh—I dare say he's forgotten already. He must have lots of patients to think about; his head must be full of people's life histories.'

Francesca opened the tin of beans. 'Yes, of course, only I wish I need never see him again.'

To her secret unacknowledged chagrin, it seemed that she was to have her wish. He wasn't there the following morning, nor for the rest of the week; she told herself that it was a great relief and said so to Lucy, who said, 'Rubbish, you know you want to see him again.'

'Well—yes, perhaps. It was nice to have someone to talk to.' Francesca went on briskly, 'I wonder if it would be a good idea to go to evening classes when they start next month?'

Lucy looked at her in horror. 'Darling, you must be crazy—you mean sit for two hours learning Spanish or how to upholster a chair? I won't let you. Don't you see the kind of people who go to evening classes are very likely like us—without friends and family? Even if you got to know any of them they'd probably moan about being lonely...'

Francesca laughed. 'You know that's not quite true,' she said, 'although I do see what you mean.'

'Good. No evening classes. Doesn't Lady Mortimor have men visitors? She's always giving dinner parties…'

Francesca mentally reviewed her employer's guests; they were all past their prime. Well-to-do, self-satisfied and loud-voiced. They either ignored her in the same way as they ignored Crow or Maisie, or they made vapid remarks like, 'How are you today, little girl?' Which, since she was all of five feet ten inches tall and splendidly built, was an extremely silly thing to say.

She said, laughing, 'I can't say I've ever fancied any of them. I shall wait until you are old enough and quite grown-up, and when you've found yourself a millionaire I shall bask in your reflected glory.' She began to clear the table. 'Let's get Mum fed while the kittens are asleep—and that's another problem…'

September remained fine until the end of the month, when wind and rain tore away the last vestiges of summer. Francesca and Bobo tramped their allotted routine each morning and returned, Bobo to be fussed over once he had been dried and brushed, Francesca to hurry to her rooms, gobble breakfast and dash back again to start on the hundred and one jobs Lady Mortimor found for her to do, which were never done to that lady's satisfaction. The strict diet to which Professor Pitt-Colwyn had restricted her might be reducing her weight, but it had increased her ill humour. Francesca, supervising the making of a salad-dressing with lemon juice to accompany the thin slices of chicken which constituted her employer's lunch, wished that he had left well alone. Let the woman be as fat as butter if she wished, she reflected savagely, chopping a head of chicory while she listened to Cook detailing the menu for the dinner party that evening. A pity the professor couldn't hear that; it was dripping with calories...

Because of the dinner party the staff lunch was cold meat and potatoes in their jackets and Francesca, knowing the extra work involved in one of Lady Mortimor's large dinner parties, had hers in the kitchen and gave a hand with the preparations.

All the guests had arrived by the time she left the house that evening; Lady Mortimor, overpoweringly regal in purple velvet, had made her rearrange the flowers in the hall, polish the glasses again, much to Maisie's rage, and then go to the kitchen to make sure that Cook had remembered how to make sweet and sour sauce, which annoyed the talented woman so much that she threatened to curdle it.

'A good thing it's Sunday tomorrow,' said Francesca, eating toasted cheese while Lucy did her homework. 'And I must think of something for the kittens.' They peered at her, snug against their mother in the cardboard box, and the very idea of finding happy homes for them worried her. How was she to know if the homes were happy and what their mother would do without them?

They went to bed presently, and she dreamt of kittens and curdled sauce and Lady Mortimor in her purple, to wake unrefreshed. At least it wasn't raining, and Lucy would go with her and Bobo, and after breakfast they would go and look at the shops, have a snack somewhere and go to evensong at St Paul's.

The house was quiet as she let herself in through the side-entrance, fastened Bobo's lead and led the little dog outside to where Lucy was waiting. There was a nip in the air, but at least it wasn't raining; they set off at a good pace, crossed into the park and took the usual path. They had reached a small clump of trees where the path curved abruptly when Bobo began to bark, and a moment later Brontes came hurtling round the corner, to leap up to greet Francesca, sniff at Lucy and turn his delighted attention to Bobo, who was yapping his small head off. They had come to a halt, not wishing to be bowled over by the warmth of the big dog's attention, which gave his master ample time to join them.

'Hello—what a pleasant morning.' He sounded as though they had met recently. Francesca knew exactly how long it had been since they had last met—ten days. She bade him good-morning in a chilly voice, and when he looked at Lucy she was forced to add, 'This is my sister, Lucy. Professor Pitt-Colwyn, Lucy.'

Lucy offered a hand. 'I hoped I'd meet you one day,' she told him, 'but of course you've been away. What do you do with your dog? Does he go with you?'

'If it's possible; otherwise he stays at home and gets spoilt. You like him?'

'He's gorgeous. We've got a cat and kittens; I expect Francesca told you that—now the kittens are getting quite big we'll have to find homes for them.' She peeped at her sister's face; she looked cross. 'I'll take Bobo for a run—will Brontes come with me?'

'He'll be delighted. We'll stroll along to meet you.'

'We should be going back,' said Francesca, still very cool.

Lucy was already darting ahead and the professor appeared not to have heard her. 'I wish to talk to you, so don't be a silly girl and put on airs—'

'Well, really—' She stopped and looked up at his bland face. 'I am not putting on airs, and there is nothing for us to talk about.'

'You're very touchy—high time you left that job.' And at her indignant gasp he added, 'Just keep quiet and listen to me.'

He took her arm and began to walk after the fast retreating Lucy and the dogs. 'You would like to leave Lady Mortimor, would you not? I know of a job which might suit you. A close friend of mine died recently, leaving a widow and a small daughter. Eloise was an actress before she married—indeed, she has returned to the stage for short periods since their marriage— now she has the opportunity to go on tour with a play and is desperate to find someone to live in her house, run it for her and look after little Peggy while she is away. The tour is three or four months and then if it is successful they will go to a London theatre. You will have *carte blanche* and the services of a daily help in the house. No days off—but Peggy will be at school so that you should have a certain amount of free time. Peggy goes to a small day school, five minutes' walk from Cornel Mews—'

'That's near Lady Mortimor's—'

'Yes—don't interrupt. Eloise will come home for the very occasional weekend or day, but since the tour is largely in the north of England that isn't likely to be very often. The salary isn't bad...' He mentioned a sum which left Francesca's pretty mouth agape.

'That's—that's...just for a week? Are you sure? Lady Mortimor...I'm not properly trained.'

'You don't need to be.' He looked down his commanding nose at her. 'Will you consider it?'

'It's not permanent—and what about the cat and her kittens?'

He said smoothly, 'It will last for several months, probably longer, and you will find it easy to find another similar post once you have a good reference.'

'Lady Mortimor won't give me one.'

'I am an old friend of Eloise; I imagine that my word will carry sufficient weight. As for the cat and kittens, they may come and live in my house; Brontes will love to have them.'

'Oh, but won't your—that is, anyone mind?'

'No. I shall be seeing Eloise later; may I tell her that you are willing to go and see her?'

'I would have liked time to think about it.'

'Well, you can have ten minutes while I round up the rest of the party.'

He had gone before she could protest, walking away from her with long, easy strides.

He had said 'ten minutes' and she suspected that he had meant what he had said. It sounded a nice job and the money was far beyond her wildest expectations, and she wouldn't be at anyone's beck and call.

Prudence told her that she was probably going out of the frying pan into the fire. On the other hand, nothing venture, nothing win. When he came back presently with Lucy chattering happily and a tired Bobo and a still lively Brontes in tow, she said at once, 'All right, I'll go and see this lady if you'll give me her address. Only it will have to be in the evening.'

'Seven o'clock tomorrow evening. Mrs Vincent, two, Cornel Mews. I'll let her know. I shan't be here tomorrow; I'll see you on Tuesday. You're free for the rest of the day?'

For one delighted moment she thought he was going to suggest that they should spend it together, but all he said was, 'Goodbye,' before he started to whistle to Brontes and turned on his heel, walking with the easy air of a man who had done what he had set out to do.

Lucy tucked an arm in hers. 'Now tell me everything—why are you going to see this Mrs Vincent?'

They started to walk back and by the time they had reached the house Lucy knew all about it. They took Bobo into the kitchen and went back to their rooms to make some coffee and talk it over.

'It won't matter whether Mrs Vincent is nice or not if she's not going to be there,' observed Lucy. 'Oh, Fran, won't it be heavenly to have no one there but us—and Peggy of course—I wonder how old she is?'

'I forgot to ask...'

'All that money,' said Lucy dreamily. 'Now we can easily both get winter coats.'

'Well, I must save as much as I can. Supposing I can't find another job?'

'Never cross your bridges until you get to them,' said Lucy. 'Come on, let's go and look at the shops.' She put the kittens back in their box with their mother.

'I'm glad they'll all have a good home,' Francesca said.

'Yes. I wonder where it is?'

'Somewhere suitable for a professor,' said Francesca snappily. It still rankled that he had taken leave of her so abruptly. There was no reason why he shouldn't, of course. He had done his good deed for the day: found help for his friend and enabled her to leave Lady Mortimor's house.

'I shall enjoy giving her my notice,' she told Lucy.

IT SEEMED AS THOUGH Monday would never end but it did, tardily, after a day of Lady Mortimor's deep displeasure vented upon anyone and anything which came within her range, due to an early morning visit to her hairdresser who had put the wrong coloured streaks in her hair. Francesca had been ordered to make another appointment immediately so that this might be remedied at once, but unfortunately the hairdresser had no cancellations. Francesca, relaying this unwelcome news, had the receiver snatched from her and listened to her employer demanding the instant dismissal of the girl who had done her hair that morning, a demand which was naturally enough refused and added to Lady Mortimor's wrath.

'Why not get Ethel to shampoo your hair and re-set it?' Francesca suggested, and was told not to be so stupid, and after that there was no hope of doing anything right... She was tired and a little cross by the time she got to their rooms to find Lucy ready with a pot of tea.

'You drink that up,' she told Francesca bracingly.

'Put on that brown jacket and skirt—I know they're old, but they're elegant—and do do your face.' She glanced at the clock. 'You've twenty minutes.'

It was exactly seven o'clock when she rang the bell of the charming little cottage in Cornel Mews. Its door was a rich dark red and there were bay trees in tubs on either side of it, and its one downstairs window was curtained in ruffled white net. She crossed her fingers for luck and took a deep breath as the door was opened.

The woman standing there was small and slim and as pretty as a picture. Her dark hair was in a fashionable tangle and she wore the kind of make-up it was difficult to separate from natural colouring. She wore a loose shirt over a very narrow short skirt and high-heeled suede boots and she could have been any age between twenty and thirty. She was in fact thirty-five.

'Miss Haley—do come in, Renier has told me all about you...' She ushered Francesca into a narrow hall and opened a door into a surprisingly large living-room. 'Sit down and do have a drink while we get to know each other.'

Francesca sat, took the sherry she was offered and, since for the moment she had had no chance to say a word, she stayed silent.

'Did Renier explain?' asked Mrs Vincent. 'You know what men are, they never listen.'

It was time she said something, thought Francesca. 'He told me that you were going on tour and needed someone to look after your daughter and keep house for you.'

'Bless the darling, he had it right.' Mrs Vincent

curled up in a vast armchair with her drink. 'It's just the details—'

'You don't know anything about me,' protested Francesca.

'Oh, but I do, my daily woman is sister to Lady Mortimor's cook; besides, Renier said you were a sensible young woman with a sense of responsibility, and that's good enough for me. When can you come? I'm off at the end of next week.' She didn't give Francesca a chance to speak. 'Is the money all right? All the bills will go to my solicitor, who'll deal with them, and he'll send you a weekly cheque to cover household expenses and your salary. If you need advice or anything he'll deal with it.'

Francesca got a word in at last. 'Your daughter— how old is she? Can she meet me before I come? I have a sister who would have to live here with me.'

'That's fine. She's up in the nursery; I'll get her down.'

Mrs Vincent went out of the room and called up the narrow stairs, and presently a small girl came into the room. She was one of the plainest children Francesca had ever set eyes on: lank, pale hair, a long, thin face, small, dark eyes and an unhappy little mouth.

'She's six years old,' said Mrs Vincent in a detached way. 'Goes to school of course—very bright, so I've been told. Shake hands with Miss Haley, Peggy. She's coming to stay with you while I'm away.'

The child shook hands with Francesca and Francesca kept the small paw in her own for a moment. 'I shall like coming here to live with you,' she said gently. 'I've a sister, too…' She remembered something. 'Have you a cat or a dog to look after?'

The child shook her head. Her mother answered for her. 'My last nanny wouldn't have them in the house, though it's all one to me.' She laughed. 'I'm not here long enough to mind.'

'Then could I bring a kitten with me? Perhaps you would like one of your very own to look after, Peggy?'

The child smiled for the first time; there was an endearing gap in her teeth. 'For my own?' she asked.

'If your mother will allow that.'

'Oh, let the child have a pet if she wants.' Mrs Vincent added unexpectedly, 'She takes after her father.'

A remark which made everything clear to Francesca; a lovely, fragile creature like Mrs Vincent would find this plain, silent child a handicap now that she was going back on the stage. Probably she loved her dearly, but she wasn't going to let her interfere with her career. She went pink when Mrs Vincent said, 'I've been left comfortably off, but I've no intention of dwindling into a lonely widowhood,' because she might have read her thoughts. She smiled suddenly. 'I shall wait for a decent interval and get married again.'

Francesca watched Peggy's small face; it was stony with misery. She said quickly, 'I'll bring the kitten when I come, shall I? And you can choose a name for it—it's a little boy cat; he's black and white with yellow eyes.'

Peggy slipped a small hand into hers. 'Really? Will he live here with us?'

'Of course, for this will be his home, won't it?'

Eloise poured herself another drink. 'You have no

idea what a relief this is—may I call you Francesca? Now when can we expect you?'

'References?' ventured Francesca.

'Renier says you're OK. That's good enough for me; I told you that.'

'I shall have to give a week's notice to Lady Mortimor. I can do that tomorrow.'

'Good. I can expect you in a week's time. Give me a ring and let me know what time of day you'll be coming and I'll make a point of being in. Now have you time to go round the cottage with me?'

It was a small place, but very comfortably furnished with a well-planned kitchen and, on the ground floor, the living-room and, on the floor above, two good-sized bedrooms and a smaller room with a small bathroom leading from it. 'This is the nursery,' said Mrs Vincent. 'Peggy plays here—she's got masses of toys; she's quite happy to amuse herself.'

Francesca wondered about that although she said nothing. 'How long will you be away?' she asked.

'Oh, my dear, how am I to know? The tour will last three months at least, and with luck will end up at a London theatre; if it doesn't I shall get my agent to find me something else.'

'Yes, of course. Has Peggy any grandparents or cousins who may want to visit?'

'My parents are in America; Jeff's live in Wiltshire, almost Somerset, actually. We don't see much of them.' Something in her voice stopped Francesca from asking any more questions, and presently she bade Mrs Vincent goodbye, and bent to shake Peggy's hand.

'You won't forget the kitten?'

'No, I'll bring him with me, I promise.'

Back in her little sitting-room she told Lucy everything. 'It's a dear little house, you'll love it. I think Peggy is lonely—she's withdrawn—perhaps she misses her father; I don't know how long ago he died. I promised her a kitten—the black and white one. Mrs Vincent didn't mind.'

'You don't like her much, do you?' asked Lucy shrewdly.

'Well, she's charming and friendly and easy-going, but she didn't seem very interested in Peggy. Perhaps it's hard to stay at home quietly with a small child if you've been used to theatre friends, and perhaps when her husband was alive they went out a lot.'

'It'll be better than Lady Mortimor's, anyway. We had better start packing up tomorrow, and don't forget Professor Pitt-Colwyn is going to take mother cat and the other kittens. Shall you meet him tomorrow?'

'He said he would be there.' She frowned. 'I must be careful what I say about Mrs Vincent; he said he was a close friend of her husband so I expect he is a close friend of hers as well.'

'Do you suppose she's got her eye on him?'

'Don't be vulgar, Lucy. I should think it was very likely, although for all we know he's married already.'

'You'd better ask him—'

'Indeed I will not.'

He was in the park, waiting for her when she got there the next morning with Bobo. It was a bright day with more than a hint of the coming winter's chill and Francesca, an elderly cardigan over her blouse and skirt, wished she had worn something warmer.

He wasted no time on good-mornings but said, 'You're cold; why didn't you wear something sensible? We had better walk briskly.'

He marched her off at a fine pace, with Bobo keeping up with difficulty and Brontes circling around them. 'Well? You saw Eloise Vincent? Are you going to take the job?'

'Yes, I'm going to give Lady Mortimor my notice this morning and let Mrs Vincent know when I'll be going to her.'

'You saw Peggy?'

'Yes.'

He looked down at her thoughtfully. 'And...?'

'She's a quiet little girl, isn't she? I said I would take one of our kittens there for her to look after; her mother said that I might. You will take the mother cat and the other kittens, won't you?'

'Certainly I will. When will it be convenient for me to collect them? One evening? Let me see, I'm free on Thursday after six o'clock. Where exactly do you live?'

'Well, over the garage at the back of the house. There's a side-door; there's no knocker or bell, you just have to thump.'

'Then shall we say between six o'clock and half-past six? Have you a basket?'

'No, I'll get a cardboard box from the kitchen.'

'No need. I'll bring a basket with me. You're quite happy about this job?'

'Yes, thank you. You see, it's much more money and it will be so nice not to be...that is, it will be nice to be on our own.'

'That I can well believe. Are you scared of Lady Mortimor?'

She gave his question careful thought. 'No, not in the least, but she is sometimes rather rude if anything has annoyed her. I have longed to shout back at her but I didn't dare—she would have given me the sack.'

'Well, now you can bawl her out as much as you like, though I don't suppose you will; you've been too well brought up.'

He had spoken lightly, but when she looked at him she saw the mocking little smile. He must think her a spineless creature, dwindling into a dull spinsterhood. He had been kind, but his pity angered her. After all, she hadn't asked him for help. She said in her quiet voice, 'I have to go. Thank you for your help, and we'll have mother cat and the kittens ready for you when you come.' She gave him a stiff smile. 'Goodbye, Professor Pitt-Colwyn.'

She would contrive to be out when he called on Thursday evening, she decided as she made her way back to the house.

She couldn't have chosen a worse time in which to give in her notice. Lady Mortimor had been to a bridge party on the previous day and lost money, something she couldn't bear to do, and over and above that her dressmaker had telephoned to say that the dress she had wanted delivered that morning was not finished. Francesca went into the room in time to hear her employer declaring that it was no concern of hers if the girl working on it was ill, the dress was to be delivered by two o'clock that afternoon. She glanced up when she saw Francesca. 'Better still, I'll send round a girl to collect it and it had better be ready.

'You heard that,' she snapped. 'That stupid woman having the cheek to say I can't have the dress today. I intend to wear it to the Smithers' drinks party this evening. You'll fetch it after lunch.'

She sat down at the little writing-table and glanced through the letters there. 'Bills,' she said peevishly. 'These tradespeople always wanting their money. You'd better see to them, I suppose, Francesca.' She got up. 'I've a hair appointment—see that they're ready for me when I get back.'

Francesca picked up the letters. 'Lady Mortimor, I wish to give you a week's notice as from today.' She laid an envelope on the desk. 'I have put it in writing.'

Lady Mortimor looked as though she had been hit on the head. Her eyes popped from her head, her mouth gaped. When she had her breath she said, 'What nonsense is this? You must be mad, girl. A cushy job and a flat of your own...I won't hear of it.'

'There's nothing you can do about it,' Francesca pointed out reasonably. 'It isn't a cushy job, it's very badly paid, and it surely isn't a flat—it's two small rooms with a minute kitchen and a shower which doesn't work half the time.'

'You'll have difficulty in getting work, I'll see to that. I'll not give you a reference.'

'That won't be necessary. I already have a job to go to and your reference won't be required.'

'Then you can go now, do you hear, you ungrateful girl?'

'Just as you say, Lady Mortimor. You will have to

give me two weeks' wages, one in lieu of notice.' She watched her employer's complexion becoming alarmingly red. 'And whom shall I ask to arrange the dinner party for Saturday? And your lunch party on Sunday? Shall I let Ethel have the bills to check? And there will be the invitations for the charity tea party you are giving next week.'

Francesca paused for breath, astonished at herself. Really she had been most unpleasant and deserved to be thrown out of the house for rudeness. She realised that she wouldn't mind that in the least.

Lady Mortimor knew when she was worsted. 'You will remain until the following week.'

'Tuesday evening,' Francesca interpolated gently, ignoring the woman's glare.

'You will send an advertisement to the usual papers this morning. I require letters in the first instance; interviews can be arranged later to suit me.'

'Certainly, Lady Mortimor. Am I to state the salary?'

'No. The flat goes with the job, of course.' She swept to the door. 'It may interest you to know that you have ruined my day. Such ingratitude has cut me to the quick.'

Francesca forbore from saying that, for someone of Lady Mortimor's ample, corseted figure, the cut would have to be really deep.

Naturally a kind girl and seldom critical of other people, she felt guilty once she was alone. She had been most dreadfully rude; she felt thoroughly ashamed of herself. She had almost finished the bills when Maisie came in with her coffee.

'Cor, miss, what a lark—you going away. Mr Crow was just in the hall passing as you might say and 'eard it all. He said as 'ow you gave as good as you got and good luck to you, we all says—treated you something shameful, she 'as, and you a lady and all.'

'Why, Maisie, how very kind of you all. I'm afraid I was very rude…'

'A bit of plain speaking never 'urt no one, miss. I 'opes 'owever that 'oever takes yer place is capable of a bit of talking back.'

Francesca drank her coffee, feeling cheerful again. She wasn't going to apologise, but she would behave as she always had done, however unpleasant Lady Mortimor might choose to be.

She chose to be very unpleasant. It was a good thing that there were no signs of the professor the next morning for she might have burst into tears all over him and wallowed in self-pity, but by Thursday evening she didn't care any more and allowed Lady Mortimor's ill temper and spiteful remarks to flow over her head. Heedful of her decision, she took care not to get to the rooms until well after seven o'clock, only to find the professor sitting in comfort in the only easy-chair in the place, drinking tea from a mug while Brontes brooded in a fatherly fashion over mother cat and the kittens in their box.

'There you are,' said Lucy as Francesca went in. 'We thought you'd never come. There's still tea in the pot. But Renier's eaten all the biscuits; he didn't have time for lunch. Have you had a beastly day?'

'Well, a bit sticky. I say, isn't Brontes sweet?'

The professor had got up from his chair and pushed

her gently into it, and had gone to sit on the small wooden chair which creaked under his weight. He said now, 'I shall be away for the next ten days or so; I hope you settle down with Peggy.' His hooded gaze swept over her tired face. 'It's time you had a change, and I think you will find she will be much nicer to live with than your Lady Mortimor.' He got up. 'I must be going.' He scooped the cat and kittens into the basket he had brought with him, while Lucy cuddled the other kitten on her lap. 'I'll take good care of them,' he said. He smiled at them both. *'Tot ziens.'* And when Francesca made an effort to rise he said, 'No, I'll see myself out.'

The room seemed very empty once he had gone.

CHAPTER THREE

THE WEEK SEEMED never-ending, and Lady Mortimor was determined to get the last ounce of work out of Francesca before she left. There had been several answers to the advertisement, but so far the applicants had refused the job. They had turned up their noses at the so-called flat and two of them had exploded with laughter when they had been told their salary. They were, they had pointed out, secretary-companions, not dog minders or errand girls. Lady Mortimor actually had been shaken. 'You will have to remain until someone suitable can take your place,' she had said the day before Francesca was due to leave.

'That won't be possible,' said Francesca. 'I start my new job immediately I leave here. One of the agencies might have help for you, but only on a daily or weekly basis.'

Lady Mortimor glared at her. 'I am aware of that, but I have no intention of paying the exorbitant fees they ask.' She hesitated. 'I am prepared to overlook your rudeness, Francesca. I am sure that you could arrange to go to this new job, say, in a weeks' time?'

'I am very sorry, Lady Mortimor, but that is impossible.'

She watched her employer sweep out of the room

in a towering rage, and went back to making out the last of the cheques for the tradesmen.

The last day was a nightmare she refused to dwell upon. Lady Mortimor gave her not a moment to herself, and when six o'clock came declared that half the things she had told Francesca to do were still not done. Francesca listened quietly, allowing the tirade to flow over her head. 'There is nothing of importance left to do,' she pointed out. 'Whoever can come in place of me can deal with anything I've overlooked. Goodbye, Lady Mortimor.'

She closed the door quietly on her erstwhile employer's angry voice. She had a happier send-off from the staff, and Crow presented her with a potted plant from them all and wished her well. 'For we're all sure you deserve it, miss,' he said solemnly.

She went to join Lucy, and, after a meal, packed the last of their belongings. A taxi would take them the short distance to Cornel Mews in the morning.

Eloise Vincent was waiting for them when they arrived mid-morning. Peggy was at school, she told them. 'My daily woman will fetch her after lunch. I'm up to my eyes packing; I'm off this evening. I've written down all the names and addresses you might need and a phone number in case you should need me urgently, but for heaven's sake don't ring unless it's something dire.' She led the way upstairs. 'You each have a room; I'll leave you to unpack.' She glanced at the cat basket Lucy was holding. 'Is this the kitten? I dare say Peggy will like having him. There's coffee in the kitchen; help yourselves, will you? Lucy's bed is made up. I'm sorry I haven't put clean sheets on the other bed; the room's been turned out, but I had to empty cupboards and drawers—you won't mind doing it?'

She smiled charmingly and went downstairs, leaving them to inspect their new quarters. The rooms were prettily furnished and to have a room of one's own would be bliss. They unpacked and hung everything away and, with the kitten still in his basket, went downstairs. Mrs Wells, the daily cleaner, was in the kitchen. She was a pleasant-faced, middle-aged woman who poured coffee for them, found a saucer of milk for the kitten and offered to do anything to help. 'I've been here quite a while, before poor Dr Vincent died, so I know all there is to know about the place. I come in the mornings—eight o'clock—and go again after lunch,' she offered biscuits, 'though I said I'd fetch Peggy from school before I go home today.'

'Can't we do that?' asked Francesca. 'We have to get to know her, and it's a chance to see where the school is.'

'Well, now, that would be nice. It's at the end of Cornel Road, just round the corner in Sefton Park Street. Mrs Vincent hoped you wouldn't mind having a snack lunch—the fridge is well stocked and you can cook this evening. She is going out to lunch with a friend, but she'll be back by two o'clock and aims to leave around six o'clock—being fetched by car.'

Francesca thought of the questions she wanted answered before Mrs Vincent left. She put down her coffee-cup. 'Perhaps I could talk to her now?'

Eloise Vincent was in the sitting-room, sitting at her desk, a telephone book before her, the receiver in her hand. She looked up and smiled as Francesca went in. 'Settling in?' she asked. 'Mrs Wells is a fount of knowledge if you've any questions.'

'Yes. She's been most helpful. Mrs Vincent, could you spare a moment? Just to tell me what time Peggy goes to bed, if there's anything she won't eat, which friends is she allowed to play with while you are away…?'

'Oh, dear, what a lot of questions. She goes to bed about seven o'clock, I suppose. She eats her dinner at school and I've been giving her tea about five o'clock. I don't know about her friends. My husband used to take her with him when he went to see his friends; they haven't been here, although on her birthday we had a party, of course—'

'May I have the names of your doctor and dentist?'

Mrs Vincent laughed. 'Oh, get Renier if anything is worrying you. He's Peggy's godfather; he's fond of her. She's never ill, anyway. Now, you really must excuse me—Mrs Wells can tell you anything else you may want to know.'

It was obvious to Francesca that Mrs Vincent had no more time for her. She went back to the kitchen and did a thorough tour of its cupboards and shelves, went through the linen cupboard with Mrs Wells and, when Mrs Vincent had left for her lunch appointment, sat down with Mrs Wells and Lucy to eat sandwiches and drink more coffee.

Peggy came out of school at three o'clock, and both of them went to fetch her since Mrs Vincent wasn't back. The children came out in twos and threes and Peggy was one of the last, walking slowly and alone.

They went to meet her and she seemed pleased to see them, walking between them, holding their hands, answering their cheerful questions about school politely. Only when Francesca said, 'The kitten's waiting for you,' did she brighten. They spent the rest of the short walk discussing suitable names for him.

Mrs Vincent was back and there was a car before the door, which was being loaded with her luggage by a tall, middle-aged man. He said, 'Hello, Peggy,' without stopping what he was doing.

She said, 'Hello, Mr Seymour,' in a small wooden voice, all her animation gone again.

'You'd better go and say goodbye to your mother,' he told her over his shoulder. 'We're off in a few minutes.'

The three of them went inside and found Mrs Vincent in the sitting-room, making a last-minute phone call. 'Darlings,' she cried in her light, pretty voice, 'I'm going now. Come and say goodbye to your old mother, Peggy, and promise to be a good girl while I'm away. I'll send you lots of postcards and when I can I will telephone to you.' She kissed her small daughter and turned to Francesca. 'I'll be trying to keep in touch,' she said. 'I'm sure you'll do a marvellous job. Let me know how you are getting on from time to time.'

She smiled, looking so pretty and appealing that Francesca smiled back, quelling the uneasy feeling that Eloise Vincent was only too delighted to be starting her theatrical career once more and couldn't wait to get away.

She was prepared for Peggy's tears once her mother

had gone, but the child's face had remained impassive. 'May I have the kitten now?' she asked, almost before they were out of sight.

She and the small creature took to each other at once. She sat happily in the sitting-room with him on her small, bony knees, talking to him and stroking his head with a small, gentle hand. 'I shall call him Tom,' she told Francesca.

'That's a nice name.'

'Daddy used to read me a story about Tom Kitten…' The small voice quavered and Francesca said quickly, 'Shall we talk about your daddy? I'd like to know all about him.'

So that was the trouble, she reflected, listening to the child's rambling description of her father and the fun they had had together. Peggy had loved him dearly and there had been no one to talk to her about him. She let the child chat on, the small face animated, and then said gently, 'What nice things you have to remember about him, Peggy, and of course he'll never go away; he'll always be there inside your head.'

'I like you,' said Peggy.

It took a few days to settle into a routine. Lucy went to school each morning and Francesca took Peggy to her school shortly afterwards, going back to make the beds and shop and wash and iron while Mrs Wells gave the house what she called a good tidy up. Tom settled down without any nonsense, aware by now that he belonged to Peggy and no one else, sitting beside her chair at meals and sleeping at the foot of her bed.

There had been no news of Mrs Vincent. Francesca wasn't sure where she was, for the promised list of the various towns the company would be appearing in hadn't turned up. It was a relief that at the end of the week there was a cheque in the post with her salary and a housekeeping allowance.

It was two days later, after they had had tea and Francesca was on the floor in the kitchen, showing Peggy how to play marbles while Tom pranced around them both, that the front doorbell was rung.

'I'll go,' called Lucy, in the sitting-room with her homework, and a moment later Professor Pitt-Colwyn's voice sent Peggy flying to the kitchen door. He caught her in his arms and kissed her soundly. 'Hello, love, I thought it was time I came to see how you were getting on...'

He watched Francesca get up off the floor and brush down her skirt. 'Marbles—am I in time for a game?' and then he added, 'Good evening, Francesca.'

She was surprised at how glad she was to see him. 'Good evening, Professor.' She scanned his face and saw that he was tired. 'Shall we go into the sitting-room? I'll make a cup of coffee while you and Peggy have a talk—she wants to show you Tom.'

He looked down at the small, earnest face staring up at him. 'A splendid idea—shall we be disturbing Lucy?'

'I've just finished,' said Lucy. 'I'll help Fran get the coffee—'

'A sandwich with it?' asked Francesca.

'That would be very nice.'

'Have you had no lunch or tea?'

'A rather busy day.' He smiled, and she could see that he wasn't going to talk about it.

She made a pot of coffee, cut a plateful of cold beef sandwiches and bore the tray into the sitting-room. Peggy was sitting on the professor's knee and Tom had curled upon her small lap. Francesca was astonished to hear the child's happy voice, talking nineteen to the dozen.

'We are talking about Peggy's father,' said the professor deliberately.

Francesca said at once, 'He must have been a marvellous dad. Peggy has told us a little about him.' She poured him a cup and gave it to him. 'You stay there, darling. Here's your milk, and take care not to spill it over your godfather's trousers.'

She passed the sandwiches too, and watched him eat the lot. 'There's a cake I made this afternoon,' she suggested.

He ate several slices of that too, listening to Peggy's chatter, knowing just when to make some remark to make her giggle. Francesca let her bedtime go by, for the little girl was really happy. It was the professor who said at last, 'It's way past your bedtime, Peggy,' and when she wound her arms round his neck he said, 'If you go to bed like the good girl you are, I'll come and take you to the zoo on Saturday afternoon.'

'Fran and Lucy too?'

'Of course. Tom can mind the house and we'll come back here and have an enormous tea.'

She slid off his knee. Kissed him goodnight then, and went to stand by Francesca's chair. 'Will we?' she asked. 'Will we, really?'

'If your godfather says so, then of course we will,

and I'll make a simply enormous cake and we'll have crumpets dripping with butter.'

'Could Lucy put her to bed?' asked the professor. 'We might have a chat?'

'Of course I can.' Lucy scooped up the kitten and handed him to Peggy. 'And Fran will come and tuck you up when you're in bed.'

Peggy went happily enough, her hand in Lucy's and the kitten tucked under one arm. Francesca, suddenly shy, offered more coffee.

'Any problems?' asked the professor.

She thought before she answered. 'No, I don't think so. I should have liked to have known a bit more about Peggy before Mrs Vincent left, but there wasn't much time. Mrs Wells is a great help with things like shopping and so on. Peggy doesn't seem to have any friends...do you suppose it would be all right if I invited one or two children for tea one day? I think she is a very shy little girl.'

'She is a very unhappy little girl. She loved her father very much and she misses him; she likes to talk about him. I think that Eloise didn't understand that and the child is too small to carry so much hidden grief.' He glanced at her. 'She told me that she talks to you and Lucy about him.'

'Yes, he is still alive to her, isn't he? If you're sure that's the right thing to do?'

'Quite sure. By all means see if you can get some children round to play with her. Has she no friends at all at school?'

'Oh, one or two speak to her but she doesn't seem to have any special friends, but I'll do my best. She has masses of toys and it would be nice if she were to share them.'

'Have you heard from Eloise?'

'Me? No. She said she would be too busy rehearsing to write for a while.'

'I'm going to Cheltenham to see the opening show next week. If you think of anything you want to know about, let me know before then.'

'Thank you. She left everything beautifully organised. I expect she's a very good actress?'

He didn't answer, and she wondered uncomfortably if she had said something about Mrs Vincent which might have annoyed him. She couldn't think of anything but if he was in love with her, and she supposed that he was, he would be touchy about her. Lucy came in then.

'Peggy's bathed and in bed; she 's waiting for you to say goodnight—both of you.'

The child wreathed her arms round Francesca's neck. 'I love you, Fran.'

'Thank you, darling. I love you too, and Tom of course. Now go to sleep quickly, won't you? Because he's asleep already.'

The professor was hugged in his turn, and he was reminded of his promise to take them to the zoo on Saturday, then he was kissed goodnight. 'Now tuck me in, please, Fran.'

So she was tucked in and he stood in the little room, leaning against the wall, watching, his eyes half closed.

Back in the sitting-room he said, 'I must be off. Thanks for the coffee and sandwiches.'

'It made Peggy very happy to see you,' Francesca said. The thought that it had made her very happy too was sternly dismissed. 'You will have a good meal before you go to bed, won't you?'

He looked as though he were going to laugh. 'Indeed I will.' He smiled at Lucy and dropped a large hand on Francesca's shoulder for a moment and went away. Lucy went to the window to watch him drive away, but Francesca busied herself with the cups and saucers.

'I shall enjoy the zoo,' said Lucy.

'Yes, it should be fun; Peggy will love it. Lucy, I must do something about finding her some friends...'

'Well, gossip around when you go to get her from school. I dare say our Eloise discouraged them—children are noisy and they make a mess...'

'You're probably right, but don't call her that, dear—we might forget and say something—I mean, I think he's in love with her, don't you? He's going all the way to Cheltenham for the opening night.'

They were in the kitchen, washing up the coffee-cups.

'That doesn't mean that he's in love with her. What shall we have for supper? It's a bit late.'

The following day Francesca made a few tentative overtures to the mothers and nannies taking the children to school. They were friendly enough, and she made a point of letting them know that Mrs Vincent had gone away for a time and that she was looking after Peggy. She said no more than that, but it was, she thought, the thin end of the wedge...

She wasn't sure, but she thought that maybe the

children had been discouraged from getting friendly with Peggy, a child too shy to assert herself with the making of friends. It might take some time, but it would be nice if she could get to know a few children while her mother was away, so that by the time she got back home Peggy would have established a circle of little friends. Already the child was livelier, learning to play the games small children played, spending long hours with Francesca or Lucy rearranging the elaborate doll's house, planning new outfits for the expensive dolls she had. 'Woollies for the winter,' explained Francesca, getting knitting needles and wool and starting on miniature sweaters and cardigans.

They all went shopping the next day, and it was apparent that Peggy had never been to Woolworth's. They spent a long time there while she trotted from one counter to the other, deciding how to spend the pocket money Francesca had given her. After the rigours of Lady Mortimor's household, life was very pleasant. Francesca, going about her chores in the little house, planning meals, playing with Peggy, sitting in the evenings sewing or knitting, with Lucy doing her homework at the table, felt that life was delightful. They had a home, well, not a permanent one, but still a home for the time being—enough money, the prospect of having some new clothes and of adding to their tiny capital at the bank. She was almost content.

The professor came for them after lunch on Saturday, bundled them briskly into his car, and drove to the zoo. It was a mild autumn day, unexpected after several days of chilly rain. Francesca, in her good suit, her burnished hair gleaming in the sunshine, sat beside him in the car making polite small talk, while Lucy and Peggy in the back giggled and chattered together. The professor, who had been up most of the night with a very ill patient, allowed the happy chatter from the back seat to flow over his tired head and listened to Francesca's pretty voice, not hearing a word she said but enjoying the sound of it.

The afternoon was a success; they wandered along, stopping to look at whatever caught their eyes, with Peggy skipping between them until she caught sight of the camels, who were padding along with their burden of small children.

The professor fished some money out of his pocket and gave it to Lucy. 'You two have a ride; Francesca and I are going to rest our feet. We'll be here when you get back.'

'You make me feel very elderly—bunions and dropped arches and arthritic knees,' protested Francesca, laughing as they sat down on an empty bench.

'You, my dear girl, will never be elderly. That is an attitude of mind.' He spoke lightly, not looking at her. 'You have settled down quite happily, I hope?'

'Oh, yes, and Lucy and Peggy get on famously.'

'So I have noticed. And you, Francesca, you mother them both.'

She was vexed to feel her cheeks grow hot. She asked stiffly, 'How is Brontes? And mother cat and the kittens?'

'He has adopted them. You must come and see them. The children are at school during the day? You will be free for lunch one day? I'll give you a ring.'

'Is that an invitation?' asked Francesca frostily.

'Certainly it is. You want to come, don't you?'

She had no intention of saying so. 'I shall be very glad to see mother cat and the kittens again.'

His stern mouth twitched a little. 'I shall be there too; I hope you will be glad to see me.'

'Well, of course.' She opened her handbag and looked inside and closed it again for something to do. She would be very glad to see him again, only he mustn't be allowed to know that. He was merely being friendly, filling in his days until Eloise Vincent should return. She wished that she knew more about him; she voiced the wish without meaning to and instantly wanted it unsaid.

'You flatter me.' He told her blandly, 'Really there is nothing much to tell. I work—as most men work. Perhaps I am fortunate in liking that work.'

'Do you go to a hospital every day or have a surgery?'

'I go to several hospitals and I have consulting-rooms.'

She persisted. 'If you are a professor, do you teach the students?'

'Yes. To the best of my ability!' He added gently, 'I examine them too, and from time to time I travel. Mostly to examine students in hospitals in other countries. I have a very competent secretary and a nurse to help me—'

'I'm sorry, I've been very rude; I can't think why I asked you about your work or—or anything.' She had gone pink again and she wouldn't look at him, so that the long, curling lashes, a shade darker than her hair, lay on her cheeks. She looked quite beautiful and he studied her with pleasure, saying nothing. It was a great relief to her when Lucy and Peggy came running towards them. Caught up in the excited chatter from Peggy, she forgot the awkward moment.

They went back to the little house in the Mews presently and had their tea: fairy cakes and a gingerbread, little sandwiches and chocolate biscuits. 'It's like my birthday,' said Peggy, her small, plain face wreathed in smiles.

The professor stayed for an hour after tea, playing ludo on the floor in front of the sitting-room fire. When he got to his feet, towering over them, he observed pleasantly, 'A very nice afternoon—we must do it again some time.' He kissed his small god-daughter, put a friendly arm around Lucy's shoulders, and went to the door with Francesca.

'I'll phone you,' was all he said, 'and thanks for the tea.'

IT WAS several days later when she had a phone call. A rather prim voice enquired if she were Miss Haley and went on to ask if she would lunch with Professor Pitt-Colwyn in two days' time. 'If it wouldn't inconvenience you,' went on the voice, 'would you go to the Regent hospital at noon and ask for the professor?'

Francesca agreed. Were they going to eat at the hospital? she wondered, and what should she wear? It would have to be the brown suit again. Her winter coat was too shabby and although there was some money now Lucy needed a coat far more than she did. She would wash her hair and do her nails, she decided, and buy a new lipstick.

The Regent hospital was in the East End. It was a hideous building, heavily embellished with fancy brickwork of the Victorian era, brooding over a network of shabby streets. Francesca got off the bus opposite its entrance and presented herself at the reception desk inside the entrance hall.

The clerk appeared to know who she was, for she lifted the phone and spoke into it, and a moment later beckoned to one of the porters.

'If you would wait for a few minutes, Miss Haley, the porter will show you...'

Francesca followed the man, wishing that she hadn't come; she couldn't imagine the professor in this vast, echoing building. Probably he had forgotten that he had invited her and was deep in some highly urgent operation. Come to think of it, she didn't know if he was a surgeon or a physician. She sat down in a small room at the back of the entrance hall, facing a long corridor. It was empty and after a minute or two she was tempted to get up and go home, but all at once there were people in it, walking towards her: the professor, towering above the posse of people trying to keep up with him, a short, stout ward sister, two or three young men in short white coats, an older man in a long white coat, a tall, stern-looking woman with a pile of folders under one arm and, bringing up the rear, a worried-looking nurse carrying more folders.

The professor paused in the doorway of the room she was in, filling it entirely with his bulk. 'Ah, there you are,' he observed in a voice which suggested that she had been in hiding and he had just discovered her. 'Give me five minutes...'

He had gone and everyone else with him, jostling each other to keep up.

He reappeared not ten minutes later, elegant in a dark grey suit and a silk tie which had probably cost as much as her best shoes. They had been her best for some time now, and she hardly ever wore them for they pinched abominably.

'Kind of you to come here,' he told her breezily. 'I wasn't sure of the exact time at which I could be free. Shall we go?'

She walked beside him, out to the space reserved for consultants' cars and got into the car, easing her feet surreptitiously out of her shoes. The professor, watching out of the corner of his eye, turned a chuckle into a cough and remarked upon the weather.

He drove west, weaving his way through the small side-streets until she, quite bewildered by the one-way traffic, saw that they were in Shaftesbury Avenue. But only briefly; he turned into side-streets again and ten minutes or so later turned yet again into a narrow street, its trees bare of leaves now, the houses on either side elegant Regency, each with a very small garden before it, steps leading up to doorways topped by equally elegant fanlights. The professor stopped the car and got out to open her door. 'I thought we might lunch at home,' he told her. 'Brontes is anxious to see you again.'

'You live here?' asked Francesca. A silly question, but she had been surprised; it was, she guessed, five minutes away from Mrs Vincent's cottage.

'Yes.' He took her arm and marched her up the

steps as the door was opened by a dignified middle-aged man in a black jacket and pin-striped trousers.

'Ah, Peak. Francesca, this is Peak, who sees that this place runs on oiled wheels. Mrs Peak is my house-keeper. Peak, this is Miss Haley. Show her where she can leave her coat, will you?' He picked up his bag. 'I'll be in the drawing-room, Francesca.'

In the charming little cloakroom concealed beneath the curving staircase, she poked at her hair, added more lipstick and deplored the suit; she had better take off the jacket otherwise it might look as though she were ready to dart out of the house again. Her blouse wasn't new either, but it was ivory silk, laundered and pressed with great care, and the belt around her slender waist was soft leather. Her feet still hurt, but she would be able to ease them out of her shoes again once they were sitting at the table. She went back into the narrow hall and the professor appeared at a half-open door.

'Come and have a drink before lunch.' He held the door wide and Brontes stuck his great head round it, delighted to see her.

The room was long and narrow, with a bay window overlooking the street and a charming Adam fireplace. The chairs were large and deep and well cushioned, and there was a scattering of small lamp tables as well as a handsome bow-fronted display cabinet embellished with marquetry, its shelves filled with silver and porcelain. The professor went to the rent table under the window. He asked, 'Sherry for you? And do sit down.'

She sat, and was aware that mother cat and her kittens were cosily curled up together in one of the easy chairs. She said, 'Oh, they seem very much at home.'

He handed her the sherry. 'Brontes has seen to that; he is their devoted guardian angel.'

She sipped her sherry, very aware of him sitting opposite her, Brontes pressed up against him, both of them watching her. Her tongue, as it sometimes did, ran away with her. 'Do you want to tell me something? Is that why you asked me to lunch?'

'Yes, to both your questions, but it can wait.' He settled back in his great chair. 'Your sister is a bright child; has she any ideas about the future?' It was a casual question and she answered readily enough.

'She's clever; she's set her heart on GCSEs, A levels, and a university.'

'Some discerning young man will snap her up long before then.' He smiled at her. 'And why aren't you married?'

It was unexpected. 'Well, I—I...that is, they weren't the right ones. None of them the right man.'

This muddled statement he received with a gentle smile. 'Have you any messages for Eloise?'

'If you would tell her that Peggy seems happy and is doing well at school and that everything is fine. She hasn't written or phoned, but I expect she's very busy.'

'Undoubtedly,' he agreed gravely. Peak came then to tell them that lunch was ready, and she went with the professor to a smaller room at the back of the house, which overlooked a surprisingly large garden. 'You've got trees, how lovely,' she exclaimed. 'It must look beautiful in the spring.'

They lunched off iced melon, baked salmon in a

pastry case and a coffee *bavarois* and, while they ate, the professor kept the conversation quite firmly in his hands; impersonal topics, the kind of talk one might have had with a stranger sharing one's table in a restaurant, thought Francesca peevishly. Back in the drawing-room, drinking coffee from paper-thin cups, she said suddenly, 'I wish you would talk about your work—you looked different at the hospital; it's a side of you that I know nothing about.' She put down her cup. 'I'm sorry, I'm being nosy again.' She looked at her feet, aching in the shoes she longed to kick off. 'Only I'm interested,' she mumbled.

'I have an appointment at half-past two,' he told her. 'I'll drive you back as I go to my rooms, which means that we have half an hour. Do take off those shoes and curl up comfortably.'

'Oh, how did you know? I don't wear them very often and they're a bit tight. You don't mind?'

'Not in the least. What do you want to know about my work, Francesca?'

'Well, I know that you're a professor and a consultant, but are you a surgeon or a physician? You said you went to other hospitals and that you travelled. Why?'

'I'm a surgeon, open-heart surgery valve replacements, by-passes, transplants. Most of my work is at Regent's, but I operate at all the big provincial hospitals if I'm needed. I have a private practice and an out-patients clinic twice a week. I work in Leiden too, occasionally in Germany and the States, and from time to time in the Middle East.'

'Leiden,' said Francesca. 'You said *"tot ziens"* one morning in the park; we looked it up—it's Dutch.'

'My mother is a Dutchwoman; she lives just outside Leiden. I spend a good deal of time there. My father was British; he died two years ago.'

He looked at her, half smiling, one eyebrow raised in a gentle way. The half-smile widened and she thought it was mocking, and went red. He must think her a half-wit with no manners. She plunged into a muddled speech. 'I don't know why I had to be so rude, I do apologise, I have no excuse, if I were you I wouldn't want to speak to me again—'

He said gently, 'But I'm not you, and fortunately I see no reason why I shouldn't speak to you again. For one thing, it may be necessary from time to time. I did tell Eloise that I would keep an eye on Peggy.'

'Yes, of course. I—I expect that you would like to go now.' She sat up straight and crammed her feet back into her shoes and then stood up. 'Thank you for my lunch—it was delicious.'

He appeared not to notice how awkward she felt. Only as he stopped in Cornel Mews and got out to take the key from her and open the door of the cottage did he say, 'We must have another talk some time, Francesca,' and he bent to kiss her cheek as she went past him into the hall.

CHAPTER FOUR

FRANCESCA WAS sitting by the fire, reading to Peggy, when Lucy came in. 'Well, did you have a good lunch? What did you eat?'

Francesca recited the menu.

'Nice—to think I was chewing on liver and bacon... Where did you go?'

'To his house; it's quite close by.'

Lucy flung down her school books and knelt down by the fire. 'Tell me everything,' she demanded.

When Francesca had finished she said, 'He must be very rich. I expect he's clever too. I wonder what his mum's like.'

'How's school?'

'OK.' Lucy dug into a pocket. 'There's a letter for you, but don't take any notice of it; I don't want to go...'

The words were bravely said but palpably not true. A party of pupils was being organised to go skiing two weeks before Christmas. Two weeks in Switzerland with proper tuition and accompanied by teachers. The fare and the expenses totalled a sum which Francesca had no hope of finding.

'Oh, Lucy, I'm so sorry. If it's any consolation I'll get the money by hook or by crook for next winter.'

She glanced at her sister's resolutely cheerful face. 'All your friends are going?'

'Well, most of them, but I really don't mind, Fran. We can have a lovely time here, getting ready for Christmas.'

So nothing more was said about it, although Francesca sat up late, doing sums which, however hard she tried, never added up to enough money to pay for Lucy's skiing holiday. There was enough money set aside for her school fees, of course, but that wasn't to be touched. She went to bed finally with a headache.

There was no postcard from Mrs Vincent; nor was there a phone call. Francesca reminded herself that the professor would be with her, and most likely he would bring back something for Peggy when he returned. The child showed no concern at the absence of news from her mother, although it seemed to Francesca that she was looking pale and seemed listless; even Tom's antics were met with only a half-hearted response. Francesca consulted Mrs Wells. 'I think she should see a doctor. She isn't eating much either. I wonder if she's missing her mother...'

Mrs Wells gave her an old-fashioned look. 'I'm not one for telling tales out of school, but 'er mum never 'as had no time for 'er. Disappointed she was; she so pretty and charming and Peggy as plain as a pikestaff. No, you don't need to fret yerself about that, Miss Haley; little Peggy don't love 'er mum all that much. She was 'appier when her granny and grandpa came to visit. That was when Dr Vincent was alive—loved the child they did, and she loved them.'

So Francesca had done nothing for a few more days,

although Peggy didn't seem any better. She had made up her mind to get a doctor by now. If only the professor had phoned, she could have asked his advice, but he, of course, would be wherever Mrs Vincent was. She fetched Peggy from school, gave her her tea which she didn't want and, as soon as Lucy came home, took the child upstairs to bed. Peggy felt hot and she wished she could take her temperature, but there was a singular lack of first-aid equipment in the house, and she blamed herself for not having attended to that. She sat the child on her lap and started to undress her, and as she took off her clothes she saw the rash. The small, thin back was covered with red spots. She finished the undressing, washed the pale little face, and brushed the mousy hair and tucked the child up in bed. 'A nice glass of cold milk,' she suggested, 'and Lucy shall bring it up to you.'

'Tom—I want Tom,' said Peggy in a small voice. 'I've got a pain in my head.'

'You shall have Tom, my dear,' said Francesca and sped downstairs, told Lucy, and went to the phone. Even if the professor were still away, surely that nice man Peak would have a phone number or, failing that, know of a local doctor.

She dialled the number Mrs Vincent had left in her desk and Peak answered.

'Peak, did Professor Pitt-Colwyn leave a phone number? I need to speak to him—Peggy's ill.'

'A moment, Miss Haley,' and a second later the professor's voice, very calm, sounded in her ear.

'Francesca?'

'Oh, so you are there,' she said fiercely. 'Peggy's

ill; there's a rash all over her back and she feels sick and listless. She's feverish, but I can't find a thermometer anywhere and I don't know where there's a doctor and I've not heard a word since Mrs Vincent went away—'

'Peggy's in bed? Good. I'll be with you in about ten minutes.' He rang off and she spent a moment with the unhappy thought that she had been anything but calm and sensible; she had even been rather rude...and he had sounded impassive and impersonal, as though she were a patient to be dealt with efficiently. Though I'm not the patient, she thought in a muddled way as she went back to Peggy and sent Lucy downstairs to open the door for the professor, and then sat down on the side of the bed to hold the tearful child in her arms.

She didn't hear him come in; for such a big man he was both quick and silent. She was only aware of him when he put two hands on her shoulders and eased her away from Peggy and took her place.

He was unhurried and perfectly calm and apparently unworried and it was several minutes before he examined the child, took her temperature and then sat back while Francesca made her comfortable again. 'Have you had chicken-pox?' He glanced at Francesca.

'Me? Oh, yes, years ago; so has Lucy.'

'And so have I, and now so has Peggy.' He took the small, limp hand in his. 'You'll feel better very soon, Peggy. Everyone has chicken-pox, you know, but it only lasts a few days. You will take the medicine Francesca will give you and then you'll sleep as soundly as Tom and in the morning I'll come and see you again.'

'I don't want Mummy to come home—'

'Well, love, there really is no need. Francesca will look after you, and as soon as you feel better we'll decide what is to happen next, shall we?' He kissed the hot little head. 'Lucy will come and sit with you until Francesca brings your medicine. *Tot ziens.*'

Peggy managed a watery smile and said, *'Tot ziens.'*

In the sitting-room Francesca asked anxiously, 'She's not ill, is she? I mean, ill enough to let her mother know? She said she didn't want to be—that is, there was no need to ring her unless there was something serious.'

When he didn't answer she added, 'I'm sorry if I was rude on the phone; I was worried and I thought you were away.'

'Now why should you think that?'

'You said you were going to Cheltenham.'

'As indeed I did go.' He was writing a prescription as he spoke. 'Don't worry, Peggy is quite all right. She has a temperature but, having chicken-pox, that is only to be expected. Get this tomorrow morning and see that she takes it three times a day.' He took a bottle from his bag and shook out a tablet. 'This will dissolve in hot milk; it will make her more comfortable and she should sleep.'

He closed his bag and stood up. 'I'll call in on my way to the hospital in the morning, but if you're worried don't hesitate to phone me; I'll come at once.' At the door he turned. 'And don't worry about her mother. I'll be seeing her again in a day or so and then I can reassure her.'

Francesca saw him to the door and wished him a polite goodnight. If it hadn't been imperative that she should see to Peggy at once, she would have gone somewhere quiet and had a good cry. She wasn't sure why she wanted to do this and there really wasn't time to think about it.

Peggy slept all night and Francesca was up and dressed and giving the little girl a drink of lemonade when the professor arrived. He was in flannels and a thick sweater and he hadn't shaved, and she said at once, 'You've been up all night.'

'Not quite all of it. How is Peggy?'

They went to look at her together and he pronounced himself content with her progress. There were more spots now, of course, but her temperature was down a little and she greeted him cheerfully enough. 'Anything in moderation if she's hungry,' he told Francesca, 'and get the elixir started as soon as you can.'

'Thank you for coming. Lucy's made tea—we haven't had our breakfast yet. You'll have a cup?'

He refused pleasantly. 'I must get home and shower and change; I've an out-patients clinic at ten o'clock.'

She opened the door onto a chilly morning.

'I'll look in some time this evening.' He was gone with a casual nod.

It was late in the afternoon when Francesca had a phone call from Peggy's grandmother in Wiltshire. It was a nice, motherly voice with no hint of fussing. 'Renier telephoned. Poor little Peggy, but we are so glad to know that she is being so well looked after. I suppose you haven't heard from her mother?'

'Well, no, the professor said that he would be seeing her and that there was no need to let her know. Peggy is feeling much better and he is looking after her so well, so please don't be anxious.'

'She's our only grandchild and so like our son. He was Renier's friend, you know. They were at university together and school together—he was best man at their wedding and is godfather to Peggy.'

'Would you like to speak to Peggy? She's awake. I'll carry her across to the other bedroom; there's a phone there...'

'That would be delightful. Shall I ring off or wait?'

'If you would wait—I'll be very quick...'

The conversation went on for some time, with Peggy on Francesca's lap, talking non-stop and getting too excited. Presently Francesca whispered, 'Look, Peggy, ask Granny if you can telephone her each day about teatime, and if she says "yes" say goodbye now.'

A satisfactory arrangement for all parties.

The professor came in the evening, once more the epitome of the well-dressed gentleman. He was coolly polite to Francesca, spent ten minutes with Peggy, who was tired and a little peevish now, pronounced himself satisfied and, after only the briefest of conversations, went away again.

'No need to come in the morning,' he observed, 'but I'll take a look about this time tomorrow.'

The next day he told Francesca that Peggy might get up in her dressing-gown and roam the house.

'Keep her warm, she needs a week or so before she goes back to school. You're dealing with the spots, aren't you? She mustn't scratch.'

The next day he told her that he would be seeing Eloise on the following day.

'How nice,' said Francesca tartly. 'I'm sure you will be able to reassure her. Peggy's granny has been phoning each afternoon; she sounds just like a granny...' A silly remark, she realised, but she went on, 'Peggy's very fond of her.'

'Yes, I know. I shall do my best to persuade Eloise to let her go and stay with her for a few days. You will have to go too, of course.'

'But what about Lucy?'

'I imagine that it could be arranged for her to board for a week or so? Eloise will pay, of course. Would Lucy mind?'

'I think she would love it...but it will be quite an expense.'

'Not for Eloise, and Peggy will need someone with her.'

'What about Tom?'

'I'm sure that her grandmother will make him welcome. I'll let you know.'

He made his usual abrupt departure.

'Most unsatisfactory,' said Francesca to the empty room. She told Lucy, of course, who found it a marvellous idea. 'They have such fun, the boarders—and almost all of my friends are boarders. Do you suppose Mrs Vincent will pay for me?'

'Professor Pitt-Colwyn seemed to think she would. He's going to let me know...'

'Well, of course,' said Lucy airily. 'If they're in love they'll do anything to please each other. I bet you anything that he'll be back in a few days with everything arranged.'

She was right. Several days later he arrived at teatime, just as they were sitting on the floor in front of the fire, toasting crumpets.

Peggy, no longer spotty but decidedly pasty-faced, rushed to meet him.

'Where have you been? I missed you. Francesca and Lucy missed you too.'

He picked her up and kissed her. 'Well, now I'm here, may I have a cup of tea and one of those crumpets? There's a parcel in the hall for you, too.' He put her down. 'Run and get it; it's from your mother.'

'Will you have a cup of tea?' asked Francesca in a hostess voice and, at his mocking smile and nod, went on, 'Peggy seems to be quite well again, no temperature for three days, but she's so pale…'

She came into the room then with the parcel and began to unwrap it without much enthusiasm. A doll— a magnificent creature, elaborately dressed.

'How very beautiful,' said Francesca. 'You must give her a name. What a lovely present from Mummy.'

'She's like all my other dolls and I don't like any of them. I like my teddy and Tom.' Peggy put the doll carefully on a chair and climbed on to the professor's lap. 'I had a crumpet,' she told him, 'but I can have some of yours, can't I?'

'Provided you don't drip butter all over me and Francesca allows it.'

Francesca passed a large paper serviette over without a word, and poured the fresh tea Lucy had made. That young lady settled herself on the rug before the fire once again and sank her teeth into a crumpet.

'Do tell,' she said. 'Is—?' She caught the professor's eye. 'Oh, yes, of course,' and went on airily, 'Did you have a nice time wherever you went?'

The professor, who had spent exactly twenty-four hours in Birmingham—a city he disliked—only four of which had been in Eloise's company, replied blandly that indeed he had had a most interesting time, as he had a flying visit to Edinburgh and, since heart transplants had often to be dealt with at the most awkward of hours, an all-night session there and, upon his return, another operation in the early hours of the morning at Regent's. Francesca, unaware of this, of course, allowed her imagination to run riot.

She said waspishly, 'I expect a man in your position can take a holiday more or less when he likes. Have another crumpet?'

He took one and allowed Peggy to bite from it before demolishing it.

'There are no more crumpets, I'm afraid,' said Francesca coldly, 'but there is plenty of bread. I can make toast…'

He was sitting back with his eyes closed. 'Delicious—well buttered and spread with Marmite. You know the way to a man's heart, Francesca.'

He opened one eye and smiled at her, but she pretended not to see that and went away to fetch some bread and a pot of Marmite. She put the kettle on again too, foreseeing yet another pot of tea.

The other three were talking about Christmas and

laughing a great deal when she got back, and it wasn't until he had at last eaten everything he had been offered that he exchanged a glance with Lucy, who got up at once. 'Peggy! Help me take everything into the kitchen, will you, and we'll wash up? You can have an apron and do the washing; I'll dry.'

Peggy scrambled off the professor's knee. 'You'll not go away?'

'No. What is more, if I'm allowed to, I'll stay until you're in your bed.'

Left alone with him, Francesca cast around in her head for a suitable topic of conversation and came up with, 'Did Mrs Vincent give you any messages for me?'

'None. She thinks it a splendid idea that Peggy should go to her grandmother's for a week or so and that you will go with her. She is quite willing to pay for Lucy to stay at school during that time since she is inconveniencing you. She has asked me to make the arrangements and deal with the travelling and payment of bills and so forth. Oh, and she wishes Mrs Wells to come each day as usual while you're away.'

'Tom Kitten...?'

'He can surely go with you; I can't imagine that Peggy will go without him.'

'No. I'm sure she wouldn't. You reassured Mrs Vincent about Peggy not being well? She's not worried?'

The professor had a brief memory of Eloise's pretty face turning petulant at the threat of her new, exciting life being disrupted. 'No,' he said quietly. 'She is content to leave Peggy in your charge.'

'When are we to go?'

'Sunday morning. That gives you three days in which to pack and leave everything as you would wish it here. I'll telephone Mrs Vincent and talk to her about it; I know that she will be delighted.'

'It won't be too much work for her?'

'She and Mr Vincent have plenty of help. Besides, they love Peggy.'

'Am I to ask Lucy's headmistress if she can board for a week or two?'

'I'll attend to that as well.'

Lucy and Peggy came back then. 'I've washed up,' piped Peggy importantly, 'and now I'm going to have a bath and go to bed. I'll be so very very quick and if you like you can see where my spots were.'

'I look forward to that,' he assured her gravely. 'In ten minutes' time.'

He went as soon as Peggy, bathed and in her nightgown, had solemnly shown him the faint scars from her spots and then bidden him a sleepy goodnight.

His goodbyes were brief, with the remark that he would telephone some time on Saturday to make final arrangements for Sunday.

Lucy was over the moon; she was popular at school and had many friends and, although she had never said so, Francesca was aware that she would like to have been a boarder, and, as for Peggy, when she was told there was no containing her excitement. Something of their pleasure rubbed off on to Francesca and she found herself looking forward to the visit. The future seemed uncertain: there was still no word from Mrs Vincent, although Peggy had had a postcard from Carlisle. There had been no message on it, merely a scrawled, 'Hope you are being a good girl, love Mummy.'

Francesca's efforts to get Peggy to make a crayon drawing for her mother or buy a postcard to send to her came to nought. She wrote to Mrs Vincent's solicitor, enclosing a letter to her and asking him to forward it. She gave a faithful account of Peggy's progress and enclosed an accurate rendering of the money she had spent from the housekeeping allowance, assured her that the little girl was quite well again and asked her to let her know if there was anything special she wished done. The solicitor replied immediately; he understood from Mrs Vincent that it was most unlikely that she would be returning home for some time and Miss Haley was to do whatever she thought was best for Peggy. It wasn't very satisfactory, but Francesca realised that she would have to make the best of it. At least she could call upon the professor again if anything went wrong, and, now that they were going to stay with Peggy's grandparents for a while, they would surely accept responsibility for the child.

The professor telephoned quite early on Saturday morning; he would take Lucy to her school and at the same time have a word with the headmistress. 'Just to make sure that everything is in order,' he explained in what Francesca described to herself as his soothing voice.

'Should I go with you?' she wanted to know.

'No need. I dare say you've already had a few words with her.'

Francesca, feeling guilty, said that yes, she had.

'Just about her clothes and so on,' she said placatingly, and was answered by a mocking grunt.

He arrived on the doorstep in the afternoon with Brontes sitting on the back seat, greeted her with casual civility, assured Peggy that he would take her to her granny's in the morning, waited while Lucy bade Francesca goodbye at some length and then drove her away, refusing politely to return for tea. 'I'm expecting a call from Eloise,' he explained, watching Francesca's face.

Lucy telephoned in the evening; she sounded happy and any doubts that Francesca might have had about her sister's feeling homesick were swept away. She promised to phone herself when they arrived at Peggy's grandparents' house and went away to finish packing.

The professor arrived in time for coffee which Mrs Wells, who had popped round to take the keys and lock up, had ready. He was in an affable mood, answering Peggy's questions with patience while Brontes brooded in a kindly fashion over Tom. Francesca drank her coffee and had nothing to say, conscious that just having the professor there was all she wanted; he annoyed her excessively at times and she didn't think that he liked her overmuch but, all the same, when he was around she felt that there was no need for her to worry about anything. The future was vague—once Mrs Vincent came home she would be out of work again—but then in the meantime she was saving almost every penny of her wages and she liked her job. Moreover, she had become very fond of Peggy.

Rather to her surprise, she was told to sit in the front of the car. 'Brontes will take care of Peggy,' said the professor. 'Tom can sit in the middle in his basket.'

She stayed prudently silent until they joined the M4 where he put a large, well-shod foot down and allowed the car to slide past everything else in the fast lane. 'Just where are we going?' she asked a shade tartly.

'Oh, dear, did I not tell you? But you do know Wiltshire?' When she nodded he added, 'Just on the other side of the Berkshire border. Marlborough is the nearest town. The village is called Nether Tawscombe. They live in the Old Rectory, a charming old place.'

'You've been there before?'

He laughed shortly. 'I spent a number of school holidays there with Jeff and later, when we were at Cambridge and medical school, we spent a good deal of time there.'

'Then he got married,' prompted Francesca.

'Yes. Eloise was never happy there; she dislikes the country.'

Something in his voice stopped her from saying anything more; she turned round to see how the occupants of the back seat were getting on. Peggy had an arm round Brontes's great neck, she had stuck the fingers of her other hand through the mesh in front of Tom's basket and wore an expression of happiness which turned her plain little face into near prettiness. Francesca, who had had secret doubts about the visit, knew that she had been mistaken.

They arrived at Nether Tawscombe in time for lunch. The one village street was empty under the thin, wintry sunshine, but the houses which lined it looked charming. They got larger as the street went uphill until it reached the church, surrounded by a church-yard and ringed around by fair-sized houses. The Old Rectory was close by; an open gate led to a low, ram-bling house with diamond-paned windows and a solid front door.

As the professor stopped before it, it was opened and an elderly man came to meet them. She stood a little on one side until Peggy's excited greetings were over and the two men had shaken hands. She was led indoors while the professor saw to their baggage. The hall was stone-flagged, long and narrow, with a door opening on to the garden at the back of the house at its end. Brontes had made straight for it and had been joined by a black Labrador, who had rushed out of an open doorway as a grey-haired lady, cosily plump, had come into the hall.

Peggy screamed with delight and flung herself at her grandmother, and Mr Vincent said to Francesca, 'Always had a soft spot for each other—haven't had her to stay for a long time. This is delightful, Miss—er…?'

'Would you call me Francesca, please? Peggy does.'

Mrs Vincent came to take her hand then, with a warmth which caused sudden tears to prick her eye-lids, for the last few years she had been without that kindly warmth…

That the professor was an old friend and welcome guest was evident: he hugged Mrs Vincent, asked which rooms the bags were to go to, and went up the wide staircase with the air of a man who knew his way about blindfold.

Mrs Vincent saw Francesca's eyes follow him and said comfortably, 'We've known Renier for many years. He and our son were friends; he spent many a school holiday here and Jeff went over to Holland. He's a good man, but I suspect you've discovered that for yourself, Miss…may I call you Francesca?'

'Oh, yes, please. What would you like me to do? Take Peggy upstairs and tidy her for lunch? She's so happy and excited.'

'Yes, dear. You do exactly what you've been doing. We know so little about her day-to-day life now that her father is dead—he brought her here very often, you see.'

No mention of Eloise, reflected Francesca. It wasn't her business, of course. She bore Peggy away upstairs to a couple of low-ceilinged rooms with a communicating door and windows overlooking the wintry garden beyond. After London, even the elegant part of London, it was sheer bliss.

The professor stayed to lunch and she was mystified to hear him say that no, he wasn't going back to London.

'Having a quiet weekend at Pomfritt Cleeve? Splendid,' observed Mr Vincent, and most annoyingly said no more about it.

Renier took his leave soon after lunch, saying goodbye to Francesca last of all, patting her shoulder in an avuncular fashion and remarking casually that he would probably see her at some time. She stood in the hall with everyone else, wishing with all her heart that she were going with him. For that was where she wanted to be, she realised with breathtaking surprise, with him all the time, forever and ever, and, now she came to think about it, she had been in love with him for quite some time, only she had never allowed herself to think about it. Now he was going; not that that would make any difference—he had always treated her at best with friendliness, more often than not with an uninterested politeness. She looked away so that she didn't see him go through the door.

However sad the state of her heart, she had little time to brood over it. Peggy was a different child, behaving like any normal six-year-old would behave, playing endless games with the Labrador and Tom, racing around the large garden with Francesca in laughing pursuit, going for rides on the elderly donkey who lived in the paddock behind the house, going to the shops in Marlborough with her grandmother and Francesca. She had quickly acquired a splendid appetite and slept the moment her small head touched the pillow. A good thing too, thought Francesca, for by bedtime she was tired herself. She loved her days in the quiet village and Mr and Mrs Vincent treated her like a daughter. Sometimes she felt guilty that she should be living so comfortably while Lucy was in London, although she thought that her sister, from all accounts, was as happy as she was herself. They missed each other, but Francesca had the sense to see that it was good for Lucy to learn independence. She tried not to think of the professor too often and she felt that she was succeeding, until after a week or so Lucy wrote her usual letter and mentioned that he had been to see her at the school and had taken her out to tea. 'To the Ritz, no less!' scrawled Lucy, with a lot of exclamation marks.

The professor, having returned Lucy to her school, went to his home and sat down in his great chair by the fire with Brontes pressed against his knee and mother cat and the kittens asleep in their basket to keep him company. Tea with Lucy had been rewarding and he had made no bones about asking questions, although he had put them in such a way that she hadn't been aware of how much she was telling him. Indeed, she had confided in him that her headmistress had offered her a place in a group of girls from her class going to Switzerland for a skiing holiday. 'But of course I can't go,' she had told him. 'It's a lot of money and Fran couldn't possibly afford it—I mean, we both have to have new winter coats, and if Mrs Vincent comes back we'll have to move again, won't we?'

He had agreed with her gravely, at the same time prising out as much information about the trip as he could. He stroked Brontes's great head. 'I shall have to pay another visit to Eloise,' he told the dog. 'Now how can I fit that in next week?'

Presently he picked up the telephone on the table beside him and dialled a number.

A week, ten days went by. Peggy was so happy that Francesca began to worry about their return; she saw that the child loved her grandparents and they in turn loved her. They didn't spoil her, but she was treated with a real affection which Francesca felt she had never had from her mother. One morning when Peggy had gone off with her grandfather, leaving Francesca to catch up on the washing and ironing of the child's wardrobe, Mrs Vincent came to sit with her in the little room behind the kitchen where the ironing was done. 'You must be wondering why we don't mention Peggy's mother. Oh, I know we talk about her because Peggy must not forget her mother, but you see Eloise never wanted her and when she was born she turned against her—you see she takes after my son, and Eloise was so pretty. She said that her friends would laugh at such an ugly child. It upset Jeff, but she was fortunate—he was a loyal husband; he took Peggy around with him as much as possible and they adored each other. It was a pity that Peggy overheard her mother telling someone one day that she wished the child had not been born. She never told her father, bless the child, but she did tell Mrs Wells, who told me. There is nothing I would like better than to have Peggy to live with us always.'

'Have you suggested it to Eloise?'

'No; you see she will probably marry again and he might like to have Peggy for a daughter.'

Francesca thought Mrs Vincent was talking about the professor. She said woodenly, 'Yes, I dare say that would be very likely.'

It seemed as though it might be true, for the very next day he arrived just as they were sitting down to lunch.

Francesca, going out to the kitchen to ask Bertha, the housekeeper, if she could grill another few chops for their unexpected guest, was glad of her errand: it gave her time to assume the politely cool manner she could hide behind. It was difficult to maintain it,

though, for when she got back to the dining-room it
was to hear him telling the Vincents that he was on
his way to see Eloise. 'I shall be glad of a word with
you, sir,' he told Mr Vincent, 'as my visit concerns
Peggy, and I think you should know why I am going.'

Francesca ate her chop—sawdust and ashes in her
mouth. Afterwards she couldn't remember eating it;
nor could she remember what part she took in the conversation during the meal. It must have been normal,
for no one looked at her in surprise. She couldn't wait
for the professor to be gone, and as though he knew
that he sat over coffee, teasing Peggy and having a
perfectly unnecessary conversation with Mrs Vincent
about the uses of the old-fashioned remedies she used
for minor ailments.

He got up at length and went away with Mr Vincent
to the study, to emerge half an hour later and, amid a
great chorus of goodbyes, take his leave.

This time Francesca watched him go; when next she
saw him he would most likely be engaged to Eloise—
even married. She was vague about special licences
but, the professor being the man he was, she had no
doubt that if he wished to procure one at a moment's
notice he would find a way to do so.

It was three days later when Mr Vincent remarked
to his wife, 'Renier phoned. He has got his way. He's
back in London, but too busy to come down and see
us for a few days.'

Mrs Vincent beamed. 'Tell me later—how delightful; he must be very happy.' Francesca, making a Plas-
ticine cat for Peggy, did her best to feel happy, because he was happy, and one should be glad to know

that someone one loved was happy, shouldn't one? She found it hard work.

He came at the end of the week, walking in unannounced during a wet afternoon. He looked tired; he worked too hard, thought Francesca lovingly, scanning the weary lines on his handsome face. He also looked smug—something she found hard to understand.

CHAPTER FIVE

RENIER HAD HAD LUNCH, he assured Mrs Vincent, before going with Mr Vincent to the study again. When they came back into the sitting-room the older man said, 'Well, my dear, it's all settled. Which of us shall tell Peggy?'

'What?' asked Peggy, all ears. 'Is—is it something nice? Like I can stay here forever?'

'You clever girl to guess,' said Mrs Vincent, and gave her a hug. 'That's exactly what you are going to do—live here with Grandpa and me and go to school every day.'

Peggy flung herself at her grandfather. 'Really, truly? I may stay here with you? I won't have to go back to Mummy? She doesn't want me, you know.'

'Well, darling, your mummy is a very busy person and being on stage is very hard work. You can go and see her whenever you want to,' said Mrs Vincent.

'Shan't want to. Where will Francesca go?'

Francesca went on fixing a tail to another cat and didn't look up. 'If there is no objection, I think it might be a good idea if I took her somewhere quiet and explained everything to her,' said the professor.

He added gently, 'Get your coat, Francesca, and come with me.'

'Now that is a good idea,' said Mrs Vincent. 'Run along, dear; Renier will explain everything to you so much better than we can.'

There was no point in refusing; she fetched her old Burberry and went out to the car with him, to be greeted with pleasure by Brontes, who was roaming the garden. The professor opened the door and stuffed her gently into her seat, got in beside her and, with Brontes's great head wedged between their shoulders, drove off.

'Where am I going?' asked Francesca coldly.

'Pomfritt Cleeve. I have a cottage there. We can talk quietly.'

'What about? Surely you could have told me at Mrs Vincent's house?'

'No, this concerns you as well as Peggy.'

He had turned off the main road into a narrow, high-hedged lane going downhill, and presently she saw a cluster of lights through the gathering dusk. A minute or so later they had reached the village—one street with a church halfway along, a shop or two, and small, old cottages, well maintained—before he turned into another narrow lane, and after a hundred yards or so drove through a propped-open gate and stopped before a thatched cottage of some size. There were lights in the windows and the door was thrown open as she got out of the car, hesitating for a moment, giving Brontes time to rush through the door with a delighted bark, almost knocking down the stout little lady standing there. She said, 'Good doggie,' in a soft, West Country voice and then added, 'Come on in out of the cold, sir, and the young lady. There's a good fire in the sitting-room and tea in ten minutes.'

The professor flung an arm around her cosy person and kissed her soundly. 'Blossom, how very nice to see you again—and something smells delicious.'

He caught Francesca gently by the arm. 'Francesca, this is Blossom, who lives here and looks after the cottage for me. Blossom, this is Miss Haley. Take her away so that she can tidy herself if she wants to, and we'll have tea in ten minutes, just as you say.'

The cottage, decided Francesca, wasn't a cottage really. It might look like one, but it was far too big to warrant such a name, although there was nothing grand about it. The sitting-room to which she was presently shown was low-ceilinged with comfortable chairs and tables dotted around on the polished floor. There was a low table before the fire and sofas on either side of it. She sat opposite her host, pouring tea into delicate china cups and eating scones warm from the oven and, having been well brought up, made light conversation.

However, not for long. 'Let us dispense with the small talk,' said the professor, 'and get down to facts. Eloise is quite happy to allow Peggy to live with her grandparents. She will of course be free to see the child whenever she wishes, but she will remarry very shortly and intends to stay on the stage, so it isn't likely that she will visit Peggy more than once in a while. Mrs Vincent will employ her old nanny's daughter to look after Peggy, so you may expect to leave as soon as she arrives.' Francesca gave a gasp, but he went on, 'Don't interrupt, I have not yet finished. Lucy has been told that she may join a school party going to Switzerland to ski—I have seen her headmistress and she will join the party.'

'Now look here,' said Francesca, and was hushed once more.

'I haven't said anything to you, for I knew that you would refuse to do anything about it. The child deserves a holiday and, as for the costs, you can repay me when you are able.'

'But I haven't got a job,' said Francesca wildly. 'I never heard such arrogance—going behind my back and making plans and arranging things—'

'Ah, yes, as to arrangements for yourself, Eloise is quite agreeable to your remaining at the cottage for a few days so that you can pack your things.'

She goggled at him, bereft of words. That she loved him dearly went without saying, but at the moment she wished for something solid to throw at him. 'You have been busy, haven't you?' she said nastily.

'Yes, indeed I have. I shall drive Lucy over to Zeebrugge to meet the school party there; you would like to come with us, no doubt.'

'How can I? I'll have to look for a job—'

'Well, as to that, I have a proposal to make.' He was sitting back, watching her, smiling faintly.

'Well, I don't want to hear it,' she declared roundly. 'I shan't listen to anything more you may say—'

'Perhaps this isn't the right time, after all. You are cross, are you not? But there is really nothing you can do about it, is there? You will break young Lucy's heart if you refuse to let her go to Switzerland—'

'She had no skiing clothes.'

'Now she has all she needs—a Christmas present.'

She all but ground her teeth. 'And I suppose you're going to get married?'

'That is my intention.'

Rage and despair almost choked her, and she allowed rage to take over.

'I hope you will be very happy.' Her voice was icy and not quite steady.

'I am certain of that.'

'I'd like to go back.' He agreed at once, which was a good thing—otherwise she might have burst into tears. Where was she to go? And there was Lucy to think of when she got back from Switzerland. Would she have time to get a job by then? And would her small hoard of money be sufficient to keep them until she had found work again? There were so many questions to be answered. Perhaps she should have listened to this proposal he had mentioned—it could have been another job—but pride wouldn't allow her to utter another word. She bade Blossom goodbye, complimented her on her scones and got into the car; it smelled comfortingly of leather and, very faintly, of Brontes.

Strangely enough, the great bulk of the professor beside her was comforting too, although she could think of no good reason why it should be.

Back at the Vincent's house after a silent drive, he bade them goodbye, bent his great height to Peggy's hug, observed cheerfully to Francesca that he would be in touch, and left.

She had no idea what he had said to the Vincents, but from what they said she gathered that they understood her to have a settled future, and there seemed no point in enlightening them. Peggy, chattering excitedly as Francesca put her to bed, seemed to think that she would see her as often as she wanted, and Francesca said nothing to disillusion her. The future was her own problem.

She left the Vincents two days later, and was driven back to the mews cottage by Mr Vincent. She hated leaving the quiet village. Moreover, she had grown very fond of Peggy who, even while bidding her a tearful goodbye, was full of plans to see her again, which were seconded by her grandmother. She had responded suitably and kept up a cheerful conversation with her companion as they drove but, once he had left her at the empty house, with the observation that they would be seeing each other shortly, she sat down in the kitchen and had a good cry. She felt better after that, made a cup of tea, and unpacked before starting on the task of re-packing Lucy's cases as well as her own. There had been a brief letter for her before she left the Vincents', telling her that they would be crossing over to Zeebrugge in two days' time, and would she be ready to leave by nine o'clock in the morning and not a minute later?

Mrs Wells had kept the place spotless, and there was a note on the kitchen table saying that she would come in the morning; there was a little ironing and nothing else to do but pack. She was halfway through that when Lucy phoned.

'You're back. Isn't it exciting? I can't believe it's true. I'm coming home tomorrow afternoon. The bus leaves here in the evening, but Renier says he'll take us to Zeebrugge early the next day and I can join the others there. Isn't he a darling?' She didn't wait for Francesca's answer, which was just as well. 'Oh, Fran, I do love being a boarder. I know I can't be, but you have no idea what fun it is. I've been asked to lots of parties at Christmas, too.'

Francesca let her talk. There was time enough to worry over the problem of Christmas; she still had almost three weeks to find a job and somewhere for them to live, too.

'You're very quiet,' said Lucy suddenly.

'I've had a busy day; I'm packing for us both now—I'll do the rest tomorrow. I've got to talk to Mrs Wells, too.'

'I'll help you. You are looking forward to the trip, aren't you?'

'Tremendously,' said Francesca with her fingers crossed. 'See you tomorrow, Lucy.'

By the time Lucy arrived, she had done everything that was necessary. Mrs Wells had been more than helpful, arranging to come early in the morning to take the keys and lock up. The solicitor had been dealt with, she had been to the bank and taken out as much money as she dared, found their passports—unused since they had been on holiday in France with their parents—and, finally, written a letter to Mrs Vincent which she had enclosed in a letter to the solicitor. There was nothing more to do but have a good gossip and go to bed.

The Bentley purred to a halt outside the cottage at precisely nine o'clock, then the professor got out, wished them an affable good-morning, put Francesca's overnight bag and Lucy's case in the boot, enquired as to what had been done with the rest of their luggage—safely with Mrs Wells—and urged them to get in. 'You go in front, Lucy,' said Francesca and nipped into the back seat, not seeing his smile, and resolutely looked out of the window all the way to Dover, trying not to listen to the cheerful talk between the other two.

Five hours later they were in Zeebrugge, driving to the hotel where the rest of the party had spent the night, and it was only then that she realised that she had no idea what was to happen next. There wasn't any time to think about it; the bus was ready to leave. It was only after a hasty goodbye to Lucy, when she was watching the party drive away, that the full awkwardness of the situation dawned upon her. 'Whatever am I going to do?' She had turned on the professor, her voice shrill with sudden fright. 'When is there a boat back?'

He took her arm. 'We are going to my home in Holland for the night. My mother will be delighted to meet you.'

'I must get back—I have to find a job.'

He took no notice, merely urged her gently into the car, got in beside her and drove off.

'This is ridiculous…I've been a fool—I thought we would be going straight back. I'm to spend the night at Mrs Wells's house.'

'We will telephone her.' His voice was soothing as well as matter-of-fact. 'We shall soon be home.'

They were already through Brugge and on the motorway, bypassing Antwerp, crossing into Holland, and racing up the Dutch motorways to Tilburg, Nijmegen and on past Arnhem. The wintry afternoon was turning to an early dusk and, save for a brief halt for coffee and sandwiches, they hadn't stopped. Francesca, trying to make sense of the situation, sat silent, her mind addled with tiredness and worry and a deep-seated misery, because once they were back in England there would be no reason to see the professor ever again. The thought cast her in such deep gloom that she barely noticed the country had changed; the road ran through trees and thick shrubbery with a light glimpsed here and there. The professor turned off the road through a gateway, slowed along a narrow, sanded drive and stopped before the house at its end. He leaned over, undid her safety belt, got out and helped her out too, and she stood for a moment, looking at the dark bulk of the house. It was square and solid, its big windows lighted, frost sparkling on the iron balcony above the porch.

She said in a forlorn voice, 'I should never have come with you. I should never have let you take over my life, and Lucy's, too. I'm very grateful for your help; you have been kind and I expect it suited you and Eloise. I can't think why you've brought me here.'

'You wouldn't listen to my proposal at Pomfritt Cleeve,' the professor had come very close, 'I can see that I shall have to try again.' He put his arms around her and held her very close. 'You are a stubborn, proud girl with a beautiful head full of muddled thoughts, and I love you to distraction. I fell in love with you the first time I saw you, and what is all this nonsense about Eloise? I don't even like the woman, but something had to be done about Peggy. Now you will listen, my darling, while I make you a proposal. Will you marry me?'

What with his great arms around her and her heart thumping against her ribs, Francesca hadn't much breath—only just enough to say, 'Yes, oh, yes, Renier,' before he bent to kiss her.

A CHRISTMAS WISH

CHAPTER ONE

THE dim and dusty Records Office, tucked away in the depths of the hospital, was hardly a cheerful place in which to work, but the girl going back and forth between the long rows of shelves sounded cheerful enough, singing a medley of tunes as she sorted the folders into their right places with the ease of long practice.

She was a tall girl with a splendid shape, a beautiful face and a head of tawny hair which glowed under the neon lights, wearing a blouse and skirt and a cardigan which, although well-fitting, lacked any pretensions to high fashion.

Presently, her arms full, she went to the table against one of the whitewashed walls and laid them down, still singing—quite loudly since there was nobody there but herself, and she was far from the busy wards. 'Oh, what a beautiful morning...' she trilled, very slightly out of tune, and then stopped as the door was opened.

The door was a long way from the table; she had ample time to study the man coming towards her. He came unhurriedly, very tall and large in a beautifully tailored suit, fair hair already silver at the edges and a handsome face with heavy-lidded eyes. She hadn't seen him before, but then she seldom if ever went up to the hospital. When he was near enough she said cheerfully, 'Hello, do you want something?'

His good morning was uttered in a quiet voice. He laid a folder on the table. 'Yes, I asked for Eliza Brown's notes, not Elizabeth Brown's.'

'Oh, so sorry. I'll get them.' She picked up the discarded folder and went down one of the narrow passages between the shelves, found the folder, replaced the discarded one and went back to the table.

'Here it is. I hope it wasn't too inconvenient for you...'

'It was.' His voice was dry, and she went a little pink. 'Do you work here alone?'

'Me? Oh, no. Debbie has got the day off to go to the dentist.'

'And do you always sing as you work?'

'Why not? It's quiet down here, you know, and dim and dusty. If I didn't sing I might start screaming.'

'Then why not look for other employment?' He was leaning against the wall, in no hurry to be gone.

She gave him a tolerant look. 'We—that is, clerks and suchlike—are two a penny. Once we get a job we hang on to it...'

'Until you marry?' he suggested in his quiet voice.

'Well, yes.'

He picked up the folder. 'Thank you, Miss...?'

'Harding.' She smiled at him, for he seemed rather nice—a new member of the medical staff; a surgeon, since Mrs Eliza Brown was on the surgical landing. He nodded pleasantly and she watched him walk away; she wasn't likely to see him again. A pity, she reflected, making a neat pile of her folders ready for someone to fetch them from Outpatients.

The nurse from Outpatients was in a bad temper. Sister, she confided, was in a mood and there was no pleasing her, and the waiting-room was stuffed to the ceiling. 'And I've got a date this evening,' she moaned. 'At the rate we're going we'll be here all night, as well as all afternoon.'

'Perhaps Sister will have a date too,' comforted Miss Harding.

'Her? She's old—almost forty, I should think.'

The nurse flounced away, and was replaced almost at once by a tall, thin girl with a long face.

'Hi, Olivia.' She had a nice grin. 'How's trade? I want Lacey Cutter's notes. They're missing. I bet Debbie got our lot out yesterday—she may look like everyone's dream of a fairy on the Christmas tree, but she's not heart and soul in her job, is she?'

Olivia went across to the nearest shelf and began poking around. 'She's really rather a dear and so young... Here you are...'

'Well, you sound like her granny. She must be all of nineteen or so.'

'Twenty, and I'm twenty-seven—on the verge of twenty-eight.'

'Time you settled down. How's the boyfriend?'

'Very well, thank you. We'll have to wait for a bit, though.'

'That's rotten bad luck. I say, there's a new man on Surgical—a consultant all the way from somewhere or other in Holland—come to reorganise Mrs Brown's insides. It seems he's perfected a way of doing something or other; our Mr Jenks asked him here so that he can pick up some ideas.' She started for the door. 'He's nice.'

Olivia agreed silently. She didn't allow her thoughts to dwell upon him, though. For one thing she had too much to do and for another she had plenty of things—personal things—to think about. Rodney, for instance. She and Rodney had been friends for years, long before her father had died and left her mother poor, so that they had had to leave their home in Dorset and come to London to live with her grandmother in the small flat on the fringe of Islington. That had been four years ago, and Olivia had found herself a job almost at once to augment the two older ladies' income. It wasn't very well paid but, beyond an expensive education, she had no training of any sort and it was well within her scope. Indeed, after a couple of months she had realised that it was work which held no future, and longed to have the chance to train for something which would enable her to use her brain, but that was impossible. Making ends meet, even with her wages added, was a constant worry to her mother, and she couldn't add to that.

If her grandmother had been more amenable it might have been possible, but Mrs Fitzgibbon, having offered them a home, considered that she had done her duty and saw no reason to forgo her glass of sherry, her special tea from Fortnum and Mason, and her weekly visit to the hairdresser, with a taxi to take her there and back. She had sent away her daily cleaner too, saying that her daughter was quite capable of keeping the flat tidy, but graciously allowed a woman to come once a week to do the heavy housework.

It wasn't an ideal situation, but Olivia could see no way out of it. Nor could she see any chance of marrying Rodney, a rising young man on the Stock Exchange, who had reiterated time and again that once he had got his flat exactly as he wanted it, and bought a new car, they would marry. Four years, thought Olivia, sitting at the table eating sandwiches and drinking pale and tepid tea from a flask, and there's always something—and anyway, how can I marry him and leave Mother? She'll be Granny's slave.

The day's work came to an end and she got into her raincoat, tied a scarf over her glorious hair, locked the door and took the key along to the porter's lodge. She stood in the entrance for a moment, breathing in the chill of the evening, and made for the bus-stop.

It was an awkward journey to and from the hospital, and the buses at that time of day were packed. Olivia, her junoesque proportions squeezed between a stout matron carrying a bag full of things with sharp edges and a small, thin man with a sniff, allowed her thoughts to wander to the pleasanter aspects of life. New clothes—it was high time she had something different to wear when she went out with Rodney; a legacy from some unknown person; finding a treasure-trove in the tiny strip of garden behind her grandmother's flat; being taken out to dinner and dancing at one of the best hotels—the Savoy for instance—suitably dressed, of course, to eat delicious food and dance the night away. She realised with something of a shock that it wasn't Rodney's face on her imaginary

partner but that of the man who had asked why she
sang while she worked. This won't do, she told herself, and frowned so fiercely that the thin man recoiled.

The street where her grandmother had her flat was
suited to that old-fashioned word 'genteel'. The tiny
front gardens were all alike—laurel bushes, a strip of
grass and two steps leading to the front door behind
which was another smaller door, leading to the flat
above. All the windows had net curtains and, beyond
distant good mornings and good evenings, no one who
lived there spoke to anyone else.

Olivia hated it; she had spent the first year that they
were there planning ways of leaving it, but her mother
felt it to be her duty to stay with Granny since she had
offered them a home and Olivia, a devoted daughter,
found it impossible to leave her mother there though
she disliked it, she suspected, just as much as she did.

She got out her key, unlocked the door, and went
into the little hall, hung her outdoor things on the old-
fashioned oak stand and went through to the sitting-
room. Her mother looked up with a smile.

'Hello, love. Have you had a busy day?'

Olivia bent to kiss her cheek. 'Just nicely so,' she
said cheerfully, and crossed the small room to greet
her grandmother. Mrs Fitzgibbon was sitting very upright in a Regency mahogany open armchair with a
leather seat and wooden arms, by no means comfortable but the old lady had inherited it from her mother,
who had acquired it from some vague relation who
had been married to a baronet, a fact which seemed to
ensure its comfort from Mrs Fitzgibbon's point of
view. She said severely now, 'Really, Olivia, your hair

is badly in need of a brush, and is that plastic bag you're carrying really necessary? When I was a gel…'

Olivia interrupted her quickly. 'I called in at Mr Patel's as I got off the bus—he had some nice lettuces; you like a salad with your supper…'

She made a small comic face at her mother and went to her room—very small, just room for the narrow bed, the old-fashioned wardrobe and a small chest of drawers with an old-fashioned looking-glass on it. Rodney had phoned to say that he would come for her at around seven o'clock so she poked around, deciding what she would wear, and then, undecided, went to the kitchen to start the supper. Lamb chops, mashed potatoes and carrots. There were a couple of tomatoes in the fridge and a rather wizened apple. She contrived a small salad with the lettuce, laid the table in the poky dining-room beside the kitchen, and went to pour her grandmother's sherry. She poured a glass for her mother too, ignoring her grandmother's sharp look.

She went back to the kitchen and the phone rang. It was probably Rodney, to say that he would be earlier than they had arranged. She turned down the gas and went into the hall where the phone was. It *was* Rodney. His faintly pompous, 'Hello, Olivia,' sounded rather more so than usual, but it was one of the things she had decided didn't matter.

Her own 'hello' was cheerful. 'If you're coming earlier than you said, I won't be ready…'

'Well, as a matter of fact, I can't come, Olivia— something's turned up and I can't get away.'

'Oh, bad luck. Let's go out tomorrow instead.'

She felt faintly uneasy at his hesitancy. 'It's a long job,' he said finally, 'I may have to go away…'

She was instantly sympathetic. 'Big business and very hush-hush?' she wanted to know. 'Well, if it's going to give you a leg-up, I won't crumble. You don't know when you're going?'

'No, no, nothing's settled yet. I'll give you a ring. Can't stay any longer now.'

She was disappointed but still cheerful. 'Don't get overworked…' His goodbye interrupted her, and she put the phone down with the feeling that something was wrong. My imagination, she told herself, and went to stretch the supper to allow for another person and then tell her mother that she wouldn't be going out after all.

Her grandmother, listening, observed tartly, 'You can't rely on the young men of today. Rodney's eyes are too close together.'

Which was difficult to refute, for they were.

The week wore on. Debbie enlivened the days with her chatter, confiding with a good deal of giggling the carrying on of her various boyfriends, while Olivia patiently did most of the filing and hurriedly resorted Debbie's careless efforts.

'You ought to go out more often,' declared Debbie as they drank their mid-morning coffee. 'Never mind that Rodney of yours,' she added with an unconscious lack of concern, 'it would do him good. He ought to be taking you out somewhere every blessed moment he's free. Give him a ring and say you want to go out this evening; there's a smashing film on at the Odeon in Leicester Square.'

'He's not here. I mean he's had to go away—something to do with his firm.'

'Don't you know where he is?'

'No idea.'

'Ring wherever he works and ask for his address. He's not MI5 or anything hush-hush is he?'

'No—something in the Stock Exchange.'

Olivia got up and went back to the shelves with a pile of folders just as the door opened.

Here he was again, as elegant as she remembered him and as calm. She left Debbie to ask him if she could help him.

'Indeed you can. Once again I have here Mrs Elizabeth Brown's notes, but it is Mrs Eliza Brown who is my patient.'

Debbie beamed at him. 'Oh, sorry—that's me. I make mistakes all the time—only Olivia puts them right and covers up for me. It's a dull job, you know.'

'I can appreciate that.' He looked past her and wished Olivia a bland good morning. 'Olivia,' he added, and before she could answer that he said, 'And you, young lady, what is your name?'

'Debbie—what's yours? You aren't on the staff, are you? Have you come here to brush up your technique or something?'

'Or something?' He smiled a little. 'And my name is van der Eisler.'

'Foreign,' said Debbie. 'You wouldn't know it except you're on the large side. Got friends here?'

'Er, yes, I have.'

Olivia, feverishly seeking Mrs Eliza Brown's notes, clutched them thankfully and took them to him. He took them from her with a brief nod. 'I mustn't keep you from your work,' he observed. He sounded as though he had already dismissed them from his thoughts.

As he closed the door behind him Debbie said, 'Olivia, why did you hide? Isn't he great? A pity you found the notes just as I was going to suggest that he might like me to show him round the town.'

Olivia said sharply, 'You wouldn't, Debbie—he might be someone fearfully important.'

'Him? If he were, he wouldn't come down to this hole, would he? He'd send a nurse. I think he rather liked me.'

'Why not? You're pretty and amusing, and you can look small and helpless at the drop of a hat...'

'Yes, I know, but you're not just pretty, Olivia, you're beautiful. Even if you are—well, amply curved.'

Olivia laughed then. 'Yes, I know, and as strong as a horse. Even if I were to faint there wouldn't be any-one strong enough to pick me up off the floor.'

'He could—strong enough to carry a grand piano upstairs without a single puff...'

'I'm not a grand piano!' laughed Olivia. 'Look, we'd better get on, it's almost time for our dinner-break.'

They went to the canteen in turn and Debbie, going first, came back with disquieting news. 'You know that girl who works in the secretary's office?'

'Mary Gates,' said Olivia. 'What's happened to her—got engaged?'

'No, no. She told me something she'd overheard.

There's not enough money—they are planning to make redundancies—one's going to have to do the work of two. Olivia, supposing it's me who goes? Whatever shall I do? With Dad out of work, Mother's part-time job barely pays the rent.'

Olivia said matter-of-factly, 'Well, we don't know anything yet, do we? They could have been talking about another hospital—and I don't see how they could get rid of one of us.'

'Well, I do. You're too nice, Olivia. Do you suppose these people who sit around talking over super food and drink care a damn if they cut back on jobs, just as long as they can save some money for some pet scheme or other? We aren't people to them, just stat-stat...'

'Statistics,' supplied Olivia. 'Debbie, don't worry. If—and I say it's a big if—one of us is given the sack it will be me; they have to pay me more because I'm older. You're not yet twenty-one so you earn less.'

Debbie looked relieved and then asked, 'But what will you do?'

'Oh, I can turn my hand to anything,' said Olivia airily, and took herself off to the canteen. She shared a table with two clerks from Admissions, older than herself, competent, hard-working ladies both.

'There's a nasty rumour going round,' one of them said to Olivia as she sat down. 'They're cutting down, starting with the domestics and then us.'

'Is it just a rumour or for real?'

'We're to get letters tomorrow, warning us, and at the end of next week we shall get notes in our pay envelopes if we're to be made redundant.'

Olivia pushed shepherd's pie and two veg around the plate. Something would have to be done about Debbie. Her own wages would be missed at home, but they wouldn't starve and they had a roof over their heads whereas Debbie's family would be in sore straits. She ate prunes and custard, drank the strong tea, and went along to the secretary's office.

He wasn't there, but his PA was—a nice girl, who Olivia knew slightly. 'I want you to help me,' said Olivia in a no-nonsense voice.

She was listened to without interruption, then the PA said, 'I'll do my best—shall I say that you've got another job lined up? The hospital manager will be delighted; he's going to be very unpopular.'

Olivia went back to her work, and spent the rest of the day doing her best to reassure Debbie.

It was pay-day in the morning and, sure enough, everyone had a letter in their pay-packet, setting out the need to retrench, cut costs and improve hospital services.

'How will they do that if there aren't enough of us to go round?' demanded Debbie. 'I shan't dare tell my mum.'

'Not until next week,' cautioned Olivia. 'You haven't got the sack yet.'

The next week crawled to its end and Olivia opened her pay packet to find a note advising her that she had been given a week's notice. Although she had been fairly sure that she would be the one to go, it was still a blow—mitigated to a certain extent by Debbie's relief. 'Though how I'll manage on my own, I don't know,' she told Olivia. 'I'm always filing things wrong.'

'No, you aren't. Besides, you'll be extra careful now.'

'What about you? Have you got a job to go to?'

'Not yet, but we can manage quite well until I find something else. Look, Debbie, we've got next week—let's check the shelves together so that everything is OK before I go.'

She hadn't told her mother yet; that could wait until she had actually left. Thank heaven, she reflected, that it's spring. We can economise on the heating if only we can get Grandmother to co-operate, and not go round the flat turning on lights that aren't needed and switching on the electric fires and then forgetting them. It was, after all, her flat—something of which she reminded them constantly.

They worked like beavers during the next week, and although Olivia was glad that she need no longer work in the dreary underground room she was sorry to leave Debbie. She put a brave face on it, however, assured her that she had her eye on several likely jobs, collected her pay-packet for the last time and went home. The bus was as usual crowded, so she stood, not noticing her feet being trodden on, or the elderly lady with the sharp elbows which kept catching her in the ribs. She was regretting leaving without seeing that nice man who had been so friendly. Doubtless back in Holland by now, she thought, and forgotten all about us.

She waited until they had had their supper before she told her mother and grandmother that she had lost her job. Her mother was instantly sympathetic. 'Of course you'll find something else much nicer,' she said, 'and until you do we can manage quite well…'

Her grandmother wasn't as easy to placate. 'Well, what do you expect?' she wanted to know. 'You're not really trained for anything, and quite right too. No gel should have to go out to work—not people of our background…' Mrs Fitzgibbon, connected by marriage to the elderly baronet and his family who never took any notice of her, was inclined to give herself airs.

'All the same,' she went on, 'of course you must find something else at once. I, for one, have no intention of living in penury; heaven knows I have sacrificed a great deal so that both of you should have a home and comfort.' She stared at her granddaughter with beady eyes. 'Well, Olivia, perhaps that young man of yours will marry you now.'

'Perhaps he will,' said Olivia brightly, thinking to herself that perhaps he wouldn't—she hadn't heard from him for almost three weeks—and anyway, the last time they had been out together he had told her that he had his eye on a new car. The nasty thought that perhaps the new car might receive priority over herself crossed her mind. Rodney had never been over-loving, and she had told herself that it was because they had known each other for some time and his feelings had become a trifle dulled. Perhaps it was a good thing that they hadn't seen each other for a few weeks; he might look at her with new eyes and ask her to marry him. Something he had not as yet done, although there was a kind of unspoken understanding between them. Anyway, now was not the time to worry about that. A job was the first thing she must think about.

She had been given good references but it seemed that her skills as a filing-clerk weren't much in demand. She went out each day, armed with the details of suitable jobs culled from the newspapers, and had no luck at all; she couldn't use a word-processor; she had no idea how to work with a computer, and a cash register was a closed book as far as she was concerned. The week was almost up when Rodney phoned. He sounded—she thought for a word—excited, and she wondered why. Then he said, 'I want to talk to you, Olivia, can we meet somewhere? You know how it is if I come and see you at your grandmother's place...'

'Where do you suggest? I've things to tell you too.'

'Yes?' He didn't sound very interested. 'Meet me at that French place in Essex Road this evening. Seven o'clock.'

He rang off before she could agree.

He had sounded different she reflected as she went to tell her mother that she would be out that evening. Mrs Fitzgibbon, reading the newspaper by the window, put it down. 'And high time too,' she observed. 'Let us hope that he will propose.' She picked up her paper again, 'One less mouth to feed,' she muttered nastily.

Perhaps you get like that when you're old, thought Olivia, and gave her mother a cheerful wink. It was of no use getting annoyed, and she knew that her grandmother's waspish tongue was far kinder to her mother, an only daughter who had married the wrong man—in her grandmother's eyes at least—and it was because Olivia was more like her father than her mother that her grandmother disliked her. If she had been slender and graceful and gentle, like her mother, it might have been a different kettle of fish...

She dressed with care presently, anxious to look her best for Rodney. The jacket and skirt, even though they were four years old, were more or less dateless, as was the silk blouse which went with them. She didn't look too bad, she conceded to herself, studying her person in her wardrobe mirror, only she wished that she were small and dainty. She pulled a face at her lovely reflection, gave her hair a final pat, and bade her mother goodbye.

'Take a key,' ordered her grandmother. 'We don't want to be wakened at all hours.'

Olivia said nothing. She couldn't remember a single evening when Rodney hadn't driven her back well before eleven o'clock.

Perhaps, she mused, sitting in an almost empty bus, she and Rodney had known each other for too long. Although surely when you were in love that wouldn't matter? The thought that perhaps she wasn't in love with him took her breath. Of course she was. She was very fond of him; she liked him, they had enjoyed cosy little dinners in out of the way restaurants and had gone to the theatre together and she had been to his flat. Only once, though. It was by the river in a new block of flats with astronomical rents, and appeared to her to be completely furnished, although Rodney had listed a whole lot of things which he still had to have. Only then, he had told her, would he contemplate settling down to married life.

It was a short walk from the bus-stop and she was punctual but he was already there, sitting at a table for two in the corner of the narrow room. He got up when he saw her and said 'hello' in a hearty way, not at all in his usual manner.

She sat down composedly and smiled at him. 'Hello, Rodney. Was your trip successful?'

'Trip? What...? Oh, yes, very. What would you like to drink?'

Why did she have the feeling that she was going to need something to bolster her up presently? 'Gin and tonic,' she told him. A drink she disliked but Debbie, who knew about these things, had assured her once that there was nothing like it to pull a girl together.

Rodney looked surprised. 'That's not like you, Olivia.'

She didn't reply to that. 'Tell me what you've been doing, and why do you want to talk, Rodney? It's lovely to see you, but you sounded so—so urgent on the phone.'

He had no time to answer because the waiter handed them the menus and they both studied them. At least Olivia appeared to be studying hers, but actually she was wondering about Rodney. She asked for mushrooms in a garlic sauce and a Dover sole with a salad, and took a heartening sip of her drink. It was horrible but she saw what Debbie meant. She took another sip.

Their talk was trivial as they ate. Whatever it was Rodney had to tell her would doubtless be told over their coffee. He was an amusing companion, going from one topic to the next and never once mentioning his own work. Nor did he ask her about her own job or what she had been doing. She would tell him presently, she decided, and suppressed peevish surprise when he waved away the waiter with his trolley of desserts and ordered coffee. She was a girl with a healthy appetite and she had had her eye on the peach pavlova.

She poured the coffee and caught Rodney's eye. 'Well?' she asked pleasantly. 'Out with it, my dear. Have you been made redundant—I…'

'Olivia, we've known each other a long time—we've been good friends—you may even have expected us to marry. I find this very difficult to say…'

'Well, have a go!' she encouraged in a matter-of-fact voice which quite concealed her shock. 'As you say, we've been friends for a long time.'

'Perhaps you've guessed.' Rodney was having difficulty in coming to the point.

'Well, no, I can't say I have.'

'The truth is I haven't been away—I wanted to tell you but it was too difficult. I'm in love. We're going to be married very shortly…'

'Before you get your new car?' asked Olivia. Silly, but what else to say?

'Yes, yes, of course. She's worth a dozen new cars. She's wonderful.'

She looked at him across the table. Her grandmother was quite right: his eyes were too close together.

She smiled her sweetest smile. 'Why, Rodney, how could I possibly have thought such a thing? I'm thinking of getting married myself.'

'You could have told me…'

She gave him a limpid look. He looked awkward and added, 'What's he like? Has he got a good job? When are you getting married?'

'Handsome. He has a profession and we intend to marry quite soon. Enough about me, Rodney, tell me about the girl you're going to marry. Is she pretty? Dark? Fair?'

'Quite pretty. I suppose you'd call her fair. Her father's chairman of several big companies.'

'Now that is nice—a wife with money-bags.'

He looked astounded. 'Olivia, how can you say such a thing? We're old friends—I can't believe my ears.'

'Old friends can say what they like to each other, Rodney. If I stay here much longer I might say a great deal more, so I'll go.'

He got to his feet as she stood up. 'You can't,' he spluttered. 'I'll drive you back; it's the least I can do.'

'Don't be a pompous ass,' said Olivia pleasantly, and walked out of the bistro and started along the street to the bus-stop.

Sitting in the bus presently, she decided that her heart wasn't broken. Her pride had a nasty dent in it, though, and she felt a sadness which would probably turn into self-pity unless she did something about it. Of course it happened to thousands of girls, and she had to admit that she had thought of him as part of her pleasant life before her father had died, hoping that somehow or other she could turn back the clock by marrying him. She had been fond of him, accepted him as more than a friend, and although she had been in and out of love several times she had never given her whole heart; she had supposed that she would do that when they married.

'How silly can you get?' muttered Olivia, and the severe-looking couple sitting in front of her turned round to stare.

'I counted my chickens before they were hatched,' she told them gravely, and since it was her stop got off the bus.

'It must be the gin and tonic,' she said to herself. 'Or perhaps I'm in shock.' She unlocked the front door and went in. 'I'll make a strong cup of tea.'

The sitting-room door was half open. 'You're home early, darling,' said her mother. 'Is Rodney with you?'

Olivia poked her head round the door. 'I came home by bus. I'm going to make a cup of tea—would you like one?' She glanced across the room to her grandmother. 'And you, Granny?'

'You have refused him,' said Mrs Fitzgibbon accusingly. 'It is time you learnt on which side your bread is buttered, Olivia.'

'You're quite right, Granny, his eyes are too close together, and he's going to marry the daughter of a chairman of several large companies.'

'Do not be flippant, Olivia. What do you intend to do?'

'Put the kettle on and have a cup of tea,' said Olivia.

'You're not upset, darling?' asked her mother anxiously. 'We all thought he wanted to marry you.'

Olivia left the door and went to drop a kiss on her mother's cheek.

'I'm not a bit upset, love.' She spoke with matter-of-fact cheerfulness because her mother did look upset. Unlike her daughter she was a small, frail little woman, who had been cherished all her married life and was still bewildered by the lack of it, despite Olivia's care of her. 'I'll make the tea.'

She sat between the two of them presently, listening to her grandmother complaining about the lack of money, her lack of a job, and now her inability to get herself a husband. 'You're such a big girl,' observed Mrs Fitzgibbon snappily.

Olivia, used to this kind of talk and not listening to it, drank her tea and presently took herself off, washing the tea things in the kitchen, laying her grandmother's breakfast tray and their own breakfast, before she at last closed the door of her room.

Now, at last, she could cry her eyes out in peace.

CHAPTER TWO

DEBBIE looked up from the piles of folders on the table in the Records Office as the door opened and Mr van der Eisler came in. Her disconsolate face broke into a smile at the sight of him, although she asked with a touch of wariness, 'Oh, hello—have I sent the wrong notes up again? I can't get anything right, and now that Olivia's not here to sort things out for me I seem to be in a muddle the whole time.'

He came unhurriedly to the table and glanced at the untidy piles on it. 'I expect it will get easier once you have got used to being on your own. And I do want some notes, but there's no hurry. Do you have to file these before you go home?'

She nodded. 'It's almost five o'clock and I daren't leave them until the morning; there'll be some bossy old sister coming down and wanting to know where this and that is. Interfering so-and-sos.'

'Ten minutes' work at the most,' declared Mr van der Eisler. 'I'll sort them into alphabetical order, you file them.'

'Cor—you mean you'll give a hand? But no one ever does...'

He was already busy, and after a moment she did as he suggested.

'I expect you miss Olivia,' he observed presently.

'You bet I do.'

'Does she come to see you?' His voice was casual.

'No, worse luck. Doesn't live near here. Her granny's got a flat Islington way; she and her mum have to live with her since her dad died, left them badly off. Not that Olivia told me much—shut up like an oyster when it came to her private life.' She laughed. 'Not like me.'

He handed her another pile of folders. 'You live near the hospital?'

'Five minutes walk. Me dad's out of work, Mum's part-time at the supermarket. Was I scared that I'd get the sack? Olivia didn't tell me, but the girl in the office said as how she had another job to go to. This wasn't her cup of tea. Been to one of those la-di-da schools, I dare say. Always spoke posh, if you see what I mean.'

Mr van der Eisler agreed that he saw. 'Not many jobs going in Islington, I should have thought.'

'Not where her granny lives—one of those dull streets with rows of houses with net curtains. Had a soppy name too—Sylvester Crescent.'

Mr van der Eisler's heavy lids drooped over the gleam in his eyes.

'Very fanciful,' he agreed. He handed over the last pile, waited while Debbie filed the folders away and came back to the table, made his request for the notes he needed, listened with a kind smile to her thanks and, with the folder under his arm, took himself off.

Debbie, bundling herself into her jacket, addressed

the tidy shelves. 'Now there's a real gent for you. That was a nice chat too—no one knows how dull it is down here these days.'

Mr van der Eisler, discussing the next day's list with the senior surgical registrar and the theatre sister, wrung from that lady a reluctant assent to begin operating at eight o'clock in the morning instead of an hour later, gave her a smile to set her elderly heart beating a good deal faster, and took his leave.

'That man could wring blood from a stone,' declared Sister. 'I'm sure I don't know why I let him get away with it...'

The registrar laughed. 'Go one with you, you know you'd agree to open theatre at six a.m. He's a splendid man and a first-rate surgeon. He's been here several weeks now, hasn't he? Handed over several new techniques, shared his ideas with Mr Jenks—between them they've perfected them—look at Mrs Eliza Brown.'

'He'll be leaving soon, I suppose.'

'Yes, and Mr Jenks is going back with him for a week or two.' He turned to leave. 'He'll be back, I've no doubt—goes all over the place—got an international reputation already. Not bad for a man of thirty-six.'

He wandered away to look out of a window, in time to see Mr van der Eisler's grey Bentley edge out of the hospital forecourt.

'I wonder where he goes?' he reflected aloud.

Mr van der Eisler was going to Islington to cast his eye over Sylvester Crescent. He found it eventually, tooling patiently up and down identical streets of identical houses, and drove its length until he came to Mr Patel's shop, still open.

Mr van der Eisler, who never purchased food for his excellently run household, nevertheless purchased a tin of baked beans, and engaged Mr Patel in casual conversation. Naturally enough the talk led to observations about Islington and Sylvester Crescent in particular.

'A quiet area,' observed Mr van der Eisler. 'Flats, I suppose, and elderly people.'

'You are right, sir.' Mr Patel, with no customers in the offing, was glad of a chat. 'Many elderly ladies and gentlemen. It is not a street for the young—and an awkward journey to the day's work. There is Miss Harding, who lives with her grandmother Mrs Fitzgibbon at number twenty-six, but I see her each morning now, and I think she must no longer work.' He sighed. 'Such a beautiful young lady too. It is dull here for the young.'

Mr van der Eisler murmured suitably, remarked that Mr Patel and his shop must be a boon and a blessing to the neighbourhood, professed himself pleased with his purchase, paid for it and got back into his car. Number twenty-six was in the middle of the row of houses and there was a chink of light showing between the heavy curtains pulled across the windows on the ground floor.

He drove back to the quiet, elegant street near Sloane Square and let himself into his ground-floor flat to be met in the hall by his housekeeper.

'You're late, sir. Your dinner's ready and I'll be so

bold as to say that it won't keep for more than five minutes.'

'Excellent timing, Becky.' He patted her plump shoulder and added, 'Here's something for you to amuse yourself with.'

He handed her the bag and she looked inside. 'Mr Haso, whatever will you do next? Since when have you eaten baked beans?' She gave him a suspicious glance. 'What did you want to buy it for?'

'Well, I needed to ask for some information and the best place was the local corner shop.'

Miss Rebecca Potts, elderly now, and long since retired as his nanny, was his devoted housekeeper whenever he was in London, and she knew better than to ask him why he wanted to know something. All the same, she gave him a sharp look. 'I'll dish up,' she told him severely. 'You've time for a drink.'

He picked up his bag and went down the hall to his study and sat down in the leather armchair drawn up to the fire. A drink in his hand, he sat quietly, busy with his thoughts, until Becky knocked on the door.

It was two days before he had the opportunity to return to Sylvester Crescent. He had no plan as to what he intended doing, only the vague idea of seeing Olivia going to or from the shops or, failing that, calling at her grandmother's flat with some trumped-up story about Debbie. Perhaps, he thought ruefully, once he had met her again, he would be able to get her off his mind.

He saw her as he turned the car into Sylvester Crescent, coming towards him in her well-worn jacket and skirt, her bright hair a splash of colour in the sober street, a shopping basket over her arm. He slowed the car and stopped as she drew abreast of it.

The quick colour swept over her face when she saw him but she said composedly, 'Why, good morning, Mr van der Eisler. Have you a patient to visit?'

Mr van der Eisler, an upright and godfearing man, could on occasion lie like a trooper when it was necessary, and he considered that this was necessary. 'No, no, I have a few hours with nothing to do. I am looking for a suitable flat for a friend who will be coming to London for a few months.'

He got out of the car and stood beside her. 'A most delightful surprise to meet you again. I was in the Records Office only the other day and Debbie was telling me how much she missed you. She tells me that you have another job—how fortunate…'

'Yes, isn't it?' She caught his eye and something in his look made her add, 'Well, no, I haven't actually. I told her that because she was worried about getting the sack. Is she managing?'

'Tolerably well.' He smiled down at her, looking so kind that she had a sudden urge to tell him about her grandmother, whose nasty little digs about her not getting a job had done nothing to make her fruitless efforts easier to bear. Instead she said briskly, 'It's nice meeting you, but don't let me keep you from your house-hunting.'

Mr van der Eisler, never a man to be deterred from his purpose, stood his ground. 'As to that—' he began, and was interrupted by the sudden appearance of Rodney, who had pulled in behind the Bentley and was grabbing Olivia by the arm.

'Olivia—I had to come and see you…'

Olivia removed her arm. 'Why?' she asked coldly.

'Oh, old friends and all that, you know. Wouldn't like you to think badly of me—you did walk off in a huff…' He glanced at Mr van der Eisler towering over him, a look of only the faintest interest upon his face. 'I say,' Rodney went on, 'is this the lucky man?' He shook hands, beaming. 'Olivia said she was going to get married—described you to a T. Well, everything works out for the best, doesn't it?' He patted Olivia's shoulder. 'You don't know what a relief it is to see you so happy. Can't stop now. My regards to your mother. Bye, old girl.'

He flashed a smile at them both, got back into his car, and drove away without looking back.

Olivia looked at her feet and wished she could stop blushing, and Mr van der Eisler looked at the top of her head and admired her hair.

'I can explain,' said Olivia to her shoes. 'It wasn't you I described; I said he was very large and had a profession and a great deal of money.' She added crossly, 'Well, that's what any girl would say, isn't it?'

Mr van der Eisler, used to unravelling his patients' meanderings, hit the nail on the head accurately. 'Any girl worth her salt,' he agreed gravely. 'Did you actually intend to marry this—this fellow?'

'Well, you see, I've known him for years, long before Father died and we had to move here, and somehow he seemed part of my life then and I didn't want to give that up—do you see what I mean?'

She looked at him then. He looked just as a favourite uncle or cousin might have looked: a safe recipient of her woes, ready to give sound advice. She said breathlessly, 'I'm sorry, I can't think why I'm boring you with all this. Please forgive me—he—Rodney was something of a shock.'

He took her basket from her. 'Get in the car,' he suggested mildly. 'We will have a cup of coffee before you do your shopping.'

'No, no, thank you. I can't keep you standing around any longer. I must get the fish…'

As she was speaking she found herself being urged gently into the Bentley. 'Tell me where we can get coffee—I passed some shops further back.'

'There's the Coffee-Pot, about five minutes' walk away—so it's close by. Aren't I wasting your time?' she asked uneasily.

'Certainly not. In fact, while we are having it I shall pick your brains as to the best way of finding a flat.'

The café was in a side-street. He parked the car, opened her door for her, and followed her into the half-empty place. It was small, with half a dozen tables with pink formica tops, and the chairs looked fragile. Mr van der Eisler, a man of some seventeen stones in weight, sat down gingerly. He mistrusted the chairs and he mistrusted the coffee which, when it came, justified his doubts, but Olivia, happy to be doing something different in her otherwise rather dull days, drank hers with every appearance of enjoyment and, while she did, explained in a matter-of-fact way about living with Granny.

'I dare say you are glad to have a brief holiday,' he

suggested, and handed her the plate of Rich Tea biscuits which had come with the coffee.

'Well, no, not really. I mean, I do need a job as soon as possible, only I'm not trained for anything really useful…' She went on in a bright voice, 'Of course I shall find something soon, I'm sure.'

'Undoubtedly,' he agreed, and went on to talk of other things. He had had years of calming timid patients, so he set about putting Olivia at her ease before mentioning casually that he would be going back to Holland very shortly.

'Oh—but will you come back here?'

'Yes. I'm an honorary consultant at Jerome's, so I'm frequently over here. I do have beds in several hospitals in Holland—I divide my time between the two.' He drank the last of the coffee with relief. 'Do you plan to stay with your grandmother for the foreseeable future?'

'Until I can get a job where Mother and I can live together. Only I'm not sure what kind of job. There are lots of advertisements for housekeepers and minders, although I'm not sure what a minder is and I'm not good enough at housekeeping, although I could do domestic work…'

He studied the lovely face opposite him and shook his head. 'I hardly think you're suitable for that.'

Which dampened her spirits, although she didn't let him see that. 'I really have to go. It has been nice meeting you again and I do hope you find a nice flat for your friend.'

He paid the bill and they went outside, and she held out a hand as they stood on the pavement. 'Goodbye,

Mr van der Eisler. Please give Debbie my love if ever you should see her. Please don't tell her that I haven't got a job yet.'

She walked away quickly, wishing that she could spend the whole day with him; he had seemed like an old friend and she lacked friends.

By the time she reached the fishmonger's the fillets of plaice that her grandmother had fancied for dinner that evening had been sold and she had to buy a whole large plaice and have it filleted, which cost a good deal more money. Olivia, her head rather too full of Mr van der Eisler, didn't care.

Naturally enough, when she returned to the flat she was asked why she had spent half the morning doing a small amount of shopping. 'Loitering around drinking coffee, I suppose,' said Mrs Fitzgibbon accusingly.

'I met someone I knew at the hospital; we had coffee together,' said Olivia. She didn't mention Rodney.

Mr van der Eisler drove himself back to his home, ate the lunch Becky had ready for him, and went to the hospital to take a ward-round. None of the students trailing him from one patient to the next had the least suspicion that one corner of his brilliant mind was grappling with the problem of Olivia while he posed courteous questions to each of them in turn.

Olivia had let fall the information that her grandmother had once lived in a small village in Wiltshire, and in that county was the school where his small goddaughter was a boarder, since her own grandmother lived near enough to it for her to visit frequently during term-time. In the holidays she went back to Holland to her widowed mother, who had sent her to an English school because her dead husband had wanted that. Might there be a possibility of Mrs Fitzgibbon and Nel's grandmother being acquainted, or at least having mutual friends? It was worth a try...

'Now,' he said in his placid way, 'which of you gentlemen will explain to me the exact reasons which make it necessary for me to operate upon Miss Forbes?'

He smiled down at the woman lying in bed and added, 'And restoring her to normal good health once more?' He sounded so confident that she smiled back at him.

It was several days before Mr van der Eisler was free to drive down to Wiltshire. His small goddaughter's grandmother lived in a village some five or six miles from Bradford-on-Avon and on that particular morning there was more than a hint of spring in the air. The sky was blue—albeit rather pale, the sun shone—as yet without much warmth, and the countryside was tipped with green. Slowing down to turn off the road on to a narrow country lane leading to Earleigh Gilford, he told himself that he was wasting his time: Olivia had probably got herself a job by now and the chance of her grandmother knowing Lady Brennon was so remote as to be hopeless.

He had phoned ahead and they met as old friends, for both of them had been charged with the care of Nel during term-time. Lady Brennon was a youthful sixty, living in a charming little Georgian villa on the edge of the village, busy with her garden and her painting, her dogs and the various village committees on which she sat.

'So nice to see you, Haso.' She looked sad for a moment. 'It seems a long time since Rob's wedding and your coming here as his best man. I miss him still, you know. Thank heavens we have little Nel.'

They went into the house together and he asked, 'Is she here for the weekend?'

'Yes, she'll be here on Saturday. There's no chance of your staying until then?'

'I'm afraid not. I'll try and get down before the Easter holidays. In fact, I might be able to arrange things so I can drive her over to Holland.'

'That would be splendid.' Lady Brennon poured their coffee. 'The child's very fond of you. Rita phoned this week; she said that you had been to see her when you were in Holland. Was she happy?'

'I believe so. She likes her work and she has her friends. She misses Nel, but she wants to carry out Rob's wishes.'

'Of course. Probably she will change her mind and come to live here later on.'

'Perhaps.' He put down his cup. 'Lady Brennon, did you know a Mrs Fitzgibbon—oh, it would be some years ago? I believe she lived somewhere near Bradford-on-Avon.' He dredged up the bits and pieces of information that Olivia had let drop. 'I believe her daughter married a man called Harding—rather a grand wedding in Bath Abbey…'

'Fitzgibbon? The name rings a bell. You know her? She is a friend of yours? Rather an elderly one…'

'No. No. I have never met her.'

'Then I can tell you that she was a most disagreeable woman—I remember her very well—bullied her daughter, a rather sweet little thing. Married against her wishes, I believe. I met her several times. The daughter had a little girl—the husband died, I believe, it was in the *Telegraph* a few years ago. Dear me, it must be almost thirty years since we met.'

She gave Haso an enquiring look. 'May I know why you are interested in her?'

'I have met her granddaughter—she was working at Jerome's as a filing clerk, got made redundant and can't find work. She and her mother live with Mrs Fitzgibbon and I gather are not happy there. Olivia has said very little about herself, and I am barely acquainted with her, but she got herself sacked so that the girl she worked with, who desperately needs the money, could keep her job, and I wondered if you knew of anything…' He smiled then. 'I have no personal interest in her; it is only that I feel that she deserves a better chance.'

'Is she educated?'

'Yes. Intelligent and well-mannered, speaks well, very level-headed, I should imagine. She is lacking in the essentials—typing, shorthand, computers—all that kind of thing. She had no need to work until her father died.'

'Is she very young?'

'I should guess her to be in her late twenties.' He frowned. 'I think she would make a good governess if they still have such people.'

'Not to any extent, I'm afraid. She might get a post in a private school, with the smaller children perhaps, or even taking drama classes for the older girls. What do you want me to do, Haso?'

'I'm presuming on your kindness, Lady Brennon. If you should hear of something which might suit Olivia, could you possibly find a reason to write to Mrs Fitzgibbon, mention the job, and say how you wished you knew of someone suitable to fill it? It is most unlikely, I know, but a kindly fate does occasionally step in. I don't wish her to know that I have had anything to do with it.'

'I will be most discreet. It would certainly be an ideal solution, and since it would appear to Mrs Fitzgibbon that it was through her good offices that Olivia should hear of the job she might present no difficulties. I'll ask around, my dear. There are any number of schools around here, you know.'

They talked about other things then, and Olivia wasn't mentioned again, and later, as he drove himself back to London, Mr van der Eisler's thoughts were of the week ahead of him—Liverpool and then Birmingham, then back to Holland...

It was three weeks before he returned to his London home. It was late at night on the first day of his return before he had the leisure to sit down and read his post. A good deal of it he consigned to the wastepaper basket and then put the rest aside while he read the letter from Lady Brennon. She had telephoned him, she wrote, and Becky had told her that he was away so it seemed best to write. By the greatest good fortune, she went on, Nel had told her on her half-term holiday that Miss Tomkins, who it seemed was a Jill of all trades at the school, had left suddenly and there was no one to take her place. Lady Brennon had acted with speed, recommended Olivia to the headmistress on the strength of his recommendation, and written to Mrs Fitzgibbon, using the excuse that a friend of hers had seen Olivia's mother when she was in London and that that had prompted Lady Brennon to write to her. A lie, of course, she had put in brackets. The letter continued:

'The upshot is, Haso, that your protégée is at Nel's school, working out the rest of the term, and if she proves satisfactory she is to be taken on on a termly basis and allowed to live in a small annexe of the school. Very poky, so Nel tells me, but there is room for her mother if she cares to go and live there. The salary is barely adequate but, as it has been pointed out, she has no qualifications. I hope this news will relieve you from further feelings of responsibility towards Olivia who, from Nel's account, is well-liked and apparently happy. Do phone when you can spare the time, and tell me how Rita is. Still as pretty as ever, I'm sure, and such a delightful companion. I hope you found time to see something of her.'

He smiled as he put the letter down, aware that it was Lady Brennon's dearest wish that he should marry Rita. What could be more suitable? They knew each other well, her husband had been his closest friend and he had a strong affection for Nel. It was all so suitable, and he supposed that it would be a sensible thing to do. His thoughts strayed to Olivia; when he went to school to collect Nel he would make a point of seeing her. He supposed his interest in her had been heightened by the injustice of her dismissal. Now that she was settled he could dismiss her from his mind, where she had been lurking for the past few weeks.

Lady Brennon's letter had reached Mrs Fitzgibbon at an opportune moment; there had been another letter in the post that morning, for Olivia, regretting that the post of assistant in a West End florist's had been filled. Olivia, listening to her grandmother's diatribe on the inability of young women to find suitable employment, allowed most of it to flow over her head—she knew it by heart now. Instead she wondered about Mr van der Eisler. Back in Holland, she supposed, and best forgotten.

A silence from her grandmother made her look up. The old lady was reading the letter in her hand, and when she had finished it she re-read it. She spoke. 'It is a good thing that I have a number of connections with those of a good background.' She put the letter down. 'This is a letter from an old friend who by some remote chance has written to me—you need not concern yourself as to the details.' She waited for Olivia to say something but, since she had no intention of concerning herself, she went on writing a note for the milkman and remained silent. 'There is a position at a girls' school outside Bath—making yourself useful, as far as I can see. The current holder has had to leave for some family reason and the headmistress is anxious to find someone suitable at the earliest possible moment. She suggests that you telephone and make an appointment. The headmistress is coming to London—let me see—tomorrow.'

Olivia felt her grandmother's beady eyes fixed on her. 'Just what kind of a job is it, Granny?'

'How should I know? You must bestir yourself and go and find out for yourself.'

'After I have talked to Mother. She'll be back presently, we can talk about it then.'

Mrs Harding thought it might be quite nice. 'Of course I shall miss you, love, but you'll have the school holidays.'

'Yes, Mother. If it were possible, would you come and live there if I get the job—I dare say we could rent a small house nearby.'

'Oh, darling, that would be lovely, to live in the country again.' They were in the kitchen with the door shut but all the same she lowered her voice. 'I'm sure Granny would like to have the flat to herself again. Do go and see this lady.'

So Olivia went, and since it was a fine day and quite warm she wore her jersey dress—like most of her clothes not the height of fashion but still elegant. She hoped the headmistress would like her, for although she didn't like leaving her mother she would be able to send her money and they might even take a holiday together. Her grandmother, she felt sure, would be only too glad to be rid of them both.

The headmistress, Miss Cross, was middle-aged, plump and good-natured and, when Olivia explained that she had no experience of any sort other than filing documents, waved this aside. 'Come and see how you get on,' she suggested. 'There are still several weeks of this term—almost a month. If you like the work and we like you, then I'll employ you on a termly basis. You'll live in, of course—there's a small annexe you'll have to yourself. I don't know if you have a dependant? I've no objection to a mother or sister living with you. The salary is fair, I consider, and you get your meals while you're on duty. You're not married or anything like that?'

'No, Miss Cross.'

'Then you ought to be, a lovely creature like you! Start on Saturday. Let me know what time your train gets to Bath; I'll have you met.'

Coincidence, good luck, fate—call it what you will, reflected Olivia, now something or someone had allowed her to fall on her feet. She had been at the school for two weeks and she was happy. She wasn't sure just what she could call herself, for no two days were alike, but being a practical girl she took that in her stride. She plaited small heads of hair, inspected fingernails if Matron was busy, played rounders during the games hour, took prep with the older girls, drove Miss Cross into Bath whenever she needed to go, washed the same small heads of hair, comforted those who had grazed knees and in between these tasks filled in for anyone on the staff who happened to be absent for any reason. It was a good thing that she had been good at games at school, for she found herself on several occasions tearing up and down the hockey pitch blowing her whistle. She had enjoyed it too.

The annexe had been a pleasant surprise. It was small, certainly, but there was a living-room with an alcove used as a kitchen, a shower-room and, up the narrow staircase, two bedrooms just large enough to contain a bed, a chest of drawers and a chair. Whoever had had the place before her had been clever with orange boxes, disguising them as bedside tables, bookshelves and an extra seat with a cushion neatly nailed on to it.

If Miss Cross was to keep her on then there was no reason why her mother shouldn't come and stay with her, even live with her. The school was in the country, but there was a good bus service into Bath from the village.

Olivia, on this particular Saturday morning, was rounding up the smallest of the girls ready for their weekly swimming lesson in the heated swimming-pool in the school's basement. The sports mistress would be in charge but Olivia was expected to give a hand, something she enjoyed, for she was a good swimmer and teaching the sometimes unwilling learners was a challenge. She marched them through the school and down the stairs to the basement, saw them into their swimsuits, counted heads, and handed them over to Miss Ross, a small woman with a powerful voice, before going off to get into her own swimsuit.

While Miss Ross got on with the actual teaching Olivia patrolled the pool, swimming slowly, making sure that the children were under her watchful eye, encouraging the faint-hearted to get their feet off the bottom of the pool and applauding those who were splashing their way from one side to the other. Once they were all out of the water she wrapped herself in a robe and went round checking that each child had showered, finding mislaid garments and then collecting up the sopping wet swimsuits. Only when they were all once more dressed and handed over to Miss Ross could she shower and dress herself, before hurrying back to the school to the recreation room where she was expected to dispense hot cocoa and biscuits. It should have been her half-day but the junior housemistress had gone to a wedding, which meant that Olivia would have the charge of fifteen little girls until they were in bed and hopefully asleep. On Sunday it was her turn to shepherd the whole school, under the guidance of Miss Cross and two of the senior teachers, to the village church.

Getting ready for bed that night she owned to being tired but not unhappy. The pleasure of sitting in one's own small home, drinking a last cup of tea before getting into bed, was by no means overrated. Perhaps she was a born old maid? She dismissed the idea. 'I shall be quite honest,' she told herself, since there was no one else to tell, 'I should like to marry and have a kind and loving husband and a handful of children. Never mind if there isn't enough money, just enough to live on comfortably, and keep a dog or two, and cats of course, and perhaps a donkey…'

She put down her mug and took herself upstairs to bed.

There was the opportunity to think quietly the next morning; the Reverend Bates' sermons were long and soothing, a fitting background for her thoughts, and since they were simple and blameless she didn't suppose that God would mind. The end of term was approaching, she reflected, and she would go back to

Granny's flat for almost three weeks. During that time she would have to see what her mother thought of coming to live with her, always providing Miss Cross decided to keep her. The letters from her mother had been cheerful; Olivia thought that without her her mother and grandmother lived fairly amicably together. All the same, it would be nice if her mother was to pay a visit.

She glanced down the row of childish faces under the school straw hats. Perhaps she had found her niche in life. She sighed and a small hand crept into her lap and caught at her fingers, and she made haste to smile down at the upturned little face. It was Nel, a nice child whose Granny lived not too far away. She had confided in Olivia one day that her daddy had died and Mummy lived in Holland, but she was here at school because her Daddy had wanted her to be educated in England. 'I'm half-Dutch,' she had said proudly, and instantly Mr van der Eisler's handsome features had swum before Olivia's eyes. She had wiped him out at once and suggested a game of Ludo.

With the end of term so near now there was an air of bustle and excitement at the school. Regular lessons gave way to exams, an expedition to the Roman Baths in Bath, while Miss Prosser, who taught history and geography, recited their history, and finally the school play, with its attendant rush and scurry behind the curtains, and then the last morning, with all the little girls—dressed, cases packed, forgotten articles sought for and found—waiting anxiously to be collected.

The first parents arrived soon after breakfast and after them a steady stream of cars. Olivia, finding stray children, tying shoelaces and straightening hats, remembered that she was to drive Miss Cross into Bath that afternoon. When she got back she would be able to pack her own things and by then she would know if she was to return...

Half the children had gone when Nel, standing beside her, gave a squeal of delight. 'There's Mummy and Uncle Haso.' She gave Olivia a poke to make sure that she was listening. 'We're going to Holland...'

'How nice,' said Olivia, and allowed her lovely mouth to drop open. Mr van der Eisler, accompanied by an elegantly dressed woman with fair hair cut in a boyish crop, was coming towards her.

Her surprise was so absolute that she could think of nothing to say, but Mr van der Eisler, whose surprise wasn't surprise at all but actually looked genuine, nodded in a friendly way. 'Olivia—who would have expected to see you here?'

He suffered a hug from Nel and turned to his companion. 'Rita, this is a young lady who worked at Jerome's. Nel's mother, Olivia—Mrs Brennon.'

'How nice,' said Mrs Brennon, which could have meant anything. She didn't shake hands but kissed her daughter and said, 'Shall we go, Haso? Lady Brennon will be expecting us...' She smiled briefly at Olivia. 'Goodbye. I do hope that Nel has been good.'

She didn't wait for an answer but took Nel's hand and went to the car.

Mr van der Eisler paused just long enough to ask if she was happy.

'Oh, very, thank you.' Just in case he hadn't been listening, she added, 'I have never been so happy.'

His, 'Splendid,' was uttered in a detached manner, as was his goodbye.

CHAPTER THREE

'WELL, what did you expect?' Olivia asked her face in the looking-glass in her bedroom. 'I dare say he had a job to remember you—she was very attractive, and he's fond of Nel.'

She started to pack in a half-hearted way, filling in time until Miss Cross was ready to go into Bath.

In Bath she was told to park the car and return in two hours' time, which meant that she had the leisure to look at the shops and have a cup of tea. On the way back to the school Miss Cross, who had hardly spoken, said, 'Come to my study before supper this evening, Olivia. You will be returning home tomorrow?'

'Yes, Miss Cross.' It would have been nice if she could ask if she was to be given the sack but she didn't dare. Fate had been tiresome enough without being tempted.

She had almost finished her packing when Miss Cross's maid came to summon her to the study. It was rather worse than a visit to the dentist, thought Olivia, tapping on the door, and when bidden to enter, she entered.

'Sit down Olivia.' Miss Cross looked her usual cosy self, but that was nothing to go by. 'You have been happy here?' she asked.

'Yes, Miss Cross.'

'Good. You have been most satisfactory—fitted in very well, and the children like you. I am prepared to engage you for the following term, Olivia. The same conditions will apply. You play tennis and croquet?'

'Yes, Miss Cross.'

'Good. Please return here two days before the pupils.' She consulted the desk calendar. 'That will be the fifteenth of April. Let us know the time of your arrival and you will be met at the station.' She smiled. 'You are willing to agree to these arrangements?'

'Yes, Miss Cross. I shall be happy to come back for the next term.'

'That is settled, then. I'll say goodbye now, since you will be leaving in the morning and I shall be engaged until lunchtime.'

Olivia took herself back to her room, dancing along the corridors, humming cheerfully. I may be an old maid, she reflected, but at least I'm a happy one.

It was raining when she arrived at Sylvester Crescent and the row of prim houses looked unwelcoming, but her mother was at the window looking out for her so that she forgot the sudden pang of homesickness for the school. They talked and laughed together, happy to see each other again, until Mrs Fitzgibbon came to join them.

She offered a cheek for Olivia's kiss. 'I was resting but of course your voices disturbed me. Are you back for good?'

'No, just for the Easter holidays. You look well, Granny.'

'My looks have never pitied me, I keep my sufferings to myself.'

Olivia winked at her mother and went to get the tea. Granny was only bearable if one treated her as a joke.

Her mother came into the kitchen presently. 'It's only because Granny had her nap disturbed,' she explained, looking worried. 'I'm sure she's very glad to see you, love.'

Olivia warmed the teapot. 'Yes, dear. How do you like the idea of coming to stay with me for a week or two during the term? I won't be free, of course, but there's a good bus service into Bath and I'll be there in the evenings once I'm off-duty.'

'I'd like that, darling. I won't be in the way?'

Olivia gave her parent a hug. 'Never, my dear. The country's lovely and the village is sweet—very close to Bath, of course, but it's still country.'

Life was a little dull after the bustle of school but she had saved a good deal of her salary and took her mother out and about on modest expeditions.

'This is lovely,' said Mrs Harding, perched on top of a sightseeing bus, doing the rounds of the famous landmarks. 'It all looks quite different from up here.' She turned to look at Olivia. 'I think your grandmother is quite pleased to have the flat to herself. She's been on her own for so long now, it must be tiresome for her to have me there all the time.'

Olivia nodded. 'I know, Mother. I hope that after this next term Miss Cross might take me on permanently, then you can come and live with me. The annexe is small but there's room for two. You could join

GET 2

HOW TO GET YOUR
2 FREE BOOKS AND FREE GIFT!

1. Peel off the MIRA® sticker on the front cover. Place it in the space provided at right. This automatically entitles you to receive two free books and an exciting surprise gift.

2. Send back this card and you'll get 2 "The Best of the Best™" books. These books have a combined cover price of $11.98 or more in the U.S. and $13.98 or more in Canada, but they are yours to keep absolutely FREE!

3. There's no catch. You're under no obligation to buy anything. We charge nothing – ZERO – for your first shipment. And you don't have to make any minimum number of purchases – not even one!

4. We call this line "The Best of the Best" because each month you'll receive the best books by some of today's most popular authors. These authors show up time and time again on all the major bestseller lists and their books sell out as soon as they hit the stores. You'll like the convenience of getting them delivered to your home at our special discount prices . . . and you'll love your *Heart to Heart* subscriber newsletter featuring author news, horoscopes, recipes, book reviews and much more!

SPECIAL FREE GIFT!
We'll send you a fabulous surprise gift, absolutely FREE, simply for accepting our no-risk offer!

5. We hope that after receiving your free books you'll want to remain a subscriber. But the choice is yours – to continue or cancel, anytime at all! So why not take us up on our invitation, with no risk of any kind. You'll be glad you did!

6. And remember…we'll send you a surprise gift ABSOLUTELY FREE just for giving THE BEST OF THE BEST a try.

Visit us online at
www.mirabooks.com

® and TM are registered trademark of Harlequin Enterprises Limited.

BOOKS FREE!

Hurry!

Return this card promptly to GET 2 FREE BOOKS & A FREE GIFT!

YES! Please send me the 2 FREE "The Best of the Best" books and FREE gift for which I qualify. I understand that I am under no obligation to purchase anything further, as explained on the back and on the opposite page.

385 MDL DRTA   185 MDL DR59

FIRST NAME	LAST NAME

ADDRESS

APT.#	CITY

STATE/PROV.	ZIP/POSTAL CODE

▼ DETACH AND MAIL CARD TODAY! ▼

(P-BB3-03) ©1998 MIRA BOOKS

THE BEST OF THE BEST™ — Here's How it Works:

Accepting your 2 free books and gift places you under no obligation to buy anything. You may keep the books and gift and return the shipping statement marked "cancel." If you do not cancel, about a month later we will send you 4 additional books and bill you just $4.74 each in the U.S., or $5.24 each in Canada, plus 25¢ shipping & handling per book and applicable taxes if any.* That's the complete price and — compared to cover prices starting from $5.99 each in the U.S. and $6.99 each in Canada — it's quite a bargain! You may cancel at any time, but if you choose to continue, every month we'll send you 4 more books, which you may either purchase at the discount price or return to us and cancel your subscription.

*Terms and prices subject to change without notice. Sales tax applicable in N.Y. Canadian residents will be charged applicable provincial taxes and GST. Credit or Debit balances in a customer's account(s) may be offset by any other outstanding balance owed by or to the customer.

If offer card is missing write to: The Best of the Best, 3010 Walden Ave., P.O. Box 1867, Buffalo, NY 14240-1867

BUSINESS REPLY MAIL

FIRST-CLASS MAIL   PERMIT NO. 717-003   BUFFALO, NY

POSTAGE WILL BE PAID BY ADDRESSEE

THE BEST OF THE BEST
3010 WALDEN AVE
PO BOX 1867
BUFFALO NY 14240-9952

NO POSTAGE
NECESSARY
IF MAILED
IN THE
UNITED STATES

the WI again, and help with the church flowers and do the shopping. It would be like old times.'

There were two days left of her holiday when Mrs Fitzgibbon, answering the phone, said, 'It's for you, Olivia. A man—surely not Rodney? You had better take it.'

She handed over the receiver to Olivia and sat back in her chair, shamelessly eavesdropping.

'Yes?' She spoke sharply.

'Cold steel,' said Mr van der Eisler in her ear. 'Did you think that it was Rodney?'

She turned her back on her grandmother so that that lady wouldn't see the pleased smile on her face. 'No, it's the surprise.'

'I shall be driving Nel back to her school; we'll collect you on the way.'

'Oh, but I...'

'Go back two days earlier, so Nel tells me. She is going to stay with her grandmother before she returns to school.'

'Oh—well.'

'Olivia, I must beg you to stop bleating and listen to what I have to say. We shall call for you in two days' time. Ten o'clock in the morning.'

He rang off without so much as a goodbye and she put down the receiver.

'Who was that?' demanded her grandmother. 'You didn't have much to say for yourself.'

'There was no need,' said Olivia, and went in search of her mother.

Waiting for him to arrive two mornings later, her

mother said, 'I've made some coffee, Olivia. Do you suppose he'll drink it?'

'Mother, I have no idea. He sounded so businesslike on the phone. Perhaps he's in a tearing hurry to get to Nel's granny.'

'Well, it's ready if he wants it,' said Mrs Harding. 'But I do hope he stops for just a few minutes—your grandmother is anxious to see him.'

'I was afraid of that,' said Olivia.

He was punctual, standing there at the front door, handsome, self-assured and elegant in his tweeds. Nel was hanging out of the car window and Olivia said at once, 'Oh, do come in. Nel might like a drink and the coffee's ready. Unless you're in a tearing hurry?'

'Coffee would be nice and I'm sure Nel wants to see where you live.'

He opened the car door for the little girl, who skipped up to Olivia and lifted her face for a kiss. 'I'm so glad you're coming back to school,' she declared. 'I hope you stay there forever and ever.'

Olivia stooped her splendid person. 'How very kind of you to say so, Nel. Come in and have a glass of lemonade.'

Her mother came into the hall then, and Mr van der Eisler shook her hand and smiled down at her and said all the right things in his pleasant voice before Nel was introduced too.

'There's coffee,' said Mrs Harding a little breathlessly. This marvellous man—and Olivia knew him. Her thoughts were already wrapped in bridal veils and orange blossom. 'Come in and meet my mother.'

Mrs Fitzgibbon was sitting in her chair, the uncomfortable one, and one glance at her sufficed to cause Mr van der Eisler to adopt his best bedside manner. He became all at once self-assured, deferential, and the epitome of a successful man who knew his own worth without being boastful about it.

Olivia watched her grandmother's starchy manner melt into graciousness while they drank their coffee and Nel roamed round the room, looking at photographs and ornaments. Olivia had got up to show Nel the little musical box on the side-table when she heard her grandmother remark, 'Of course, Olivia is quite unskilled. Never needed to work, and now that it is unfortunately necessary her limitations are evident. But there, I am an old woman now and must bear with life's disappointments.'

Olivia supposed that she herself was one of them and was much heartened by Mr van der Eisler's grave, 'I must beg to differ, Mrs Fitzgibbon. Olivia is fulfilling a much-needed want at Nel's school. It needs patience and kindness and understanding to care for children. I am told by the headmistress that she is worth her weight in gold.'

He turned to Mrs Harding then. 'You must be so relieved to know that Olivia is so successful. The school is a good one and the surroundings are pleasant. Perhaps you will be able to visit her?'

'Well, Olivia has asked me to go and stay with her during the term. I know I shall love it.'

Mrs Fitzgibbon sighed loudly. 'How lucky that you are young enough to go and enjoy yourself. I, alas, must stay here alone.'

Mr van der Eisler said easily, 'I'm sure you would

have no difficulty in finding a companion, Mrs Fitzgibbon.' He stood up. 'You must forgive me if we leave now. Nel's grandmother will be waiting for her.'

There was a small delay while Olivia whisked Nel upstairs, but not before the child had said in a clear little voice, 'Just in case I should get caught short before we get to Granny's house. Uncle Haso is in a hurry.'

'The age of modesty is long past,' said Mrs Fitzgibbon faintly.

'The seat's big enough for the pair of you,' said Mr van der Eisler, fastening the seatbelt round the pair of them and casting the luggage into the boot, then getting in beside them and driving away with a wave.

'I don't like your granny,' said Nel, and her godfather turned a laugh into a cough.

'She's old,' said Olivia, and added, 'I expect when you're old you sometimes say things that other people just think to themselves…'

'She said you were one of life's disappointments…'

'Yes, well, I suppose I am from her point of view. You see, she expected me to grow up small and dainty and get married when I was young.'

'Aren't you young?'

'Not very, I'm afraid.'

'Well, you're very pretty. I must see if I can find a husband for you,' said Nel importantly.

Mr van der Eisler spoke in a matter-of-fact manner. 'Most ladies prefer to choose their own husbands.'

Olivia, rather red in the face, said smartly, 'I had always thought that the men did the choosing.'

Mr van der Eisler chuckled. 'Don't you believe it.

They may be under the impression that they are doing so but it is after all the lady who decides.'

'I shall marry a prince,' said Nel, a remark which Olivia welcomed with relief since it was a topic which lasted until they were clear of the last of the suburbs and driving smoothly on the motorway.

As they neared Bath she was rather surprised when he turned off the motorway and took the Chippenham road, and still more surprised when he turned off once more into a narrow country road.

He glanced at his watch. 'On time,' he observed. 'Your granny will be waiting.'

'The school—?' began Olivia.

'After lunch. Lady Brennon asked me to bring you to lunch with her first.'

'But I don't know her.'

'Of course you don't; you've never met her,' he uttered, in such a reasonable voice that she couldn't think of an answer.

Meeting Lady Brennon, Olivia wished that she had a granny like her—smiling a welcome, delighted to see them all, hugging her small granddaughter, including Olivia in the talk. They sat down presently, in the rather old-fashioned dining-room, to crown of lamb and new potatoes and vegetables, which Lady Brennon assured her had been grown in her garden.

'You like the country?' she asked.

Olivia said that yes, she did and that she had spent her youth not so very far away from Earleigh Gilford. She offered no further details, though, and her hostess didn't question her further, and presently, after a stroll around the garden, Mr van der Eisler suggested that they should go.

Olivia got ready without any fuss and went out to the car, with Nel hanging on to her arm, after bidding Lady Brennon goodbye and thanking her with her nice manners so that that lady observed to Mr van der Eisler, 'A charming girl. Miss Cross has got herself a gem there. You did well to busy yourself with her welfare, Haso. She has no idea that it was you?'

'No, and I do not wish her to know either. I'm glad that she has found a worthwhile job.'

'You'll come back for tea before you return to town? We haven't had a talk about Rita.'

At the school he took the key to the annexe and opened the door, fetched her luggage and then inspected the small living-room, wandering slowly round, looking at the cheap and cheerful prints on its walls, peering at the bookshelves. Before the mantelpiece he stopped to pick up the card on it.

'Well, well, so Rodney has invited you to his wedding. Surely an unkind thing to do? Turning the knife in the wound, as it were?'

'Don't be absurd,' said Olivia. 'There isn't a wound. I dare say he asked me because we've known each other for a long time.'

Mr van der Eisler flipped the card with a nicely manicured fingernail. 'With companion…' He turned the card over and read aloud, '"I don't know the name of your fiancé but we hope that he will come with you".'

Olivia was very pink in the face. 'It's really none of your business…'

'Ah, but it is, Olivia. I may be only a chance acquaintance but I do not wish to see you humiliated. You intend going?'

She found herself telling him that she did. 'It's half-term so I'm free, and the wedding is at Bradford-on-Avon. I suppose she lives there.'

'I shall escort you. You will wear a pretty frock and one of those hats women wear at weddings, and I shall do you proud in a morning suit. You will linger in Rodney's memory in the best possible light—well-dressed, carefree, and safe in the knowledge that your future is secured.'

'Are you joking?' asked Olivia.

'Certainly not; marriage is no joking matter.'

She said rudely, 'How would you know, you aren't married, are you?' She wished the remark unsaid at once, but it was too late. She muttered, 'Sorry, that was dreadfully rude.'

He said silkily, 'Yes, it was. None the less, I shall accompany you to this wedding. It is the least I can do.' He put the card back and went to the door. 'We seem fated to meet unexpectedly, do we not?'

She nodded. 'Yes, but you don't need to come to the wedding, you know. You could be busy in the city or something.'

'I rather fancy seeing Rodney safely married.'

He opened the door and she held out a hand. 'Thank you very much for bringing me back. I'm most grateful.' She added, 'Nel is fortunate to have such a loving granny.'

'Yes.' He took her hand and smiled very kindly at her. 'Which cannot be said for *you*, Olivia.'

She said gruffly, 'Well, she's old, and I'm not what she hoped for.'

He bent and kissed her lightly. 'Goodbye, Olivia.'

She stood at the door and watched him drive away. The kiss had rather shaken her but she didn't let it linger in her thoughts. She went back into the living-room and picked up the wedding invitation. 'I very much dislike being pitied,' she said savagely. 'For two pins I shan't go to Rodney's wedding.'

She had no chance to brood. She settled into her little home, joined the rest of the staff for a discussion as to the term's objectives, and was detailed to check the dormitories with the matron and then, when the children arrived, to get them unpacked and settled in— several hours of hard work and bustle, followed by a number of tearful sessions with those who wanted to go home again.

The weeks, slow to pass at first, quickened their pace; she enjoyed her job despite the fact that she was at everyone's beck and call. She found herself painting scenery for the next end-of-term play, acting as ball-boy when she wasn't showing the smallest of the pupils how to hold their racquets, playing rounders, or organising games when the weather was wet. From time to time in unexpected emergencies she found herself taking a reading lesson. Not the least of her tasks was caring for the children's clothes, also helping Matron with their hair-washing, driving to the doctor or the dentist and once, when Cook was ill, cooking school dinner.

Half-term suddenly loomed, and Rodney's wedding.

She hadn't heard from Mr van der Eisler and she stifled disappointment. Still, she would go to the wedding. Miss Cross was generous with the car; she was sure that she would be allowed to borrow it since it would be half-term and there would be very few people remaining at school.

On her next day off she took herself into Bath; a suitable outfit was essential. All her summer dresses she had had for several years, and Rodney would recognise any of them. Something simple and cheap in a silvery-green, which wouldn't clash with her hair and her pansy eyes, would do nicely.

She found what she wanted after a long search. A plain, delicate green sheath with short sleeves and a modest neckline. Its fabric looked like linen although it was nothing of the sort. It was one of dozens on a rail in British Home Stores, but she guessed that the guests at Rodney's wedding would hardly shop there and wouldn't recognise it for what it was. She had her Italian sandals from better days, and a pair of good stone-coloured gloves. It was just a question of a hat.

She saw several that she liked, but their prices were well beyond her purse. Getting tired and cross, she finally found what she wanted in a department store—a perfectly plain wide-brimmed straw which she bore back to the haberdashery department so that she might match up a ribbon with the dress. The ribbon was expensive, but it transformed the hat and matched the dress exactly. She spent the rest of her day off tying it around the hat, leaving a large silky bow at the back. It might not be a model hat but it gave a very good imitation of one.

Half-term came and the school emptied for four days. Olivia, plaiting Nel's hair and making sure that her school hat was at the correct angle, was touched when the child said, 'I wish you were coming to Granny's with me, Olivia.'

'Well, that would be fun, my dear, but you'll have a lovely time with your granny. I expect she's got all kinds of treats waiting for you.'

Nel nodded. 'Do you ever have treats?' she wanted to know.

'I'm going to a wedding the day after tomorrow, and I've got a new hat.'

'Not your wedding?' asked Nel anxiously.

'No, my dear. Now off with you, Miss Cross wants you all to be in the hall by ten o'clock.'

The place was very empty without the children. The rest of the day was spent clearing up after the last of them had gone and putting everything ready for their return. The next day, with time to herself and only a handful of the staff still there, Olivia took herself off for a long walk and then spent plenty of time washing her hair and doing her nails. Miss Cross had given her permission to take the car and everything was arranged. She went into the garden behind the annexe, her hair still damp and hanging down her back, only to be called back indoors because she was wanted on the phone.

Mr van der Eisler's 'Hello, Olivia' was uttered in a voice of casual calm.

'Oh, it's you…'

'Indeed, it is I. Did I not say that I would telephone?'

'Well, yes, you did. Only it's tomorrow—I thought you'd forgotten.'

'Certainly not. Now, let us see. We need to be at the church fifteen minutes or so before the bride, do we not? Fifteen minutes to drive there, half an hour at your place for coffee and a chat. The wedding is at noon, is it not? I'll be with you at eleven o'clock.'

'Very well, I'll have coffee ready. Where are you? It sounds as though someone's washing up.'

'I've been operating; they're clearing Theatre.'

She wished she could think of something clever in answer. All she said was, 'Won't you be too tired? I mean, to drive down here tomorrow. You'll be careful?'

Mr van der Eisler suppressed a laugh. 'I will be careful, Olivia.'

'I expect you're busy. Goodbye, and thank you for ringing.'

She went back to her room and dried her hair, telling herself sternly not to get too excited, he was only doing what he had promised to do. It was kind of him. He had guessed that to go alone to Rodney's wedding would have been humiliating for her and to refuse would have been even worse—she could imagine the wagging tongues...

Mr van der Eisler went home to his dinner and then went back to the hospital again to check on his patient's condition and talk to his registrar. It was very late by the time he went to his bed and even then he lay for a time thinking about Olivia.

* * *

She was doing the same thing but since she was sleepy her thoughts were muddled and soon dissolved in sleep, and in the light of morning she dismissed them; there was too much to do.

She had her breakfast, tidied the little living-room, laid a tray for coffee and put everything ready to make sandwiches before going to dress. She didn't look too bad, she conceded, peering at her person in the spotty looking-glass behind the shower-room door. The dress would pass muster since her shoes and gloves and clutch bag were expensive, treasured leftovers from more prosperous days. The hat was a success too. She left it on the bed and went downstairs to put on the kettle and cut the sandwiches.

Just in time. The car came to a silent halt before her narrow front door and Mr van der Eisler, magnificent in a morning suit, got out.

She flung open the door. 'Hello—how very elegant you look…'

He took her hand. 'You've stolen my words, Olivia.' He studied her slowly. 'You look elegant. You also look beautiful; the bride is going to have difficulty in capturing everyone's attention once you get there.'

She went pink. 'You're joking—I hope so, it's the bride's day. We'll sit at the back…'

She led the way into the living-room, adding worriedly, 'And I'm not elegant, it's a dress from British Home Stores.' As she poured the coffee she said, 'We'll be able to slip away the moment they've left the reception. I expect you will want to get back to the hospital.'

'I have left things in the capable hands of my registrar. You are happy here, Olivia?'

'Oh, yes. Mother is coming to stay in another week or so. Wasn't it extraordinary that an old friend of Granny's should have written?'

'Indeed. Fate isn't always unkind, Olivia.'

'No. Have you been in Holland recently?'

'Yes. I came back a few days ago. I saw Debbie recently; she has become engaged to someone called Fred. Her father has a job as a part-time porter at Jerome's. So fate has been kind to her too.'

'Oh, I'm so glad. If you see her again will you tell her how happy I am? I'll write once school had settled down again.' She saw him glance at his watch. 'Is it time for us to leave? I'll get my hat.'

It took a few minutes to get it perched just so on her bright head and, although she felt fairly satisfied with the result, she felt shy as she went downstairs again.

He was standing at the window but he turned round as she went into the room. 'Charming. A wedding-hat *par excellence.*'

She had been clever, he reflected. The dress was cheap, but elegant, the hat was no milliner's model but it had style, and her gloves and shoes were beyond reproach. Mr van der Eisler, being the man he was, would have escorted her dressed in a sack and a man's cloth cap without a tremor, but he was glad for her sake that she had contrived to look so stunning.

The church, when they reached it, was already almost full and their seats at the back gave them a good view of the congregation without drawing attention to themselves. Although one or two people had turned round to look at them, recognised Olivia, studied Mr van der Eisler with deep interest and whispered to their neighbours.

Rodney was standing with his best man and didn't look round, even when the little flurry at the church door heralded the arrival of the bride.

Olivia, whose heart was as generously large as her person, felt a pang of concern at the sight of her. A rather short girl and dumpy, and decked out most unsuitably in quantities of white lace and satin. She had a long thin nose, too, and although her eyes were large and blue her mouth was discontented. On her wedding-day? thought Olivia. Perhaps her shoes pinch!

She still looked discontented as she and Rodney came down the aisle later, but Rodney looked pleased with himself, smiling and nodding to his friends. At the sight of Olivia his smile faltered for a moment, and then he grinned and winked before leading his bride out into the churchyard for the photographs.

The reception was at the bride's home, with a marquee on the lawn behind the solid redbrick residence. Rodney, decided Olivia, getting out of the car, had done well for himself.

Guests were arriving all the time and as a car drew up to park beside them a woman of Olivia's age poked her head out of its window.

'Olivia, my dear girl—someone said you were in church. Such a surprise, we all thought that you and Rodney—' She broke off as Mr van der Eisler joined Olivia.

Sarah Dowling had never been one of Olivia's

friends but an acquaintance merely, living some miles away from her home and encountered only at dances in other people's houses. 'Hello, Sarah,' she smiled, from under the brim of her hat. 'Isn't it a lovely day for a wedding? Of course we had to come to the wedding—Rodney and I are such old friends...'

Sarah had been taking stock of Mr van der Eisler. 'Is this—are you...?'

He smiled charmingly. 'Haso van der Eisler, and yes, we are.'

Olivia went a becoming pink. 'Oughtn't we to go in?' She didn't look at him as they joined the file of guests greeting the bride and groom.

Olivia shook hands with Rodney's father and mother, introduced Mr van der Eisler, and found herself face to face with Rodney.

'Olivia, old girl. So glad you could come and you've brought...?'

'Haso van der Eisler,' said Olivia calmly, and turned to shake hands with the bride. Murmuring the usual compliments, she heard Rodney.

'You'll be the next man to get caught, I suppose. We shall expect to come to the wedding, you know,' he said pompously.

She was rather surprised at the number of people who remembered her—mostly chance acquaintances whom she had met when staying with her grandmother, none of them friends. They all stayed to gossip and eye Mr van der Eisler, who bore their scrutiny with bland politeness. Olivia was sure that he was finding the whole affair tiresome and heaved a sigh of thankfulness when Rodney and his bride went away to change and presently were seen off with rose petals and confetti.

'Now we can go,' said Olivia, and made her adieux with a serenity she didn't feel, listening to Mr van der Eisler echoing her with impeccable manners. It took them some time to get to the car, for they were stopped by several people eager to discover more about her and her companion, but she fobbed them off politely and with laughing vagueness while he stood silently beside her.

She was feeling cross by the time she reached the car, and he settled her into the front seat, got in beside her, and drove off.

'Well, I'm glad that's over,' she said snappily. 'I hope you weren't too bored. I hate weddings...!'

'A nice cup of tea,' he said, in a voice to soothe the most recalcitrant child. 'There is a tea-room in Bradford-on-Avon, but I suspect that other guests will have the same idea as we have. We'll go on to Monkton—there's a cottage tea-room there. What an awkward time to have a wedding—one is scarcely sustained by vol-au-vents and things on biscuits and, one must admit, indifferent champagne.'

'Tea would be nice.' She peeped at him; his face was reassuringly calm. 'Thank you for being so nice—having to listen to all that nonsense.'

'About you and Rodney? Well, now they will have something to ponder over, won't they?'

'I did try not to give the impression that we—you...'

'You dealt with everyone beautifully, and I must

own that your hat was easily the most eye-catching there.'

'Really?' She wasn't cross any more. 'I bought it at a department store and tied a bit of ribbon round it.'

He laughed at that and after a moment she laughed with him. 'I don't know why I tell you things.'

'It's easy to talk to some people and not to others,' was all he said, then added, 'Ah, this is where we turn off for Monkton.'

The tea-room was the front room of a small cottage. The ceiling was so low that Mr van der Eisler had to bow his handsome head and the small tables were too close together for a private conversation. But, since he seemed to have no wish to talk about themselves, that didn't matter. They ate scones and jam and cream, sponge cake filled with strawberry jam and generous slabs of fruit cake, and the teapot was vast and filled with a strong brew.

'This is lovely,' said Olivia, kicking off her shoes under the table and biting into a scone. 'Actually the nicest part of the whole day.'

She licked jam off a finger and smiled at him from under the hat.

Only it didn't last long. In no time at all they were back in the car and driving to the school.

'You wouldn't like to come in?' she asked tentatively.

'Yes, I would, but I cannot—I have an engagement this evening in town.'

A remark which instantly put her on the defensive.

'Oh—I didn't know—if you had told me I could have returned straight here.'

He had got out of the car to open her door and stood with her by the open door. 'A delightful day, Olivia, and now you can consign Rodney to the past.'

'I'd already done that…'

'And have you plans for the future?'

She shook her head. 'I am content with the present.'

He took the hat off her head and bent to kiss her cheek. 'Give my love to Nel when you see her. Goodbye, Olivia.'

She stood there watching him drive away, feeling lonely.

CHAPTER FOUR

THE loneliness didn't last, of course; there was too much to do before the children came back for the second half of the term, and once they were back life became busier than ever. Olivia threw herself into her daily chores with enthusiasm, and only in the evenings, when she was on her own in the annexe, did she admit to loneliness.

It was fortunate that her mother was coming to stay for a week or ten days and, over and above that, two expeditions were planned for the pupils before the school broke up for the summer holidays. A trip to Cheddar Gorge and a second one to the Roman baths in Bath. Olivia was to go with the children on both occasions, as assistant to Miss Cutts, the history teacher—a stern lady, an excellent instructor, but given to a sharpness of tone which made her unpopular with the children. She was unpopular with Olivia too, who had been told off on several occasions and hadn't dared to answer back—it might have meant her job...

Her mother arrived on a Sunday evening and since Olivia was free she had been able to have supper ready and her small bedroom bright with flowers.

'Very nice,' pronounced Mrs Harding. 'What a dear

little place and just for you too. I don't suppose I shall see much of you, dear?'

'I get a few hours off each day and a free day once a week. I thought we might go up to Bath one day—there's a good bus service—and then if you want to go there on your own you'll know the way.' Olivia arranged the cold supper on a small table under the window. 'I have to have my midday dinner in school with the children, so if you won't mind, would you get your lunch? I'll be over most days after games and we can have tea together, then I'm free again after the children—the smallest ones—are in bed; that's at half-past seven. The evenings are light so we can go for a walk then if you like, and have supper together.' She paused. 'I hope you won't be bored, Mother?'

'My dear, you have no idea how delightful this is going to be—your grandmother has been most generous in giving us a home but I feel that we are outstaying our welcome.'

'In other words, Mother dear, Granny is behaving like an old tyrant.'

'Probably I shall be the same when I'm her age.'

'Mother, you have no idea how to be a tyrant. I do hope that Miss Cross will keep me on. This place is small but we could make it very comfortable, and we'd be on our own during the school holidays.'

Mrs Harding sighed. 'It sounds too good to be true, love, but I intend to enjoy every minute of my stay.'

Later, as they were washing up together, she asked, 'Did you go to Rodney's wedding?'

'Yes. You remember Mr van der Eisler? Well, he drove me over in his car...'

'How very kind. What was he doing here? Visiting Nel?'

'No, he—he saw the card when he brought me back after Easter and thought it would be much nicer if I had a companion to go with.'

She wrung out the dishcloth with a good deal of vigour and her mother studied the back of her head thoughtfully. 'That was indeed most thoughtful of him. So you enjoyed yourself?'

Olivia was uttering her own thoughts aloud. 'He looked quite magnificent in his morning dress; we went and had tea in a village tea-room afterwards. Why is it that wedding breakfasts aren't anything of the kind? Little bits and pieces and not nearly enough to go round.'

Mrs Harding wisely decided not to pursue the interesting subject of Mr van der Eisler. 'Was it an elegant affair? Did the bride look pretty?'

'Lots of lace and satin. I expect Rodney thought that she looked lovely.' She turned round to look at her mother. 'That sounds horrid. I dare say she's a very nice girl and I don't mind him marrying in the least. Funny, isn't it? When I thought I was in love with him.'

'Only because he was part of your life before your father died, love.'

'Yes, I realise that now. In future I shall concentrate on being a career girl.'

Her mother's murmured reply could have been anything.

They had a delightful two weeks together. Mrs Harding, freed from her mother's petty tyrany, became a cheerful housewife again, going to the village to shop, cooking delicious suppers for Olivia and taking herself off to Bath to look at the shops, and on Olivia's day off they went together to explore the delightful city. Waving her mother goodbye, Olivia vowed that, even if Miss Cross decided not to keep her on, she would find a job well away from London, where her mother could live with her. 'A housekeeper or something,' muttered Olivia, eating a solitary supper, 'there must be heaps to choose from, and at least I should get a good reference from Miss Cross.'

In two days' time two coachloads of children were to go to Cheddar Gorge, and Olivia was to go with them. Her task would be to attend to those who felt queasy, restrain the more lively and hand out the lunch packets under the stern eye of Miss Cutts, who would be travelling in the first coach with her; the second coach would contain the matron and Miss Ross—Matron and Miss Cutts didn't get on and had no hesitation in re-arranging matters to suit themselves.

Cheddar was a mere twenty miles or so and the journey was largely taken up with Miss Cutts' dry-as-dust lectures about the various ancient buildings they passed. Olivia, listening with half an ear, was aware that the small girls perched on either side of her weren't listening either—and really, why should they? She reflected, I shan't allow my daughters to be bothered with ancient monuments until they are at least ten years old. It would be different with boys, of course, they would want to know everything like that, and they would be brilliantly clever and grow up to be fine men like—well, like Mr van der Eisler. It was a good thing perhaps that Miss Cutts' voice cut through her daydreaming.

'Miss Harding, are you aware that Amelia is feeling sick? Be good enough to attend to her at once.'

Which kept Olivia busy until they reached the gorge and presently Gough's Cave, where the children were to be taken on a guided tour. Olivia found Nel beside her. 'I don't like caves,' she whispered.

Nor did Olivia, but in the face of Miss Cutts' enthusiasm nothing much could be done about that. 'We'll hold hands,' she promised. 'I think it may be rather interesting. Stalactites and stalagmites and flints and things.'

'Are they alive?' Nel wanted to know.

'No, dear—they're rock or something. You'll see…'

The tour seemed to go on forever. Long before they regained the entrance Olivia's hands and arms had been clutched by small nervous fingers, but it was amazing how soon the more timid recovered over their picnic lunch.

An instructive walk followed and Olivia, detailed to walk at the back so that she could keep an eye on the small children, allowed her thoughts to wander once more. It was a pleasant day, warm and sunny with a light breeze, and this, she told herself, was bliss compared with Sylvester Crescent and the hospital. The thought of which reminded her of Mr van der Eisler once again. I wonder what he's doing? she reflected, and started on a series of imagined situations of a highly colourful nature—operating in an atmosphere of high drama, sitting at a magnificent oak desk in a luxurious consulting-room advising some VIP, driving his beautiful motor car at a hundred miles an hour to save someone's life…!

He was doing none of these things; he was sitting behind a desk in a rather poky consulting-room in the outpatients department of a large Amsterdam hospital. He was hot and tired and rather hungry, since he had chosen to miss his lunch and start his clinic early because he had promised Rita to take her out that evening. She had phoned him that morning, saying that she wanted to talk to him about Nel, and he had suggested dinner. Now he wished that she hadn't accepted so eagerly, although he had to admit that anything to do with Nel mustn't be overlooked. He had tried to persuade Rita to make her home in England again, but in this she was adamant, being content to have Nel to live with her during the school holidays.

'After all,' she had reminded him in her gentle voice, 'her grandmother lives near the school and Nel loves her dearly, and if she came here to live with me she would be so lonely. I'm away all day and I love my job; I simply can't give it up.' She had added wistfully, 'Of course if I should meet a man who would understand this and offer me the kind of life I had before Rob died, someone who could love Nel too…' She had allowed her words to fade and then had smiled at him. 'What a good thing that I have you to advise me, Haso.'

The clinic ended, and he got into his car and drove himself to his home—an eighteenth-century gabled town mansion in a short row of similar buildings facing a narrow *gracht* leading from the Prinsengracht. It was very quiet there, a backwater in the bustling city, with trees bordering the water and a street of bricks. He parked his car, mounted the double steps to his front door, and let himself in.

The hall was narrow, with panelled walls and a high plaster ceiling. There were doors on either side and a staircase, its wooden treads worn with age, rose halfway down the hall, curving away to the floor above.

He had crossed the hall and was at a door beside the staircase when a stout man, no longer young, came through the baize door at the end of the hall.

Mr van der Eisler stopped in his stride. 'Ah, Bronger, I'm late.'

The door was pushed open and an Alsatian dog padded silently through.

'I'll take Achilles for a quick run before I go out.' He laid a hand on the dog's great head. 'I could do with some fresh air myself.'

'You'll be late back, Professor?'

'I hope not. Ask Ofke to leave some coffee on the stove for me, will you?'

He left the house again very shortly, the dog loping silently beside him. The streets were quiet in this part of the city and there was a small park nearby where Achilles raced around for some time while his master paced along its paths. Presently he whistled to the dog and they walked briskly back to his home and went, the pair of them, into the study, before Mr van der Eisler took himself upstairs to change for the evening.

Achilles was waiting for him in the hall when he

went downstairs again. 'Sorry, boy, I have to go out,' Mr van der Eisler told the dog gently and gave him a pat. 'And for some reason I have no wish to go.'

He got into his car once more. He had no wish to spend the evening with Rita; for a moment he allowed his thoughts to dwell on Olivia. Unlike Rita, whose gentle voice concealed a determination to get her own way, Olivia would speak her mind with a disregard of female wiles, cheerfully apologising afterwards if need be. Rita, he reflected, never apologised, because she never felt herself to be at fault.

He stopped before a block of flats in the more modern part of the city, got out and rang the bell of her flat.

'Haso?' Her voice was charming over the intercom. 'Come on up...'

'We're already a little late. I've a table at de Kersentuin.'

Rita joined him after about five minutes. She looked charming; she had an excellent clothes-sense, and the money to spend on a good hairdresser and beauty parlour. Mr van der Eisler helped her into the car and wondered why she didn't stir his interest in the slightest. They had got on well when Rob was alive, but he had never thought of her as anyone other than his friend's wife.

They had seen quite a lot of each other when his friend was alive and Nel was a baby, and since his death, naturally enough, they met frequently since he was one of his trustees. He had been surprised at how quickly she had returned to work as a PA to an executive in a big oil firm and how easily she had agreed to Nel going to boarding-school in England. True, Rob had wanted that, but he had envisaged Rita going to live in England too. After all, there was plenty of money...

He listened to Rita's amusing chatter, making all the right remarks, and presently, as they sat over dinner, he asked her why she had wanted to see him.

She laughed. 'Oh, nothing in particular, Haso. I suppose I was feeling lonely—you know how it is? Don't you ever wish to have a companion? A wife to come home to?'

'I'm poor company when I get home in the evening.' He smiled at her. 'Are you worried about Nel?'

'Nel? Why should I be worried about her? Her grandmother's only a few miles away from the school; she seems very happy. I had a letter from her this morning. They were taken off to Cheddar Gorge—for a treat. She didn't like the caves very much but there was someone there—one of the teachers, I presume— who didn't like them either, and they held hands. Silly child.'

'A dislike of being in an enclosed place is very common. Luckily there was someone with whom she could share her fear.'

That someone would have been Olivia, he was as sure of that as though Rita had mentioned her by name. He frowned—he really must stop thinking about the girl, she had nothing to do with his life. He said easily, 'As long as you are quite happy about Nel. She seemed perfectly content when I took her back to school.'

She handed him his coffee-cup and he went on,

'Have you any plans for the summer holidays? I suppose she'll stay for a while with Lady Brennon?'

'For as long as she likes. She can come over here, of course, but I don't want to take too much time off—I've been asked to go down to the South of France for the whole of August with the van Fonders.'

'You don't want to take Nel with you?'

'There won't be any other children there—she would be bored, my dear.' She smiled her charming smile. 'If you're in England perhaps you would collect her from school and take her to Lady Brennon's—I'm sure you want to see her again.'

Mr van der Eisler agreed; he would like to see Olivia too, although he didn't allow himself to examine this wish.

'I think it would be a good thing if Nel were to get to know you really well,' went on Rita. She met his eyes across the table. 'She does need a father.'

He said at his most bland, 'Oh, are you planning to marry again? Do I know him?'

Rita gave a little laugh to hide her annoyance. To marry Haso would settle all her problems—Nel could stay at school and, since Haso was wrapped up in his work and divided his time between the two countries, she would be free to live as she wished. He was a wealthy man, well-known in his profession, and he came from an old and respected family. Besides, he was blessed with good looks. She had set her heart on marrying him and had felt sure of getting her way. She would have to be more careful. At least she saw him frequently and there was always the excuse that she needed to know something about Nel. Perhaps she

should go over to Bath and collect the child at the end
of term? But if she suggested that, probably he would
assume that he needn't go too.

'No, of course not. I go out a good deal, you know
that, but there is no one—I still miss Rob.'

She sounded sincere and Mr van der Eisler said
kindly, 'He wouldn't want you to stay on your own
for the rest of your life, Rita. He loved you too much
for that.'

She had the good sense not to say any more but
began to talk about Nel, a subject she knew always
interested him.

It wanted a scant three weeks until the end of term,
and the whole school was occupied with preparations
of importance for the last day—prize-giving, the
school choir rendering suitable songs and the most
senior of the girls, due to leave and go on to a variety
of private schools, performing a play written by themselves. Olivia spent her days hearing lines, helping to
make the costumes and taking prep in the evenings,
so that the class mistresses could meet to discuss who
should have the prizes. She had no time to herself but
she didn't mind; life was interesting, the weather was
splendid and Miss Cross had told her that she might
return for the autumn term.

'Although I must warn you,' she had added, 'that
since you have no qualifications the Board of
Governors may wish to replace you after Christmas—
even a diploma in music or art would be sufficient. It
adds tone to the prospectus, and the parents expect
highly qualified staff in a school such as this one.' She

had sighed. 'It is a pity, Olivia, for you are a very useful member. Perhaps I shall be able to persuade them to accept you when they meet in January.'

Olivia thought it unlikely, but it was of no use worrying about it now. She had a job until Christmas, and only then would she worry. In the meantime, with certain reservations, she was happy.

On top of everything else there was the visit to the Roman baths—purely instructive; Miss Cutts had made that clear. Olivia found herself on the back seat of the school bus once more, listening to Miss Cutts' resonant voice recounting Bath's history. A pity they weren't to be allowed to see the Assembly Rooms and have tea there, reflected Olivia, longing for a cup of tea as they all got out and trooped at a snail's pace from one end to the other of the baths, stopping to admire the statue of the Emperor Hadrian overlooking the largest of the baths and listening to Miss Cutts reeling off the various measurements of the baths, expounding the beauties of the mosaic flooring, explaining how a Roman plumber had planned and fitted the lead conduit which supplied the water to the largest bath. The children listened obediently, but she could see that they had their minds on other things; the excitement of the end of term was too near to be ignored now.

That wasn't the end to the day either. It was Olivia's bedtime duty, which meant that after a hasty cup of tea she had to start collecting the smallest girls and get them bathed and into bed. They chattered like magpies, full of the things that they would do when they got home and speculation as to who would get the prizes. It was Nel who said wistfully to Olivia as she brushed her hair, 'I'm sure Mummy will come this time—I might get a prize and then she'll be proud of me.'

'I'm quite sure she's proud of you whether you get a prize or not,' Olivia assured her. 'And of course she'll come. The last day of the summer term is a very important one, isn't it? Are you looking forward to singing in the choir?'

Whereupon Nel burst into song and had to be shushed, popped into bed and tucked up.

Olivia was up early on the last day. So was everyone else, anxious to make the day a success. The first parents would arrive mid-morning and by noon, when a buffet lunch was to be served, they should all have arrived ready to take their seats in the nearby assembly hall for the entertainments and the prize-giving.

Everyone was drifting towards the dining-room when Olivia, rounding up stragglers, felt an urgent tug on her sleeve. Nel lifted a troubled face to hers. 'My Mummy hasn't come,' she whispered. 'She said she would—she promised she'd come with Granny— Granny isn't here either.'

Olivia put an arm round the small shoulders. 'There's still plenty of time, Nel—perhaps they've got held up in the traffic. I tell you what we'll do, we'll hurry to the door and make sure they aren't there...'

They reached the entrance as the Bentley came to a soundless halt and Mr van der Eisler got out, opened the door and helped Lady Brennon out. 'They've come,' shrieked Nel, and flung herself at her grandmother as Olivia beat a hasty retreat. Not fast enough, however.

'Don't go.' Mr van der Eisler spoke quietly as he turned to receive Nel's onslaught upon his vast person.

'Where's Mummy?' Nel asked suddenly.

Lady Brennon gave him a speaking look, took a few steps towards Olivia and sighed, 'Oh, dear…'

'She sends her dearest love,' said Mr van der Eisler cheerfully, 'but she just couldn't come—she has to work, you know, and she can't take a holiday whenever she wants one.'

Nel banged her small fist against his waistcoat. 'She doesn't have to work and she's got lots of money and she promised. You mustn't break a promise—Olivia told me so.' The child was near to tears. 'And it's not a holiday, it's me!'

'Ah, but I'm going to take you over to Holland in a week or two. Mummy will make sure to have a holiday then, and we'll all go out together, and we'll take Achilles with us—and Ofke's cat has had kittens. I'm sure she won't mind if you have one to keep.'

'Mummy doesn't like cats…'

'In that case, I'll have him, shall I? He'll be company for Achilles.'

He glanced at Olivia, 'Don't you think that's a good idea, Olivia?'

'Quite splendid. What fun you'll have, Nel. Now, would you like to take your grandmother to the dining-room? I'm sure you'd all like lunch.'

'You will come with us, Olivia?' asked Lady Brennon.

Olivia looked shocked. 'Me? Heavens, no! I'm

helping with the serving.' She suddenly wanted to get away from Mr van der Eisler's eyes. 'You'll excuse me?'

She made off at a great pace and in the dining-room was accosted by Miss Ross. 'There you are—where have you been? Cook has cut her hand and can't carve and we're running out of beef and ham. Go to the kitchen and slice some more as fast as you can.' She turned away to serve a parent and Olivia slid away kitchenwards. Mr van der Eisler, escorting his companions to a table near the buffet, watched her go.

Unhurriedly he collected food and drink and brought them back to the table. 'I'll be with you in a moment,' he told Lady Brennon, and wandered off to go through the same door as Olivia.

He stood a moment in the kitchen doorway, watching her. Carving was one of the things Olivia didn't know much about; a small pile of uneven slices bore witness to this, but there was no one to give her advice for Cook had retired to her room and the two kitchen-maids had gone too.

'Allow me,' said Mr van der Eisler, took the knife and two-pronged fork from her, and began to carve in a manner worthy of his calling.

'You can't come in here,' said Olivia when she had got back her breath, 'and you can't do that either.'

'But I am here, Olivia, and who but I am capable of carving this ham in the correct manner? After all, I have learned to be handy with a knife.'

'Oh, don't be absurd...'

'Don't work yourself up, dear girl. Take this dish of ham to the dining-room and I'll start on the beef.'

'You can't…'

'Now, now, off with you!'

So she picked up the dish of wafer-thin slices and hurried to the dining-room, where they were snatched from her. 'And do hurry with the beef.'

'Gratitude,' snorted Olivia, speeding back to the kitchen. Mr van der Eisler reduced the beef to a pile of evenly cut slices, took one, and sat down on the table to eat it.

'You can't…' began Olivia.

'That is the third time you have said that. Run along with the beef, there's a good girl, and then come back here.'

'I…' She caught his eye and did as she was bid, and presently returned.

'On which day do you return to Sylvester Crescent?' he asked her.

'Oh, I have to stay for another day, to tidy up, you know, and leave everything just so.'

'I'm staying with Lady Brennon for a day or two. I'll pick you up and drive you back—I've to be in London myself.'

'Yes, but…'

'But what? Is there some young man waiting for you?'

'A young man? Me? Heavens above! I don't have time to say more than good morning to the milkman—and there aren't any young men around.'

'A pity. Never mind. I'll come for you about ten o'clock in the morning. Are you going away for your holidays?'

'No. I—we—that is, we shall stay with Granny.'

'And what will you do all day?'

She was suddenly cross. 'I don't know—I have not the least idea. I must go.'

'Run along,' said Mr van der Eisler, and carved himself another slice of beef.

Parents were leaving the dining-room and making their way to the assembly hall. Olivia began to clear the plates and glasses and presently went round to the back of the stage to make sure that the choir were all present and looking presentable. The senior girls' play was already in progress and when that was over there would be a brief display of dancing before the choir. She laced up shoes, tied hair-ribbons and stilled child-ish nerves, and went to peep at the audience through a spyhole in the curtain. Lady Brennon and Mr van der Eisler were sitting in the second row. Lady Brennon was smiling gently; her companion looked as though he might be asleep.

The play over, the dancing done to great applause, the choir was coaxed into a semi-circle, the music mis-tress struck up a chord, and they were off, speeding the boat over to Skye with tremendous verve.

Olivia, in the wings acting as prompt, thought that if Mr van der Eisler had been dozing, that should have roused him nicely.

They sang a bit of Gilbert and Sullivan next, and then a rather sad song about snow. The choir hadn't liked it but the music mistress had decided that they were to sing it. They got through the first verse well enough, moaning 'Oh, snow' with enthusiasm, but somehow they lost the thread during the second and Olivia had to do some prompting. Several small faces turned to look at her in panic, the music mistress thumped out the last few bars and since no one sang began on them again. Olivia began to sing the words very softly and in a moment a relieved chorus of small voices took over from her. It had been only a slight hitch in an otherwise perfect performance and the applause was deafening.

It was later, as the children began to leave with their parents, that Mr van der Eisler went in search of Olivia. He found her on her hands and knees, grovelling under a schoolroom cupboard.

'I must say,' he remarked pleasantly, 'that you look nice from any angle, Olivia.'

She rose to her splendid height, very red in the face. 'I'm looking for a lost tennis racquet. What do you want?'

'You do not mince your words. To remind you that I shall be waiting for you at ten o'clock on the day after tomorrow.' He smiled and nodded and turned to go. 'You have a pretty singing voice,' he observed as he left the room.

She spent the next day doing whatever she was told to do and then going to the annexe to pack her own things. Her thoughts were muddled. On the one hand she felt a pleasurable excitement at the thought of seeing Mr van der Eisler again, but this was strangely mitigated by her doubts as to whether she should allow herself to be drawn into some kind of friendship with him. Perhaps just this once, she told herself weakly—she wasn't likely to see much of him anyway; he had said that he was taking Nel back to Holland with him and perhaps her mother would bring her back next term. Besides she had a strong suspicion that he and Nel's mother intended to marry.

He was just being kind, she decided. What could be more normal than to offer a lift since they were both going to London on the same day?

The thought of Sylvester Crescent depressed her. It would be lovely to see her mother again but six weeks of living with Granny was daunting.

Just before ten o'clock the next morning she locked her door, took the key along to the school porter, and went outside. The Bentley was there, with Mr van der Eisler, his hands in his pockets, strolling around the flowerbeds bordering the sweep. He saw her at once, took her case from her and put it in the boot, and then opened the car door.

'Good morning,' said Olivia pointedly.

'Don't look so cross. Will you smile if I say good morning to you?'

She laughed. 'Don't be absurd. I'm very grateful for this lift.'

He got in beside her and drove off without any fuss. 'So am I,' he told her. A remark which left her vaguely puzzled.

'I expect Nel is glad to be with her Granny?'

'She is always happy there. I'll take her over to Holland in a week's time when I go back.'

'I'm sorry she was disappointed about her mother, but she soon cheered up, didn't she?'

He grunted non-committally; he had spent a good deal of time trying to smooth over the fact of Nel's mother not coming to the school, and it had been hard work.

The grunt didn't sound very promising. Olivia stayed silent, admiring the scenery to herself and watching his hands on the wheel. They were large, blunt-fingered and beautifully kept.

They had driven for some time in a silence which was strangely companionable when he said, 'How about coffee? I don't know about you, but I was up early; Nel and I took the dogs out.'

'You like dogs?'

'Yes. My own dog, Achilles, is an Alsatian; I've had him since he was a very small puppy. I should like to have a dog here, but I don't have much time to myself when I'm in England. My housekeeper has a cat—you like cats?'

'Yes. We had two, and an Old English Sheepdog. Our cook took the cats and Shep died just before we had to leave.'

After a few moments of silence she ventured. 'Your housekeeper's cat, does it have a name?'

'Bertie.' He laughed suddenly. 'You and I don't need to make small-talk, Olivia. Here's a place where we can have coffee.'

It was a pleasant wayside inn, and they sat outside drinking their coffee in the sun. 'Tell me, what do you intend to do, Olivia?' asked Mr van der Eisler. 'You must have some plans.'

'What is the use of plans? I hope that Miss Cross will keep me on at the school and I can have Mother to stay each term. She isn't happy with Granny, you know. I have thought that I might study for something in my spare time. It would have to be something where

I could earn a living and have a home too. Am I too old to be a nurse?'

'No, but that is three years in hospital, and even when you have trained the chance of your getting a post where you could live outside hospital on your salary wouldn't be too great. I do not wish to bring up the question of Rodney, but there must have been other men in your life, Olivia.'

'Oh, yes. I had a lot of friends, and I suppose if Father hadn't died and left us awkwardly placed I might have married one of them. Although now I'm older I don't think I should have liked that.'

'No, I don't think you would. Wait for the right man, Olivia.'

'Oh, I will,' she assured him.

It was when they were back in the car, she sitting silently beside him, that she realised that there was no need for her to wait for the right man. He was here already, sitting beside her.

CHAPTER FIVE

MR VAN DER EISLER began to talk presently about nothing much, and it served to quieten her jangling nerves. She needed to go somewhere very quiet so that she could think. She mustn't see him again, of course, and she must stop thinking about him, and the sooner the better. Her thoughts were interrupted by his casual, 'Becky will have lunch ready. I hope you will lunch with me, Olivia? I'll take you home afterwards.'

So much for her good resolutions. They flew out of the window and she said happily, 'Oh! Thank you, that would be nice.' Then she added, 'But isn't it interfering with your day?'

'Not in the least. I'm free for the rest of the day.' His voice held just the right note of casualness. He lapsed into silence again and she thought uneasily that he might wonder why she didn't have something to say for herself. The weather seemed a safe topic, and the countryside, so she enlarged upon these two items at some length and he, aware that for some reason she was feeling awkward with him, allowed her to chatter in a manner quite unlike her usual self, making suitable replies in his quiet voice so that gradually she regained her normal composed manner and by the time he stopped before his house she had herself nicely in hand.

He had told Becky that he was bringing a guest to lunch and she had the door open as they reached it, a wide smile on her elderly face while she summed up Olivia with sharp eyes.

'This is Becky, my housekeeper,' he said, and 'Becky, this is Miss Olivia Harding. She works at Nel's school.'

'Now isn't that nice,' declared Becky. 'I dare say Miss Harding would like to tidy herself before lunch. I'll take her to the cloakroom while you look through your post, Mr Haso.'

Olivia, recognising the gentle tyranny of the old family retainer, followed Becky.

Mr van der Eisler was waiting for her in his sitting-room, standing by the open door leading to a small but charming garden. It was a pleasant room, furnished with a nice mixture of antiques and comfortable modern chairs, and wore the air of being well lived-in. Bertie, Becky's cat, sat washing himself on a small side-table and gave her a searching glance as she went in before continuing his toilet, and Mr van der Eisler put down the letters in his hand and invited her to sit by the window. 'There's time for a drink before lunch. Sherry? Or perhaps you would prefer something else?'

'Sherry, please.' She looked around her; the walls were almost covered by paintings—portraits as far as she could see. They sat making small-talk for a few minutes until she asked, 'May I look at your paintings? Are they your family?'

'Yes, the English side of it. My grandmother was

English and left me this flat and its contents. I came here a good deal as a boy, and later when I was at Cambridge, and I feel very much at home.'

She nodded. 'I'm sure that you must, as you were happy here.' She laughed suddenly. 'And to think that Debbie used to worry about you being lonely in London.'

'A kind-hearted child. Did you worry too, Olivia?'

'No—well, not worry exactly. I did wonder where you lived in London.' She added hastily, 'Just idle curiosity, you know.'

It wasn't too bad, she reflected, once she had gone into the room and seen him standing there. She had spent her few minutes in the cloakroom giving herself good advice and so far she was managing pretty well. True, the wish to fling herself at him and throw her arms round his neck was a strong one, but she prided herself on her good sense. She began to wander round the room, looking at each portrait—elderly gentlemen with side-whiskers, younger men with determined chins resting on snowy stocks, small, fragile-looking ladies, and several miniatures of children's heads. There were one or two portraits of younger women too, with beautiful faces and laughing eyes, and she paused before them and found him beside her. 'My grandmother and my mother. They were so unlike the earlier ladies in the family. As tall and generously built as you, and as beautiful.'

Olivia said, 'Oh,' faintly, and wondered if 'generously built' meant fat. The women in the portraits didn't look fat, just well-covered. She gave her own person a surreptitious glance, and went scarlet when he said blandly, 'No, I don't mean fat, Olivia. You need have no fears about that. You are exactly the right shape for a woman.'

She didn't look at him. Really, the conversation was straying from the coolly friendly path she had intended to tread. She said, politely cool even though her face was still pink, 'You have some charming ancestors.'

'You should see the Dutch side of the family; they must have spent half their lives being painted.'

'Were they doctors too?'

'Almost to a man.'

She faced him then. 'You must have a great deal of wisdom with such a heritage.'

Just for a moment the heavy lids lifted to show the clear blue of his eyes. 'What a very perceptive thing to say, Olivia. I do my best to carry on the family tradition.' He glanced round as the door opened and Becky came in.

'There's that naughty Bertie on your table again, and his dinner waiting for him too. If you've had your drinks, I'll serve the soup, Mr Haso.'

The dining-room was on the other side of the hall. Not a large room, it held a circular mahogany table with ribbon-back chairs around it, a side-table holding some massive silver pieces, and a Regency fireplace with a carriage clock on the mantel above it. The curtains were a rich plum velvet and the floor polished wood. A lovely room in which to have a meal, reflected Olivia, sitting down and accepting the soup Becky had set before her.

It was a good soup—watercress with a swirl of cream in its centre—and that was followed by lamb cutlets, new potatoes, and peas with baby carrots. The trifle which followed was perfection itself. Olivia, who had a good appetite and never pretended otherwise, ate every morsel.

They went back to the sitting-room for their coffee and this time she took more leisurely stock of her surroundings. The colour scheme wasn't so obvious here—the carpet on the polished wood floor was in muted blues and dull greens and pinks, and the long curtains at the windows at both ends of the room were old rose brocade, while the chairs were upholstered in the same dim colours as the carpet. There was a good deal of yew and apple-wood, and a splendid bow-fronted display cabinet with some intricate marquetry. 'But of course you'll have a study,' observed Olivia, speaking her thoughts out loud.

'Yes, and there is another small room. I don't use it but Becky tells me that my grandmother used it as her own private place, where she could sew and read and so on. It is quite a big flat. Becky has her own flatlet, and there are three bedrooms and bathrooms as well as the kitchen.'

'Did your grandmother like living in Holland?'

'Oh, yes. You see, she and my grandfather were a devoted pair; she would have lived in the middle of the desert if need be, provided she was with him. They came over here a good deal, of course, bringing the children with them, and later their grandchildren too.'

He watched the beautiful face opposite him, alight with interest, and wondered silently why he was telling her all this. Perhaps something of his thoughts showed in his usually impassive face, for Olivia said in a polite visitor's voice, 'How interesting—to have two countries, I mean.' She put her cup down. 'I expect you have things to do—I've enjoyed my lunch, thank you, and it was so kind of you to drive me back. I think I should go.'

He made no demure and after a suitable chat with Becky she followed him out to the car and was driven to Sylvester Crescent. It looked unwelcoming, with all the net curtains covering the windows and the doors tightly shut. Outside her grandmother's flat Olivia said, 'Would you like to come in?' and expected him to say no.

Instead, he said at once, 'I should like to meet your mother again,' and got out to help her out of the car and get her luggage from the boot.

By the time they reached the door her mother had it open, smiling widely. 'Darling, how lovely to see you—it seems such ages.' She kissed Olivia and held out a hand to Mr van der Eisler. 'Do please come in, Mr van der Eisler. You brought Olivia back—how kind. Have you had lunch? Or perhaps coffee?'

'We've had lunch, Mother, at Mr van der Eisler's home…'

'Then tea—it's a little early, but tea is always welcome.'

'I should love a cup,' he said surprisingly, following Mrs Harding into the drawing-room where Mrs Fitzgibbon sat in her uncomfortable chair.

She held out a hand. 'How delightful to see you again,' she said, at her most gracious. 'Do sit down and tell me what you have been doing. I get so little news here, chained as I am to this flat, and only my daughter for company.' She offered an indifferent cheek for Olivia's dutiful kiss. 'You will find it equally dull, Olivia—six weeks' holiday, I understand. I'm sure I don't know what you will do with yourself. Although your mother will be glad of some help around the house, I suppose.' She added, 'Well, now you're here you might make the tea.'

Olivia cooled down in the kitchen. It was a pity that he had chosen to come in; Granny enjoyed belittling her and usually she didn't allow it to rile her too much, but in front of Mr van der Eisler... He had no interest in her as a woman, she was sure of that, but to be held up as a tiresome fool by her grandmother might destroy the mild liking he appeared to have for her. What did it matter? she told herself fiercely, spooning tea into the pot. This was the last time they would see each other. She had heard him tell Nel that her mother would bring her back to school for the autumn term so obviously he had no other plans. Besides, that was weeks away; he would have forgotten all about her by then.

Pouring tea and handing round digestive biscuits, she had to admit that his considerable charm was making a good impression upon Granny, who enlarged upon her distant aristocratic connections at some length, much to her and her mother's discomfort. When he got up to go at last she offered him a hand, thanked him in a cool voice for giving her a lift, and uttered a conventional wish as to his future wellbeing. All without looking any higher than the middle button of his waistcoat.

'A delightful man,' observed Mrs Fitzgibbon. 'Such

a pity that you do not attract him, Olivia. I presume that he intends to marry this small girl's—Nel's—mother? He spoke of her.'

'I've no idea,' said Olivia airily, intent on pulling the wool over her grandparent's sharp eyes. 'I don't know anything about him. He was kind enough to give me a lift, Granny, that is all.'

She caught her mother's eye and that lady, about to say something, obediently didn't.

Life was dull in Sylvester Crescent and, after ten days of Mrs Fitzgibbon's lightly veiled remarks about extra mouths to feed, Olivia went looking for a job. She didn't have to go far. The Coffee-Pot needed part-time help. Four mornings a week, from ten o'clock until the regular waitress came on at one o'clock. The pay was minimal but she could keep her tips. Olivia went back to her grandmother's flat, delivered her news, and listened to a harangue from her grandmother about the humbleness of her new job.

'Honest work for an honest wage,' said Olivia cheerfully.

It wasn't all bad. True, her feet ached, and sometimes the customers were rude, but secretly she sympathised with them, for the coffee was abominable. It gave her something to do, though, and put a little money in her pocket, even after paying over a good deal of it towards her keep.

Since her afternoons were free she took her mother out to the parks or to window-shop, leaving her grandmother to play bridge with her few friends.

'Your granny would be so much happier on her own,' sighed her mother.

Olivia gave her parent's arm a sympathetic squeeze. 'If Miss Cross will take me on permanently next year you shall come and live with me, and you must come and stay next term for just as long as you would like.'

'Your grandmother might need me...'

'Pooh,' said Olivia strongly. 'She was very content until we went to live with her, and that's all nonsense about her not being able to afford help in the house.'

'You're quite happy, dear?' her mother wanted to know.

'Of course I am, love. Haven't I got everything I want—a job, money in my pocket, a pleasant place in which to work?' The memory of Mr van der Eisler made nonsense of her cheerful reply; she thought about him all day and every day, despite the fact that she wasn't likely to see him again. He would be at Jerome's, she supposed, or back in Holland...

He was in Holland, and very shortly he would return to England bringing with him Nel and her mother. Rita had agreed unwillingly to go over to England and visit her mother-in-law, but only provided that she might leave Nel with her so that she could go to her friends in the South of France. She had found Nel a nuisance, although she had taken advantage of the child being there to see as much of Haso as possible but, although he had been friendly and ready to help in any way, he had evinced no desire to spend his free time with her. Absence makes the heart grow fonder, she told herself; he would be delighted to see her again when she returned.

They were to stay for a couple of days at his flat in

London so that Rita could do some shopping, and it was Nel who gave Mr van der Eisler the excuse to go and see Olivia. He had had no intention of going, he told himself, he found her unsettling, and his growing interest in her had been brought about by circumstances and nothing more. All the same, when Nel asked him if they might go and see Olivia, he agreed. 'We might go while your mother is shopping,' he suggested.

But Rita said at once, 'Oh, but I'd love to come too—such a nice girl and so kind to Nel...'

Mrs Harding opened the door to them. 'Do come in.' She shook Rita's hand and smiled at them all. 'Have you come to see Olivia? I'm afraid she's not here. She's got a little job down at the Coffee-Pot...'

'What could be better?' exclaimed Rita. 'We can have our coffee there and talk to her at the same time.'

'Well,' said Mrs Harding doubtfully, 'she will probably be busy.'

'Oh, I'm sure she will be able to find time to have a chat. Nel's so looking forward to seeing her.'

Mr van der Eisler said smoothly, 'I dare say Olivia would rather we didn't call on her while she's working.'

However, Rita persisted. 'We've come all this way, and Nel won't be able to see her now...'

He doubted that her concern was genuine, but undoubtedly Nel was disappointed. He drove them to the Coffee-Pot, parked the car and opened the door.

Olivia had her back to them, serving coffee and buns to four people crowded round one of the little tables. They sat down, the three of them, at the only empty table, and when she turned round she saw them.

She went red and then pale, but she crossed to their table and wished them a composed good morning, smiled at Nel, and asked them if they would like coffee. The look she cast at Mr van der Eisler was reproachful, but it hid delight at seeing him again even if the circumstances were hardly what she would have wished.

'Your mother told us where you were,' he explained easily. 'Nel wanted to see you before she goes to stay with Lady Brennon. You must forgive us for taking you unawares.'

He could see that she wished to go—there were other customers. 'May we have some coffee, and perhaps a milkshake for Nel?'

She went away and Rita said, 'What a poky little place. I dare say the coffee's undrinkable. Still, I suppose if the girl's hard up it's better than nothing.'

She gave him a narrow look as she spoke—there had been something about the way he had looked at Olivia which made her uneasy. She was a beautiful girl, there was no doubt about that, but no sparkle. Rita, who had brought sparkling to a fine art, did so now at Olivia, returning with their coffee, and she could see how easily she could make Mr van der Eisler laugh...

The café emptied momentarily, and Olivia spent a minute or two talking to Nel before more customers arrived and she was kept busy, but when she saw Nel's frantic waving she went back to her.

'We're going now,' said Nel, 'but you will be at school, won't you?'

'Yes, Nel. I'll be there.'

'Such hard work it must be,' said Rita. 'But anything's better than this, I should imagine. And the coffee is vile…' She gave a little laugh. 'I say, do we leave a tip?'

Put in my place, thought Olivia. Between Granny and her, Mr van der Eisler must think me a complete nonentity. She smiled serenely while she seethed. 'Goodbye—I must go. But it was nice seeing Nel again.'

The smile took in the three of them as she turned away to take an order. Mr van der Eisler hadn't said a word. He would very much have liked to utter those which trembled on his tongue, but Olivia's dignity must be preserved at all costs before a room full of strangers, and the words he wished to utter to Rita were harsh indeed, and liable to cause some interest in those sitting around them. In the car he said blandly, 'Why were you rude, Rita, and unkind…?'

'Rude? I didn't mean to be, Haso. Oh, dear, have I upset the poor girl? My silly tongue, I'm so sorry.' She looked over her shoulder at Nel. 'Darling, when you see Olivia next term, do tell her that I didn't mean to upset her. I was joking, but we haven't all got the same sense of humour.'

'Aren't you coming to take me back to school, Mummy?' asked Nel.

'Sweetie, I'll try very hard to come, really I will, but if I'm terribly busy I may not be able to. Granny will take you back and I really will come over at the end of term.'

'Promise?'

'Promise.' She turned a smiling face to Mr van der Eisler's stern profile. 'You'll bring me over, won't you, Haso?'

'That depends on where I am and what I am doing. You can always fly to Bristol and get a car from there.'

Rita pouted charmingly. 'You know I hate travelling alone.'

He said nothing, aware that in a few days' time she would fly—quite alone—down to the South of France to join her friends. He would have liked to tax her with that, but Nel had to be kept happy; she was already getting too bright, too quick not to sense her mother's impatience with her.

He didn't stay long at Lady Brennon's but drove back to London, wishing that he had Olivia sitting beside him. What on earth had possessed the girl to work as a waitress? Was she so desperately hard-up? Was she to go on taking these dead-end jobs for the rest of her life with little or no opportunity of meeting a suitable young man who would marry her? Heaven knew that she was beautiful enough to attract them. He began to turn over in his mind the various young doctors and surgeons he knew at Jerome's, wondering how to make it possible for her to meet them. A fruitless task which got him nowhere.

He drove straight to the hospital and forgot her, and when he got back to his flat, finally, there were letters to read and answer, phone calls to make and patients' notes to study. He ate a late supper, clucked over by

Becky, and went to bed, and during the next few busy days spared her only the most cursory of thoughts.

He had something of a worldwide reputation in his particular field of surgery and an urgent summons took him to Italy, so that when the time came for Nel to return to school he was out of the country and, since Rita was still in the South of France, Nel was taken back to school by her grandmother.

Olivia, detailed to collect the children as they arrived, was confronted by a tearful Nel. 'Mummy didn't come and Uncle Haso sent me a postcard with a lot of blue sky and mountains on it. I expect they forgot...' Her small lip trembled and Lady Brennon said quickly, 'I'm sure they wouldn't forget, darling. Perhaps there wasn't a seat for them on the plane—perhaps they'll come as soon as they can. It's holiday-time, and everyone wants to travel...'

'The planes get so full,' added Olivia, anxious to avert tears.

Nel gave her the clear look that only a child could give. 'Uncle Haso has his own plane,' she said.

Olivia and Lady Brennon exchanged glances. 'Well, in that case,' said Olivia briskly, 'he may even now be on his way here. Will you say goodbye to your granny, poppet? Then I'll take you up to your dormitory—most of your best friends are in it this term.'

Nel brightened a little. 'Oh, good, and may I come and see you, Granny, at half-term?'

'Of course, my pet, but I'll be over before then to watch your sports day.'

It wasn't until Olivia was in bed that night that she

had the leisure to think her own thoughts. The day had been busy—the children's trunks to unpack, tuck to be labelled and put away, the homesick to be comforted, mislaid things to be found. She was glad that she had been too busy to think, she reflected, curled up in her bed at last. Now, tired though she was, she had to go over every word Nel and Lady Brennon had uttered about Mr van der Eisler. It was only too apparent that he was with Rita. And why should that upset her, she asked herself angrily, when she had made up her mind to forget him, never think of him again? What business was it of hers if he was to marry Rita? It would be a good thing for Nel's sake; the child was fond of him, more so than she was of her mother. The only real security she had was with her grandmother...

Olivia nodded off.

She woke in the night and had a nice comforting weep, and felt better for it. She couldn't change the way things were so she had better accept them with a good grace and make the best of what she had—a job, a frail security, and a roof over her head. Who knew? She might, any day now, meet some man who would want to marry her. But would she want to marry him?

School routine took over once more. The days followed each other with ordered speed; they got chillier too, and as the evenings darkened she had the task of overseeing the smaller children's leisure before their bedtime. There was a good deal of activity in the gym too, where those who were taking part practised for sports day. Olivia, Jill of all trades and master of none, played the piano for the rhythmic exercises, untangled the formation gymnastics when they got too involved, and soothed bruises and bumps.

It had turned quite cold by now and half-term would follow on after sports day. Her mother was coming to spend two weeks with her and since she would be free for the first week she had planned a trip to Bath—they would lunch out and have tea in the Assembly Rooms and, since she had had no reason to spend much money, they might do a little shopping. Christmas was still some way off and she dreaded spending it with her grandmother, but perhaps she and her mother would be able to spend a day out somewhere.

Parents were to arrive directly after lunch and, after the various displays, be given tea before going home again. The morning was spent on last-minute preparations and the solving of small crises as they occurred, but by one o'clock the whole school was ready—the rows of chairs in place, the trestle tables in the assembly hall covered with white cloths and piled with cups and saucers and plates.

'You will help with the tea,' said Miss Cross, pausing by Olivia as she counted sugar bowls, 'and do whatever Miss Ross wants, and be prepared to give Matron a hand if there are any mishaps.'

She went on her way and Olivia started counting the sugar bowls once more.

The children were permitted to greet their parents when they arrived so that the hall was packed with excited little girls all talking at once. Olivia, having counted heads and found them correct, took herself off to the pantry to make sure that everything was as ready as possible for tea. The occasion must go off smoothly,

Miss Cross had said. As soon as the last item was over
the parents would be ushered into the assembly hall
and the tea-urns, plates of sandwiches and cakes were
to be ready and waiting for them.

The tide of parents ebbed and flowed, and almost
at the last moment Mr van der Eisler's car drew up
before the entrance. Nel, lingering in the hall almost
in tears, rushed to meet him as he got out, opened the
door to help Lady Brennon out and then bent to swing
her in the air.

'You came, you came!' cried Nel. 'And Granny too.
Olivia said you would.' She looked around her. 'I suppose Mummy's working...'

'Yes, love, she is. Will we do instead? We're looking forward to seeing you do whatever it is...'

Nel laughed and hugged her grandmother. 'I'm in
a gym display.' She looked suddenly anxious. 'It's almost time to start.'

'Then let us go at once and sit down,' said Lady
Brennon. 'Where is your nice Olivia?'

'She's got to see to the tea as well as us. I expect
she's in one of the pantries.' She caught them both by
the hand. 'Come along—you will watch me, won't
you?'

'I shan't take my eyes off you,' promised Mr van
der Eisler.

They found seats at the end of a row, halfway
towards the back of the hall and, since there were still
some ten minutes before the first event was to take
place, he settled Lady Brennon in her seat and got up.
'I'll be back,' he assured her, and disappeared through
the nearby door.

In the hall he encountered the porter, enquired where the pantries might be, and with a brisk nod set off to find them.

Olivia, spooning tea into bowls ready for the urns, turned round to his quiet, 'Hello, Olivia.'

She felt the colour leave her cheeks and then rush back in a bright surge. She wished with all her heart that she could say something amusing and casual but all she managed was a breathless 'Oh,' and then added peevishly, 'You startled me.' She put the bowl down with a shaking hand. 'Shouldn't you be in the gym? I am glad you came.' She frowned in case she gave him the wrong impression. 'What I mean is that I'm glad you came for Nel's sake. She was so afraid no one would turn up. Is—are her grandmother and mother here too? I do hope so. She's in a rhythmic gym display, you know.' She paused for breath, aware that she was babbling.

He came into the pantry. 'And are you glad to see me again, Olivia?'

'Glad? Why should I be glad? I hadn't thought about it. You must go.'

He took no notice at all. 'I was sorry I wasn't in England to give you a lift back at the beginning of term.'

'There is an excellent train service,' she told him frostily. 'Nel told me that you were abroad.'

'Ah, yes, I sent her a postcard.'

'I hope you had a pleasant holiday...'

He smiled. 'Holiday? Ah, yes, of course. It seems a long time ago. Are you coming to watch this entertainment?'

'Of course not. I shall be helping behind the scenes and then giving a hand with the teas.' She picked up the bowl again for something to do. 'I hope you enjoy the display; please remember me to Lady Brennon. Goodbye, Mr van der Eisler.' He took his dismissal with a good grace, although he didn't return her good-bye.

As he slipped into his seat beside Lady Brennon, a few moments before the first item on the programme, she whispered, 'Did you find her?'

'Yes, but I fancy I've lost her again for the moment, although I'm not sure why.' He turned his attention to the first of the gym displays.

The afternoon went well—the gymnasts were fault-less and the younger ones performed with aplomb, knowing that their mothers and fathers were sitting there admiring their efforts. Miss Cross brought the afternoon to a close with a suitable speech and every-one surged out, bent on getting a cup of tea.

Olivia, entrenched behind an urn, did her best not to look at Mr van der Eisler, poised precariously on a small wooden chair, bowing his vast person to listen to Nel's happy chatter. Her best wasn't good enough; Matron's tart voice brought her back to reality.

'Olivia? Do you not hear what I say? Sophie Greenslade feels sick. Get her upstairs before she is, and stay with her until I come with her mother. We don't want a fuss...'

With one last lingering glance at Mr van der Eisler, Olivia led the unhappy Sophie up to her dormitory, held the bowl, cleaned the little girl up and tucked her under a blanket on her bed, looking pale but smelling sweet, so that by the time Matron and Mrs Greenslade arrived Matron was able to reassure the anxious mother that little Sophie wasn't suffering from some serious illness.

'Thank you, Olivia, you may go,' said Matron graciously.

Olivia went, as fast as her long legs could carry her. She reached the hall in time to see Lady Brennon, with Mr van der Eisler looming beside her, disappearing through the entrance.

She stood there, filled with bitter disappointment; never mind that she had decided to forget him, one more glimpse would have been nice before she began that difficult task. She looked with longing at his massive shoulders disappearing through the door. This really was the very last time she would see him…

He turned his head and saw her and came back to stand before her. 'Were you hiding?' he asked without preamble.

'Me? No. Sophie was being sick!'

'Ah.' He smiled at her and her heart turned over. 'We shall meet again,' he told her, and went away again.

A remark which made nonsense of her good resolutions, although during the course of a wakeful night she kept to her decision not to see him again. 'Not even to think of him,' she told herself. 'He was just being kind.'

He had said that they would meet again. Did he mean that he would be coming to fetch Nel at the end of term? If so, she would take care not to be anywhere near him. If necessary, she would feel ill and be ex-

cused from her duties. A headache or, better still, a
sprained ankle. On this ridiculous thought she fell into
a restless doze, to wake the next morning heavy-eyed
and pale, so that Matron asked her sharply if she was
feeling poorly.

'It will be most inconvenient if you are,' said that
lady, 'I shall want you to help me with hair-washing
this evening.'

So Olivia washed one small head after the other, an
occupation which allowed her to dream a great deal
of nonsense. Even though it was nonsense it was comforting imagining what life would be like if Mr van
der Eisler were to fall in love with her. She might not
be going to see him again but there was no harm in a
little daydreaming.

CHAPTER SIX

MRS HARDING came the next day and as the school was empty, save for the cook, the porter and the two daily maids, Olivia and her mother had the pleasant illusion that the whole place was theirs. It was cold but fine weather and they took advantage of the peace and quiet to go for long walks, finding a village pub for lunch and getting back to the annexe in time to cook their supper and spent the evening together catching up on gossip. It was apparent to Olivia that her mother wasn't happy at Sylvester Crescent. She had few friends there, indeed, mere acquaintances, who came to play bridge and rarely asked her back to their homes. Mrs Fitzgibbon was demanding too, so that Mrs Harding felt restricted. It was no good telling her to assert herself, thought Olivia, for her mother was a gentle soul, always determined to expect the best from everyone. Next year, thought Olivia, we'll make a home here. Mother can come back with me when term starts—at least she will be free to do what she likes with her days.

They sat making their plans, doing sums on scraps of paper, discussing the small things they would buy in order to make the little place like home, and Olivia,

despite her secret heartache, was glad to see her
mother so happy.

They went to Bath on the last day of the half-term,
looking at the shops and having a splendid lunch before visiting the Abbey and then treating themselves
to tea. It was a pity that once the school started again
Olivia wouldn't be free for more than an hour or so
each day, but Mrs Harding declared herself quite
happy to potter around on her own. Indeed, she looked
so much better that Olivia persuaded her to stay for
another week and took it upon herself to phone her
grandmother and tell her.

Mrs Fitzgibbon, naturally enough, was annoyed,
complaining that she was unable to manage without
her daughter's help.

'Doesn't that nice woman—Mrs Lark—come in
each day and cook and clean?' asked Olivia.

'Well, of course she does,' snapped her grandmother. 'You really don't suppose that I would wish
to do those things myself, do you?'

'No, Granny. So you're being well looked-after.
Good. Mother's very happy here and it's doing her
good—she never liked London, you know.'

'You are an impertinent girl.'

Olivia said, 'Yes, Granny,' and then rang off.

School began again and now there was excitement
in the air. Christmas was near enough for the all-
important question of presents to be the main topic
and there would be the school play at the end of term
and a concert by those who were learning some musical instrument or other.

There were the new pupils too, nicely settled in by

now but still ignorant of the festivities ahead and anxious to join in everything.

Olivia, not a skilled needlewoman, none the less sewed pantomime costumes and, under the guidance of the art mistress, painted scenery, and when there was no one else available she heard the various parts. There were a great many, for the parents would have been upset if their own particular small daughter had had no part. Those who were hopeless at learning their lines were taught a dance. It had nothing to do with the plot, but what did that matter as long as every child took part?

Nel was one of the Christmas fairies and had a speaking part—well, she had to say, 'And here is Father Christmas' before waving her wand and rejoining the other fairies.

'Mummy will be proud of me,' she assured Olivia. 'She's coming to see me—she promised.'

She sounded so doubtful that Olivia hastened to reassure her.

'You're certain?' asked Nel as Olivia, on dormitory duty, went round tucking the children up for the night. Matron didn't approve of the tucking-up, but Olivia, remembering how cosy it had been to be tucked in at bedtime, took no notice of that.

'If your Mummy promised, then she'll come,' said Olivia firmly. 'Now go to sleep like a good girl.'

'All right. Olivia...?'

She turned back. 'Yes, dear?'

'I'm going to Holland for the holidays. I hope I'll like it. Mummy has a lot of friends and I don't like the lady who looks after me when she's away.'

'Perhaps it will be another lady this time.'

'I do hope so. I wish you were coming too. We could explore together. Where would you like to go most in Amsterdam?'

'Look, love, you must settle down.' And then, seeing that the child waited for an answer, she said, 'Oh, a seat opposite that big picture in the Rijksmuseum so that I could look at it really properly.' She dropped a kiss on the small forehead. 'Goodnight.'

The end of term prize-giving and the play were to be in the very early afternoon, and this time there was to be no lunch, only coffee and sherry beforehand, and tea afterwards while the children got ready to leave with their parents. Olivia, doing two things at once and at everyone's beck and call, longed for the day to be over. She wouldn't be leaving until the following day and she wasn't really looking forward to another Christmas at her grandmother's flat but she had the New Year to look forward to, and a good deal of the holiday would be taken up with getting her mother organised to come back with her. Obedient to Miss Ross's urgent voice, she began attaching the wings to the fairies' small shoulders.

It was a cold and gloomy day and the parents crowded in, intent on coffee and drinks before finding seats in the assembly hall. Olivia, counting fairy heads, found one missing. Nel—perhaps her mother had taken her aside for a moment. Olivia darted away, intent on getting her into her right place before the curtain went up.

Nel was in the hall and Mr van der Eisler was crouching beside her, holding her close in his great arms, crumpling her wings while she sobbed into his shoulder.

'She hasn't come?' hissed Olivia, in a whisper. 'Why didn't you make her? How could you let her not come? You knew that Nel...'

Nel gave a great sniff and paused in her sobs. 'She hasn't come—promised me, she promised me—you heard her, Uncle Haso. I won't go to Holland...'

He took out a very large white handkerchief and wiped her face. 'Must I go back all alone? I was counting on your company.'

She peered up at him. 'Would you be lonely without me?'

'I certainly would. Look, Olivia's here. I expect she wants you to join the other fairies.'

Olivia spoke. 'Nel has a speaking part; she's very important to the story.'

'Then she must do her best. What is it they say? ''The show must go on''. Actresses with broken hearts always forget their sorrow and act brilliantly, don't they, Olivia?'

'Always.' She didn't look at him but bore Nel away, just in time to join the rest of the troupe before the curtain was jerked open with a certain amount of inexpertise.

The play was loudly applauded, Nel said her line without mishap, and everyone dispersed for tea and biscuits while the children changed back into their school clothes, anxious to be gone now that they had collected their prizes. All the same it took some time to get the chattering, excited children ready and sent down to where their parents were waiting. Olivia, rounding up the last of them, was accosted by a parent.

'A most enjoyable afternoon.' She was a pleasant little lady with a kind face. 'You must be tired and you are so good with the children. I'm sure we shall all be sorry to see you go, but I suppose if the Board of Governors want someone with qualifications there is no choice.' She held out her hand. 'Anyway, I do wish you the best of luck. I'm sure Miss Cross will be very sorry to lose you.'

Olivia shook the hand offered her, smiled, and heard herself saying something which must have been sensible because the little lady smiled and nodded before she went away with her small daughter.

It can't be true, thought Olivia, bustling the rest of the girls downstairs. Miss Cross would have told me. She followed more slowly, her thoughts in a turmoil, glad to see that almost everyone had gone.

Not everyone. Nel and Mr van der Eisler were standing by the door. 'Nel wants to say goodbye,' he said smoothly, and then with an abrupt change of tone, 'Olivia, what is the matter? Are you ill?'

She managed a smile. 'No, no—just a bit tired—it's been a long day but everything was very successful, wasn't it? Nel looked well as a fairy, didn't she...?' And when he didn't speak, she added, 'Are you going back to Holland straight away? I didn't see Lady Brennon.'

'She has had flu—over the worst now, but this would have tired her out. We're going there now and crossing in a day or so.'

'Mummy will be waiting for me,' said Nel. 'Uncle Haso says so.'

'Splendid. You'll have a gorgeous Christmas, I expect.'

The child nodded. 'Mummy's got a new dress for me to wear; I'm to go to some parties.' She peered up at Olivia. 'You look sad…'

'Not a bit of it,' said Olivia in a bright and brittle voice. 'Just a bit tired.' She took care not to look at Mr van der Eisler; she could feel his eyes on her. 'I must be off, there is heaps of clearing up to do.'

'If Mummy invited you, would you come and stay with me, Olivia?'

'What a lovely idea, poppet, but I really must go home. You see, I've a mother and a granny, just like you.'

'Next to Granny and Uncle Haso I like you, Olivia,' said Nel, and lifted her face for a kiss.

'And I like you…'

'And Uncle Haso?'

'And Uncle Haso.' She still didn't look at him. It was really quite difficult to bottle up the torrent of words she wished to utter. To tell him that she was to be given the sack, that she was desolate at the idea of not seeing him again, that she loved him…

She held out a prim hand. 'Goodbye, Mr van der Eisler.' She addressed his chin to be on the safe side. If she looked at him, really looked, she might burst into tears.

His handshake was brief, as was his 'Goodbye, Olivia' and a few moments later he had driven away with Nel beside him.

She stayed where she was for a while, wondering what she should do. Very soon it would be supper-time and the staff would forgather for the end-of-term glass of sherry before the meal. That mother could have been mistaken, she reflected, she might be pan-icking about nothing at all. The sensible thing to do was to behave as though it was a mistake. She went and joined the others, exchanged comments about the play and the prize-giving, listened to plans for Christmas and ate her supper sitting between Miss Ross, whom she liked, and Matron, who as usual was laying down the law about the correct method of mak-ing beds.

It was when the meal was over and they were going their separate ways that Miss Cross asked her to join her in her study. She wasn't there long; it didn't take long to give someone the sack, even if it was done with regret and kindness.

Olivia went to the annexe and began to collect up her things. There was no hurry; she was to stay for another day to help in the general tidying up, label mislaid articles of clothing, make a list of any minor damage to bedlinen, towels and tablecloths. Only then could she get on the bus to take her to her train and so to her home.

She had some money saved and Miss Cross had given her a splendid reference, and had even suggested that she should advertise for a similar post. 'A smaller school,' she had advised. 'There are any number of good private schools around the country. Several of them do without a qualified Matron, and you would do very well in such a position where qualifications are not necessary. You have had experience here. But you should start looking at once. It is probably too late for the spring term, but there is always the possibility of starting at half-term. I'm sure that you have no need to worry, Olivia.'

She worried none the less, most of the night and all the next day. She slept that night though, from sheer exhaustion. Since she had said goodbye to Miss Cross, and only the domestic staff were left now, she caught her bus and her train and, since every penny mattered now, another bus to Sylvester Crescent.

Despite the fact that Christmas was only days away, there wasn't a single Christmas tree to be seen in any of the windows shrouded in their net curtains; the only cheerful sight was Mr Patel's corner shop, bright with coloured lights and a tree ablaze with coloured ornaments and tinsel, and a counter stacked with sweets and biscuits. Bless the man, thought Olivia, as the bus crawled past. I'll go and see him tomorrow.

The air was hardly festive in Mrs Fitzgibbon's flat. True, there was a display of Christmas cards on the mantelpiece, but her granny evinced none of the Christmas spirit expected of everyone during the festive season. Olivia hugged her mother and went to kiss her grandmother's cheek.

'Back again?' asked that lady unnecessarily. 'In my day school holidays were short; education was considered important.' She studied Olivia's face. 'You look your age, Olivia.'

Olivia bit back the obvious retort, winked at her mother to show her that she didn't mind, and took her cases into her bedroom. After a minute or two her

mother joined her. 'You don't look a day older, darling,' she said earnestly, 'but you do look tired, love,
and I think you've got thinner.'

'The end of the term is always a wild scramble,
Mother. But great fun. Has Granny any plans for
Christmas?'

'Well, some friends are coming for bridge on
Christmas Eve…'

'Good, you and I will go to the midnight service.
Any plans for Christmas dinner?'

'I think your granny is ordering a chicken.' She
added, 'I bought a pudding from Marks and
Spencer…'

'Good. We'll go to Mr Patel's tomorrow and get a
bottle of wine and a box of crackers.' She added reck-
lessly, 'And after Christmas you and I will have a day
out at the sales.'

It was nice to see her mother's eyes sparkle with
pleasure. There was no need to tell her that she had
left the school just yet; she would do it after
Christmas, when she had put an advert in the papers
Miss Cross had recommended.

They went, she and her mother, to Mr Patel's shop
the next morning and bought the wine, the crackers,
and some festive-looking biscuits, and Olivia added
potato crisps, a variety of cheeses and some nuts. Her
grandmother would deplore the extravagance but, as
Mr Patel had pointed out, it was Christmas and a time
of good cheer and goodwill, and to emphasise his
point he added a small bottle of lemonade for free.

They returned to the flat in good spirits, to have
them dampened by the old lady's disapproval. They

were treated to a homily on the prudent spending of money which showed no sign of ending, so it was with relief that Olivia went to answer the doorbell.

Mr van der Eisler and Nel stood there, the little girl almost hidden under an arrangement of flowers in a basket.

Mr van der Eisler eyed Olivia keenly although his greeting was pleasantly casual. 'Nel wants to give you a Christmas present,' he explained, 'and since we're leaving in the morning we thought we should come today.'

'How very kind.' Olivia stood back to allow them to come in and added, 'What a lovely surprise.' She caught his eye and added quickly, 'The flowers, I mean.' She led the way to the sitting-room and ushered them inside. 'Would you like a cup of coffee? I was just going to get ours, and I'm sure Nel would like some lemonade.'

'Fizzy?' asked Nel.

'Very fizzy.' Mr Patel didn't sell any other kind. She handed their guests over to her mother and went to the kitchen. It was absurd how excited she felt just at the sight of him; it was a good thing he was going away tomorrow. There was no need to tell him that she wouldn't be going back to school after Christmas. 'Out of sight, out of mind,' said Olivia, and dropped the cup she was holding when Mr van der Eisler said, an inch or so from her ear, 'A very misleading statement, I have always thought.'

'Now look what you've done.' She rounded on him and found him smiling down on her so that she mumbled, 'Well, you startled me.'

'Understandably.' He was picking up the broken cup. 'Not one of your grandmother's best, I hope?'

'Well, yes, it is, but I'll tell her later…'

'Could we not throw the pieces into the dustbin and say nothing?'

She shook her head. 'Granny counts everything from time to time. She'd notice at once.'

She fetched another cup and set it on its saucer, wondering what to say next.

'Why did you look like that the other day?' he asked. 'And why are you so sad now? And don't, I beg of you, say that you don't know what I'm talking about.'

Something in his voice made her say at once, 'I'm not to go back to the school; the governors want someone with proper qualifications… It was a bit of a shock. I had hoped that I could stay on, and Mother was going to come and live there with me.'

He went to the stove and took the milk saucepan off just in time.

'My poor girl.' And when she turned her back so that he shouldn't see her threatening tears he busied himself making the coffee, and then opened cupboards until he found a packet of biscuits and arranged them on a plate. 'You haven't told your mother?'

She had turned round again, the tears swallowed. 'No, I thought I'd wait and try and find a job after Christmas.'

'Very sensible, but then you're a sensible girl, aren't you, Olivia?'

'Thank you for making the coffee.' She smiled a little. 'You don't look as though you could—what I mean is, I don't suppose you have to do it very often in your own home.'

'My housekeeper only allows me in the kitchen under her watchful eye, and you've met Becky—a tyrant if ever there was one!'

'A very kind-hearted one…'

He carried the tray into the sitting-room and sat down beside Mrs Fitzgibbon, charming her into good humour while Nel told Olivia and her mother just what a marvellous time she would have when she got to Amsterdam.

'I've a new dress,' she told them breathlessly, 'and of course it's Christmas, so Mummy won't go to her office. I expect we'll have a simply wonderful time.' She looked around her. 'You haven't got a Christmas tree—Uncle Haso has. It's in the window and people in the street can see it lighted up.'

Mrs Harding replied suitably and Olivia went away to get more coffee. The visit lasted some time but Mr van der Eisler had nothing more to say to her other than a polite goodbye and good wishes. Whether they were for Christmas or for her uncertain future she had no idea.

It was early evening and dark when she answered the doorbell again. Mr Patel stood on the doorstep with a large basket filled with tastefully arranged fruit, a large box of chocolates, and a charming floral arrangement of Christmas roses, miniature daffodils, hyacinths and jasmine.

'A surprise for you, miss,' he said cheerfully. 'I myself arranged the basket and went to the market to buy the flowers which the gentleman wished you to have. You are pleased?'

'Oh, Mr Patel, it's magnificent—how beautifully you've arranged it. It must have taken you ages.'

'Yes, indeed, but the gentleman was generous. It was a very splendid order. You will enjoy your Christmas now, miss, and may I remind you that my shop will be open until late on Christmas Eve in case you find yourself without essential food?'

'I'll remember that, Mr Patel—I expect my mother will be along to do some more shopping in the morning.'

'Always welcome and goodnight, miss.'

The cheerful little man went away and Olivia carried the basket into the sitting-room and put it on the table.

'A gift for me?' asked her grandmother.

'Well, no, Granny—it's for me,' Olivia was reading the card tucked behind the pineapple. Mr van der Eisler wished her the compliments of the season in handwriting which was barely readable. He had signed it H v d E. The card had bright red roses in one corner, but she didn't think that they signified anything.

'How very kind,' observed Mrs Harding, and looked pleased; the fruit would enliven their festive table very nicely but that wasn't why she looked pleased. She had a beautiful daughter who deserved an admirer as handsome and delightful as Mr van der Eisler. Of course there was nothing in it—there was Nel's mother, a very pretty woman and charming she had thought, although Nel had said one or two things... Of course, children did exaggerate.

Christmas came; they exchanged small gifts, cooked the chicken, ate the fruit and made up the second bridge table unwillingly on Boxing Day, when Mrs Fitzgibbon's friends came for the afternoon and evening. Olivia, who was as bad at bridge as her mother, sighed with relief as the last of them went home and she could clear the cups and glasses and plates. Their guests had eaten everything offered to them and Olivia was hungry. She did the glasses, filled a bowl with water to do the washing-up, and went to cut herself a slice of bread with a hunk of cheese on top. Her mother and grandmother had gone to bed and she didn't hurry, there was nothing planned for the following day; she would pen an advert ready to post at the first opportunity.

She finished her chores, took a chocolate from the box which her grandmother had offered round with a generous hand, and went to bed.

She was making the early morning tea when the phone rang... It was still dark and very cold and the phone was in the hall. She pulled her dressing-gown tightly round her and padded along to see who it was. A wrong number, she supposed, and her hello was abrupt.

'Have I got you out of bed,' enquired Mr van der Eisler.

'No. I'm getting the tea, and this is a fine time to phone, I must say.'

'Only because I need your help, Olivia. Nel ran away from her home—I found her and she's with me, but I must be at the hospital all day and every day for some time. She wants to go back to Lady Brennon but that has to be arranged. Bronger, who looks after my home, will fly over this morning and fetch you back here. He'll have tickets and money—have you a passport? Yes, good. He'll be with you by midday. Will you do this for me, Olivia? And for Nel? She asks for you continually.'

'Yes, of course I will. What do I bring with me? Enough for a few days?'

'Ten days—something warm. Thank you, Olivia.'

She padded back to the kitchen. The kettle was boiling merrily and she made the tea and sat down to drink hers. She was, of course, out of her mind; he had only to ask her to do something quite preposterous and she agreed without even thinking about it. Her head needed examining. All the same, she would go. She reviewed her wardrobe mentally, thought about money, and took a cup of tea to her mother.

'I heard the phone,' said that lady, with just the hint of a question in her voice.

Olivia explained. 'Do you think I'm mad?' she asked.

'Certainly not, dear. I don't imagine that Mr van der Eisler is a man to waste time on phone calls at seven o'clock in the morning unless he has good reason to do so. You do quite right to go. Poor child…!'

Olivia settled on the end of the bed. 'Only, I'm so sorry to leave you, Mother. We'd planned so much…'

'Yes, I know, love, but you won't be gone all that time, and I'll come and stay with you again.'

'Yes, of course.' Olivia picked at the cotton bedspread. 'Mother, I can't not go. You see, I'm in love with him.'

'Yes, dear.' Her mother sounded unsurprised.

Olivia pulled at a loose thread and watched it unravel. 'It's silly, really. I think he'll marry Rita—Nel's mother—it would be so suitable; she's his dead friend's widow and Nel is devoted to him. Besides, she's pretty and charming and amusing.'

'None the less you love him, Olivia. You must do whatever your heart tells you to do.'

Olivia smiled. 'Granny won't like it.'

'Granny has nothing to do with it, darling. Go and get dressed and pack a bag. I'll get breakfast. Take your Granny a cup of tea first, and don't say a word.'

So Olivia was dressed, her bag packed, her passport found, money in her purse and her winter coat laid out on the bed ready to put on by the time her grandmother came out of her room.

She looked at Olivia's neatly turned-out person. 'Why are you wearing that good skirt?' she wanted to know. 'There's no money to buy you new clothes, you know.'

Olivia handed her a cup of coffee and gave one to her mother.

'I'm going over to Holland, Granny. I've been asked to look after Nel for a week or two.'

'And where's the money coming from to pay for your fare?'

'I'm being fetched.'

As if on cue the door-knocker was thumped, and she went to answer it. A short, stout man stood on the step, very spruce as to dress, with iron-grey hair and very blue eyes.

'Miss Harding. I am Bronger, houseman to Mr van

der Eisler; I am to take you to his house in Amsterdam.' He held out a hand and crushed hers with it.

'Do please come in, we're just having coffee. Do we need to go at once or have you time for a cup?'

'That would be good, miss.' His English was fluent but strongly accented. 'If we leave in half an hour, but no later.'

She helped him off with his short, thick jacket. 'How do we go?'

'A car will come here for us, all is arranged. We fly to Schiphol and from there we drive to Amsterdam. I have left the car there.'

'Well, do come in and meet my mother and grand-mother.'

He shook hands and bowed slightly, took a chair and drank his coffee, answering Mrs Fitzgibbon's questions with politeness and telling her, in effect, nothing at all. A very discreet man, thought Olivia, liking him.

The car came and they were borne away. 'You have no need to trouble about the journey,' said Bronger. 'All is arranged.'

'In such a short time, too,' said Olivia. 'I can't think how you did it in just a few hours.'

He smiled and said nothing and presently she asked, 'May I ask you a little about Nel? She is with Mr van der Eisler, isn't she? Is there no chance that she might go home?' She paused. 'Perhaps I shouldn't ask you…'

'Mr van der Eisler has confided in me, miss. Nel refuses to go to her home; I do not know exactly why.

She left a note when she left home and most fortunately she was found within a few hours. She wishes for you and she is most upset; this is the best plan Mr van der Eisler could make in the short time he had. It is unfortunate that he has a very busy schedule at several hospitals during the next few days which he cannot change. It is good of you to come at so short a notice, miss.'

'Well, I hope I'll be able to help. Mr van der Eisler said on the phone that Nel would go back to her grandmother as soon as he could arrange that.'

Bronger nodded his grey head. 'Nel is happy with her. She is like her father was.'

They had reached the airport and the next half-hour was taken up with being processed to the plane, and once on board they didn't talk. Olivia had a great deal to think about and Bronger closed his eyes and drifted into a light doze. He must have been up very early, thought Olivia.

At Schiphol he escorted her to the main entrance, bade her wait and went away, to return within minutes driving a beautifully kept Jaguar. He got out, stowed her case, and opened the car door.

Olivia hesitated. 'May I sit with you?' she asked. 'I'd much rather.'

He looked pleased. 'A pleasure, miss.' He gave her a rare smile. 'It is a short drive to Amsterdam.'

Once in the heart of the city, Olivia looked about her eagerly. Away from the busy main streets the old houses by the canals looked as though nothing in them had altered for centuries, and when Bronger stopped before Mr van der Eisler's house she got out and stood on the narrow pavement, looking up at it.

She wasn't allowed to loiter. He mounted the double steps, opened the door and ushered her inside. At the same moment a small figure came flying down the stairs and flung herself at Olivia.

'I knew you'd come. Uncle Haso said you would. Oh, Olivia, you'll stay with me, won't you? I won't go back, I won't...'

'Now, now, poppet,' said Olivia, and hugged the child. 'Of course I'll stay, and I'm sure your uncle won't make you do anything which makes you unhappy.'

'She was horrid—she had a wart on her chin and she slapped me and told my Mummy I was disobedient and Mummy just laughed and said I'd have to change my ways... Olivia...'

Bronger took charge. 'Now, Nel, will you let miss go to her room and tidy herself? Presently you'll have your lunch with her; Ofke will have it all ready.'

A door at the end of the hall opened then, and a tall, bony woman joined them. She offered a hand to Olivia and smiled, and Bronger said, 'My wife, Ofke. She housekeeps and cooks. She speaks no English but I will help, and Nel understands Dutch—some at least.'

He said something to his wife, who nodded and led the way up the staircase. The landing was square, with doors on either side and a wide corridor running towards the back of the house. She led the way down this and opened one of the doors, beckoning Olivia to go in.

The room was square and lofty and its one large window overlooked a narrow strip of garden at the back of the house. It was furnished with a canopied bed, a rosewood table with a triple mirror on it, a tallboy in the same wood, a couple of small armchairs and a bedside table with a lovely porcelain lamp on it. The carpet and the curtains matched the soft pink of the bedspread and it was deliciously warm.

Nel ran past her. 'There's a bathroom—' she opened a door '—and a clothes closet.' She flung open another door. 'Uncle Haso let me choose.' She perched on the bed while Olivia took off her coat and hat. 'I'll tell you about how I ran away, shall I?'

'Yes, darling, I do want to know what happened. But shall we wait until we are downstairs, perhaps over lunch?'

There was no sign of Mr van der Eisler when they went downstairs and presently they had their lunch in a small, cosy room behind the vast drawing-room Olivia had glimpsed, and Nel poured out her story. It was rather garbled and Olivia had difficulty following it. The woman with the wart featured heavily in it and, so, regrettably, did Nel's mother who, it seemed, had hardly ever been at home during Christmas. She let the child talk because she could see that it was what she needed to do—perhaps later Mr van der Eisler would find the time to tell her exactly what had happened.

Nel was a little too bright-eyed, she thought, so after lunch she suggested that they went and sat by the fire in the magnificence of the drawing-room. 'And you can tell me some more,' she suggested. The chairs were large and comfortable. Nel climbed into her lap, had a little weep, and closed her eyes and presently slept. So did Olivia, worn out from the suddenness of it all.

CHAPTER SEVEN

MR VAN DER EISLER, coming quietly into his house, paused in the drawing-room doorway, put a cautionary hand on Achilles' great head, and looked his fill at the sleeping occupants of the chair. Olivia's bright hair had come a little loose from its pins and her mouth was just a little open. All the same, she looked very beautiful, sitting there, clutching Nel to her, her chin resting on the child's fair head.

He trod across the room, making no sound on the carpet, and stooped to kiss Nel's cheek and then Olivia's. Neither of them stirred as he went to sit down in his armchair on the opposite side of the great hearth. Achilles arranged himself beside his master's chair and presently sank his head on his paws and dozed. His master, tired though he was after a long list in Theatre, stayed awake, his eyes on the sleeping pair.

Olivia opened her eyes first, suddenly wide awake, staring at him over Nel's head. She whispered, 'We went to sleep—have you been here long? Why didn't you wake us up?'

He smiled and shook his head. 'I wanted to keep my dreams,' he said, and she frowned, wondering what he meant. But there was no chance to ask, for

Nel woke up then and scrambled off her lap and on to her uncle's.

'May I stay forever?' she asked him. 'I'll go to school if I must, because then I can see Granny, but I'll come back here and live with you and Olivia.'

'We'll have to think about that, Nel. I'm not sure if it would work. You see, I have to work each day and Olivia must go back to England in a little while.' He looked down at the suddenly unhappy face. 'But you shall certainly stay with Granny as often as you want to, and in two days' time I'll drive you and Olivia up to Friesland for a little holiday.'

'You won't send me back to that horrid lady? Mummy won't mind if I'm not there—I heard her tell that lady that I was an encum... a long word I can't quite remember, but I think it means that she doesn't want me.'

'I think that perhaps we can alter that, *liefje*, but we'll have to wait until I have the time to arrange things differently.'

'I don't suppose you'd like to get married?'

He laughed then. 'Well, I have been giving it serious thought just lately.'

Which would make everyone happy, reflected Olivia, excepting herself, of course. She looked up and found his eyes on her.

'I expect you would like to phone your mother, Olivia. Use the phone in my study—the last door on the opposite side of the hall. And you, my pet, must go and find Ofke and have your supper...'

'You won't go away? And Olivia? Will she put me to bed?'

'Of course,' said Olivia, and got to her feet. 'You go and have your supper while I phone home, and we'll go upstairs together.'

She was glad to get out of the room. Seeing Mr van der Eisler sitting there in his home, planning a convenient future so calmly, was turning her good sense upside-down.

By the time she had finished talking to her mother, Nel had had her supper and the next half-hour or so was taken up by getting her to bed. A long-drawn-out business which Olivia made no attempt to hasten—to spend the rest of the evening with Mr van der Eisler would be heaven but on the other hand living up to his idea of a sensible young woman was going to be difficult—but finally she could prolong the bedtime story no longer. She tucked the little girl in, kissed her and went downstairs.

Mr van der Eisler was sitting in his chair reading, with Achilles still snoozing at his feet. They both got up as she went in. 'Do sit down,' he begged her. 'Nel is a dear child, but quite exhausting. Would you like sherry?'

She accepted the crystal glass he offered her and set it down carefully on the table beside her, hoping that he hadn't seen her trembling hand. Which of course he had. She said, 'She *is* a dear little girl. Perhaps her mother could find another person to look after her? I'm sure that's her real reason for running away. The lady had a wart...' She saw his smile. 'No, I'm serious—warts and witches, you know!—and perhaps being made to eat something she didn't like... Such silly little things which need not have happened if...'

She stopped then, just in time, but he finished the sentence for her. 'If her mother had been there. You're quite right. But Rita has an excellent job at which she excels; she also meets a number of interesting people, goes to various meetings and travels—all of which are important to her.'

Not more important than looking after your small daughter, thought Olivia, although she didn't say so. 'So what do you intend to do?' she asked.

'I shall be free tomorrow afternoon. We will go and see Rita, who has agreed to be at home then. Perhaps Nel will agree to stay with her, if so all the better, but if there is still difficulty I will bring her back here for another night and the following day we will drive up to Friesland—that will be in the late afternoon, so I must ask you to look after her until then.'

'Very well. I shan't be needed in Friesland?'

'Indeed you will. My mother is more than willing to have Nel but she doesn't feel able to cope with the child. My young brother will be at home but I doubt if he will want to spend his time with Nel.'

Olivia thought of several things to say but uttered none of them. No doubt Mr van der Eisler had enough on his mind without her asking what to his mind would be foolish questions. She had almost no money, very few clothes with her, and any chances of getting a job had been knocked on the head for the time being. Such trivial matters, she reflected sourly, would mean little to him. He had arranged everything efficiently and to suit himself. If she hadn't loved him she might have flatly refused to be rushed into anything…

Bronger came in and requested that they should

dine, and over a delicious meal in the charming dining-room she became reconciled to his plans. Due, no doubt, to his placid conversation, the superb roast pheasant and the vintage claret. They had their coffee in the drawing-room and presently he excused himself on the pretext of having telephone calls to make, and left her to sit by the fire, leafing through magazines and trying to think sensibly about her future.

Since it seemed that he didn't intend to return to the drawing-room she took herself off to bed, escorted to the stairs by Bronger with the assurance that she would be called in the morning with tea.

'China or Indian, miss?' he asked, and bade her a kindly goodnight.

She slept soundly and was wakened by Nel creeping into her bed and demanding a story, only brought to its conclusion by the arrival of the morning tea, shared by the two of them. Later, dressed, they went downstairs together to find that Mr van der Eisler had already left home for the hospital, leaving a message that they were to amuse themselves that morning and be sure to be ready for him when he got back around two o'clock.

'So, what shall we do?' asked Olivia.

Nel looked surprised. 'You know already,' she said accusingly. 'We're going to look at the picture in the Rijksmuseum—you said so...'

'So I did. Stupid of me to have forgotten. I'll ask Bronger how to get there.'

'I will drive you there, miss. The professor wouldn't allow anything else.'

'Oh, wouldn't he? Professor? Is Mr van der Eisler a professor?'

'Yes, miss. Very highly thought of, too. When would you like to go, miss?'

He drove them in the dark blue Jaguar, sleek and gleaming, and set them down at the museum's entrance, handed Olivia a couple of notes with the observation that the professor had told him to deal with expenses, and told her that he would be exactly on that spot at twelve o'clock. 'There is a pleasant café inside,' he suggested. 'I wish you an enjoyable morning.'

Which it certainly was. They prowled round looking at portraits and landscapes and Olivia, who had feared that Nel might get bored, found that she was as interested as she herself was. They had their elevenses and made their way to the Nightwatch, and sat down before it. It was an enormous painting; it took them some time to pick out the many figures in it and, once they had done that, Nel insisted on making up stories about each of them—even the little dog. They sat absorbed, side by side, their heads close together while they whispered.

When Mr van der Eisler slid his vast person on to the bench beside Olivia she gave a gasp. 'Oh, heavens, have we forgotten the time?' She looked at her watch, bending her head to hide the sudden flood of colour in her face.

'No, no—the last operation had to be cancelled so I have been able to leave early. Have you been here long?'

Nel leaned across Olivia. 'Ages and ages,' she said

with satisfaction. 'Olivia's been telling me stories about the man in the picture. Will you take us home? Bronger said he'd come for us at twelve o'clock.'

'Will I do instead? I told Bronger I'd fetch you on my way back.'

'Well, of course you will, Uncle Haso. I like Bronger but I like you a lot better—so does Olivia, don't you Olivia?'

Olivia said rather coldly, 'I haven't given the matter much thought.'

'Bronger's married to Ofke,' observed Nel, 'so you can only like him a little otherwise she might mind, but Oom Haso...'

Olivia avoided Mr van der Eisler's eye and said hastily, 'Yes, yes, of course, shouldn't we be going?'

'You haven't told me about that man in the corner of the painting.'

'I think it would be nice to save him for the next time,' said Olivia briskly. 'I'm sure your uncle wants his lunch.'

Mr van der Eisler, who was quite happy where he was, saw that it might be better to agree with Olivia, who looked a little flushed and put out.

'By all means let us go home to our lunch. I dare say we shall have tea with your mother, Nel.' And at the child's quick frown he added, 'and you will have your supper in Friesland.'

A red herring which he trailed successfully all the way back to his house with Nel perched beside him, happy again.

Nel's high spirits disappeared as they got into the car again to go to her mother's flat. Her small mouth

was set in a mutinous tight line and Olivia's coaxing
was to no avail. As they stopped outside the block of
flats Nel said in a small voice, 'You promise not to
leave me here, Uncle Haso?'

'I promise, *liefje*. Your mother wants to see you and
make sure that you are happy; she won't stop you
going to Friesland with Olivia and when you have had
a holiday there perhaps you will change your mind
and go back to her. You ought to go back to school
in a week or so, but I've arranged that—you won't
need to go back until we have things sorted out here.'

'Then will you and Mummy take me back?'

'Very likely, for we need to talk to your granny.
She must be told of the plans we have for the future.'

Of course they are going to marry, thought Olivia
miserably, and had the thought substantiated by the
manner in which Rita greeted Mr van der Eisler. Arms
around his neck and looking up at him from under
long, curling—and false—eyelashes. He remained
placid, but then he wasn't a man to show his feelings,
decided Olivia, and urged Nel forward to greet her
mother.

Rita enfolded her child in a close embrace, kissed
her a great deal and murmured in a loving voice.
Olivia wasn't taken in one bit and she didn't think Nel
was either, but what Mr van der Eisler thought was
being hidden behind a passive countenance.

'Darling,' cooed Rita, 'what a lot of trouble you
have given Mummy—I'm almost out of my mind...
Now, I want you to run along and play while your
uncle and I have a talk. Juffrouw Schalk is in your
bedroom, packing some clothes for you. Take...' She

paused and smiled prettily at Olivia. 'I've forgotten your name—so stupid…'

'Olivia.'

'Of course, take Olivia with you, darling. I'm sure Juffrouw Schalk will be able to give her some useful tips.'

She flipped a hand in dismissal and turned to Mr van der Eisler as Nel led Olivia from the room. 'Don't go away,' begged the child as they crossed the hall and went into a room on the far side.

Juffrouw Schalk was there, sitting in a comfortable chair by a closed stove, and she was exactly as Olivia had pictured her—dark eyes, small and sly, a long nose, a high forehead from which dark hair was drawn back and a mean mouth, beside which was the wart. Probably she was a good and efficient woman, but Olivia could understand at once why Nel didn't like her.

Juffrouw Schalk spoke sharply in Dutch to Nel, who answered her and added in English, 'Juffrouw Schalk speaks English, Olivia.'

'Good afternoon,' said Olivia politely, and was told to sit down.

'This silly child,' said Juffrouw Schalk in thickly accented English, 'is spoilt by her English grandmother. She should go to one of our schools and learn instead of doing as she likes.'

Olivia wondered if the child had had the chance to do anything she liked while she was with her mother. 'She is a good pupil at her school and happy with her grandmother.'

'An old lady,' shrugged Juffrouw Schalk. 'Who does not punish her, I think.'

'She's not old,' shouted Nel, 'and I don't need to be punished. I'm a good girl, excepting when I'm with you. I hate you.'

'Hush, Nel,' said Olivia. 'Juffrouw Schalk doesn't mean to be unkind; she is merely expressing her opinions.'

She looked at that lady, who was red in the face and about to burst into indignant speech. 'Perhaps Nel might go to the kitchen and get a drink of milk?' she suggested, and didn't wait for an answer but sent her on the errand, aware that Juffrouw Schalk was on the point of exploding.

'You are a fool,' said that lady. 'Mrs Brennon tells me this, that you come to look after the child so that you may entice the professor. But you waste your time, miss, for they will marry soon and you will be sent packing.'

Olivia gave her a thoughtful look. 'What makes you think that I am in the least interested in Mr van der Eisler? I hardly know him. I am merely helping him out in a difficult situation—which never need have arisen if you had treated Nel with kindness.' She drew a steadying breath. 'I must say that I agree with Nel; I find you unkind and far too strict. In fact, I don't like you, Juffrouw Schalk.'

She smiled at the outraged face and walked out of the room, found her way to the kitchen and accepted a cup of tea from a comfortable woman who was plying Nel with milk and biscuits.

She was enjoying a second cup and a three-sided

conversation with Nel and the comfortable woman when the door opened and Rita came in.

'What's this I hear from Juffrouw Schalk?' she demanded. 'That you have questioned her treatment of Nel—the insolence…'

'No, no, I was quite polite to her,' said Olivia calmly, 'and what I said was true. I'm sure you must have seen that for yourself, Mrs Brennon.' She added, 'Although if you aren't at home much you would have noticed nothing.'

Nel had skipped away, to find her uncle no doubt, and Olivia watched Rita's face grow ugly with rage. Might as well be hung for a sheep as for a lamb, she thought. Mr van der Eisler, appealed to, would send her packing in the nicest possible way and Rita would weep prettily on his shoulder and tell him that she had had no idea that Juffrouw Schalk had been making her darling Nel unhappy.

'If I had the time to arrange things differently for Nel, I would do so. Unfortunately I have a most important appointment very shortly, and a dinner party this evening.' She glared at Olivia. 'But be sure that I shall not forget this. I shall speak to Mr van der Eisler and ask him to rearrange his plans for Nel.'

'I'll wait here, shall I? While you talk to him.'

Rita spoke pettishly. 'Don't be absurd. Haven't I just said that I have no time now? You'll have to go with Nel and stay with her until I can find the time to discuss this. Am I never to be allowed to live my life as I want? All this stupid fuss—Nel's only a child…'

Olivia bit back the words she longed to utter and instead thanked the comfortable woman for the tea and held the door open for Rita, who swept past her across the hall and into the room where Nel and Mr van der Eisler were standing at the window, watching the traffic in the street.

Olivia could do nothing but admire the speed with which Rita transformed herself into an ill-done-by and wistful woman.

She said in a wispy voice, 'Oh, Haso, tell me that I'm doing the right thing—I have so looked forward to these weeks with Nel and everything has gone wrong.'

Her eyes had filled with tears and Olivia wondered how she managed to do that. Crocodile tears, she decided. Rita, she suspected, was only too glad to see Nel's small back disappear through the door. It was a perfect performance; she watched Mr van der Eisler's face and wished that just once in a while he would allow his feelings to show. Certainly his voice was kind and patient.

'I am sure that when Nel has had a holiday with my mother, away from all of us, she will feel quite differently. We must talk about it later, of course, but I think that it might be best for her to return to school in a week or so, and perhaps you can arrange to be free for the Easter holidays.'

Rita pouted prettily. 'But I've already arranged...' She glanced at Olivia. 'I don't wish to discuss this before a servant.'

'If you refer to Olivia, I must point out that she is not a servant; she is looking after Nel at my request and for your convenience.'

Something in his quiet voice made Rita say reluctantly, 'I'm sorry—I'm so upset.' She wasn't too upset to look at her watch and add, 'I simply have to go—an important meeting.' She kissed Nel and then went to him and tucked a hand through his arm. 'Don't be angry with me, Haso, we'll meet and talk. You know that I depend on you utterly.'

Olivia looked away as she kissed his cheek and whispered something with a little trill of laughter. Nel, she noticed, had turned her back and was watching the street outside again. She gave her mother a dutiful kiss when bidden to do so, pressed herself close to Olivia when Juffrouw Schalk came in with her case, and hopped into the car the moment the door was opened. Nobody spoke as Mr van der Eisler drove back to his house. Only once they were inside its warm comfort did he observe, 'A cup of tea before we go, I think. Do go into the drawing-room and Bronger will bring it—I must do some phoning. I'll join you presently.'

They had almost finished when he came back, accepted a cup of tea, made a few non-committal remarks about nothing much and suggested that they should leave in ten minutes or so.

He's angry, thought Olivia, escorting Nel upstairs to fetch a forgotten teddy bear and to collect her own case. It was taken from her by a hovering Bronger, Nel and Achilles were settled on the back seat of the car, and Mr van der Eisler invited her to sit beside him.

An opportunity not to be missed; she would see precious little of him once this small upheaval had been settled. A week, she reflected, or with luck ten days before Nel would be sent back to England—and she with her, no doubt. She would see nothing of him during that time, but just being in the same country was a small comfort.

The afternoon had darkened and she had no doubt that outside the big car's comfortable warmth it was very cold.

'We shall have snow,' said Mr van der Eisler, 'probably before we reach Tierjum.'

'Just where is that?'

'A few miles east of Leeuwarden, a small village close to one of the lakes.' He didn't enlarge upon that, and she supposed that he was vexed with her for upsetting Rita. She sat very still and quiet, watching what she could see in the gathering gloom of the countryside.

They were travelling north and sure enough, as they reached the Afsluitdijk, it began to snow. Soft, feathery flakes at first, and then a whirling mass blown hither and thither by the wind.

'You're not nervous?'

She glanced at his calm profile. 'No. If I were driving, though, I should be terrified.'

'Once we're off the *dijk* the wind won't be so fierce, and we shall be at Tierjum in half an hour or so. Is Nel asleep?'

She turned her head to look. 'Yes, and so is Achilles.'

'He's devoted to her. I must do my best to come up and see her before she goes back and bring him with me.'

It seemed endless, the drive across the *dijk*—the sea *dijk* was too high for her to see the sea, but on the other side of the road it was lower, and she could see the grey waters of the Ijsselmeer roughed up by the wind; they looked cold and forbidding.

The *dijk* ended at last and although the snow was still falling relentlessly there was less wind. 'Franeker,' said Mr van der Eisler, sweeping through a small town with lighted shop windows before taking the main road to Leeuwarden. It was a motorway, she supposed, for although she could see lights from time to time there was nothing close to the road. At Leeuwarden he circumvented the town, leaving its lighted streets for the highway again, but only for a short distance, soon turning off on to a narrow brick road. Although she looked hard she could see nothing on either side of them. 'Fields,' said Mr van der Eisler briefly. 'This is a country road.'

He appeared to know it well, which was a good thing, she considered, for there were no signposts visible at the few crossings. It might be near Leeuwarden but it seemed like a distant and isolated spot. Through the snow she glimpsed lights at last, and he slowed the car to enter a village—a handful of small houses, a lighted shop, the dim outline of a church—and then another lane, to sweep the car between brick pillars and high wrought-iron gates and stop before a house whose windows blazed light. The dark evening and the snow prevented her from seeing the house clearly but she had the impression of a flat, solid front before she was urged up double steps and in through an arched doorway. Achilles loped beside her; Mr van der Eisler, with Nel in his arms, was close on her heels.

A tall, bony man with white hair opened the inner

door as they reached it and Mr van der Eisler put Nel down and clapped the older man on the shoulder, talking what to Olivia sounded utter nonsense. Dutch was bad enough, although she had begun to pick out a word here and there, but this was something different. Mr van der Eisler suddenly switched to English.

'This is Tober, Olivia. He has been with the family forever—before I was born—he is part of our lives.'

She held out a hand and said, 'How do you do?' and was a little surprised when Tober told her that he did very well in quite tolerable English. He was embraced by Nel then, before taking their coats and leading the way across the wide hall to the double doors on one side. Nel was hanging on to his hand and Achilles was trotting sedately beside him.

Very much at home, thought Olivia, and as though she had voiced her thought Mr van der Eisler said, 'Nel comes to pay us a visit each time she comes to Holland and, as for Achilles, he regards it as his second home—as indeed it is.'

They had reached the doors and Tober had opened them to reveal a large, lofty room with tall, narrow windows at one end, almost concealed by thick brocade curtains of tawny silk. The walls were hung with the same silk panels, separated by white-painted columns. The floor was polished wood and covered with silky carpets and there were massive bow-fronted display cabinets against the walls and an enormous fireplace with a stone hood. A museum, thought Olivia, and then as her eye took in the comfortable chairs, the tables with their pretty table-lamps, the pile of books on the sofa-table, the jumble of knitting cast down on a low stool and the tabby cat curled up in one of the chairs, A museum perhaps, but a lived-in one, warm and very welcoming.

Nel had darted forward to where a lady was sitting by the fire, and Olivia, propelled gently by a large hand between her shoulders, perforce followed her. The lady got to her feet, stooped to kiss Nel, and then advanced a few steps to meet them.

'Haso—how delightful to see you, my dear.' She lifted her face to receive his kiss. 'And this is Olivia. Welcome, my dear, I am so delighted to have guests.'

She held out a hand, smiling at Olivia. She was of the same height and still a beautiful woman, with bright blue eyes, iron-grey hair, brushed severely back from her forehead, and an upright figure. 'You had a good drive here? The weather can be most unpleasant at this time of year. You must have a cup of coffee before you go upstairs, and you, Nel, shall have warm milk and some of those little biscuits you like so much.'

The coffee was brought and Olivia, sitting beside her hostess before a blazing fire, felt that life just for the moment was perfect. Mr van der Eisler sat in a great wing chair with Nel on a stool beside him and Achilles already dozing at his feet; she smiled at him and his answering smile was kind. It was also impersonal.

Presently she was taken upstairs by Tober's wife, Anke, a short, stout little person, dressed severely in black and bearing all the hallmarks of an old family retainer. It was extraordinary, reflected Olivia as she followed her up the wide, curving staircase, that in this modern world Mr van der Eisler's family appeared to have no shortage of help. He was well served in his London home, and equally well here. Perhaps this house belonged to his mother—perhaps she could discover that while she was here...

She and Nel had adjoining rooms and shared a bathroom. Both were charmingly furnished in soft pastel colours and rosewood. Olivia, running a hand over the patina of the sofa-table, which did duty as a dressing-table, reflected that the house was perfect. She could hardly wait for the morning to examine it from the outside. Nel, tugging at her hand, brought her back to reality, and she tidied the pair of them and they went downstairs again. Nel, she noted, was a changed child, laughing and skipping around—a contrast to the unhappy child she had seen in Amsterdam. Perhaps when Mr van der Eisler and Rita married he would alter things.

He and his mother broke off their conversation as they went in and he said easily, 'We shall dine early as I must get back. Come and sit down and have a drink, Olivia—Nel, Anke has made some of that lemonade you like so much, and I think that you might stay up for dinner just this once.'

He was rewarded with a hug and a great many kisses. 'You really are a super uncle,' said Nel. 'It would be nice if I could live here with you and live with Granny in England.'

His mother said gently, 'But you would miss your mother, *liefje*.'

'I wouldn't, because she's never home with me, only that awful Juffrouw Schalk. She has a wart...'

'I dare say your mother will be able to find someone else without a wart…'

Nel shook her head.

'I'll talk to Mummy,' promised Mr van der Eisler, 'and see if she can find someone you'd like to be with when she's not there.'

'Olivia,' Nel cried happily. 'You wouldn't would you? Oh, do say yes.'

Mr van der Eisler spoke in a smooth voice. 'Olivia has to go back home to her mother and grandmother, Nel.'

Olivia watched the small face pucker; any moment now there would be a storm of tears. 'I dare say,' she said loudly, 'that you could come and see me sometimes—you have lots of holidays.'

Mevrouw van der Eisler agreed enthusiastically to this. 'What a splendid idea. We must talk about it while you're here. But Tober is here to tell us that dinner is on the table—I'm sure that you must be hungry.'

They dined in the splendour of a room at the back of the house, with high windows looking out over what Olivia supposed was the garden. The furniture was massive and old, and its walls were hung with rather dark portraits of handsome ancestors, staring down at the celery soup, the roast duck and the elaborate iced confection offered in Nel's honour.

Conversation flowed easily but they didn't linger at the table. Nel was sleepy by now, and Olivia suggested that she should take her up to bed.

'Of course,' agreed Mevrouw van der Eisler, 'but come down as soon as you can and have your coffee.'

So Olivia went upstairs with Nel, ran her bath while she undressed, sponged her briskly, towelled her dry and popped her into bed, already almost asleep. Even when she was free to go back downstairs she hesitated—mother and son might wish to talk together, and she had no idea how long he was staying; he had said nothing to Nel when she had kissed him goodnight. She pottered round her room, putting on more lipstick and taking it off again, and finally went slowly down the staircase.

Mr van der Eisler was in the hall, shrugging himself into his overcoat.

'There you are,' he said cheerfully, 'just in time to say goodbye.'

His words fell like so many stones. She summoned a steady voice. 'I hope you have an easy trip back,' she said brightly. 'Has it stopped snowing?'

'No, and isn't likely to for a few days, but you'll be cosy enough here. As soon as Rita and I have had a chance to talk I'll let you know what has been decided.' He came towards her and took her hand. 'I'm grateful to you, Olivia, but I won't keep you longer than is absolutely necessary. This is a sorry business, but Nel's happiness is important. At the same time one must admit that her mother has every right to her own life, but I think I can solve that for her.'

Well, of course he could, thought Olivia pettishly; he had only to marry the woman and everyone, except herself of course, would be happy.

She said in a cool, sedate voice, 'I'll take good care of Nel, Mr van der Eisler,' then edged away from him, relieved to see his mother coming from the drawing-room.

'You'll phone me, Haso?' said that lady. 'I shall be glad to see a satisfactory end to this—a suitable end too.' She added, 'I know Rob was your greatest friend…'

Olivia slipped away into the drawing-room, empty except for the cat, for Achilles was returning with his master. Tober came in with fresh coffee, smiling and nodding, and she smiled and nodded back, her ears stretched to hear the heavy front door close. If she saw Mr van der Eisler again it would be briefly, to discuss her and Nel's return to England. She might as well begin forgetting him from that moment.

The door opened and he crossed the room with rapid strides, swung her round, kissed her hard and quickly and, without a single word, went away again. She heard the door close with a dull thud and a moment later his mother came back to join her.

So much for forgetting him, reflected Olivia foggily. Now I'll have to start all over again.

CHAPTER EIGHT

MEVROUW VAN DER EISLER glanced at Olivia as she sat down. 'Oh, good, Tober brought fresh coffee. We'll have a cup and talk about Nel. I love having her here but I am grateful for someone to look after her. We've always got on well—she's a dear child, isn't she? But just with me she might get bored. Luckily Haso's young brother will be home for a few days—he's in his last year at Leiden. I've two daughters also—perhaps Haso didn't tell you?—both married, one in Canada and the other in Limburg. Dirk is twenty-four, determined to be as successful as Haso. He'll be company for you too. You haven't brothers or sisters?'

Olivia found herself being put through a gentle catechism regarding her own life. The questions were put so kindly and the answers listened to with so much sympathy that she discovered that she didn't mind.

All the same, she skirted lightly round her lack of a job and the fact that living with Granny wasn't ideal, and was glad when her hostess began to talk about the house.

'It's very old,' she observed. 'There was a house before this one—one of my husband's ancestors was a merchant with the East India Company. He made a fortune and pulled the old house down and built this one about two hundred years ago, but the grounds are very much as they were before he did that. Of course, the house belongs to Haso, but he has to spend a great deal of his time either in Amsterdam or travelling. When he marries I shall move to a smaller town-house we own in Leeuwarden.'

Three homes, thought Olivia wistfully, and said brightly, 'He must have his work cut out keeping an eye on three houses.'

'Yes. Of course he has Becky in London, who is a most capable woman, and Bronger and Ofke in Amsterdam have run the house for his father before him. Tober and Anke have been here all their lives, and I see to the business side of this place when he isn't here.'

'He's very fortunate to have such faithful people working for him.'

'Indeed, they would cheerfully die for him,' said Mevrouw van der Eisler in a matter-of-fact voice. 'As they would have done for his father.'

In bed later, Olivia remembered that. Did Rita, she wondered, realise what a splendid man she was to marry? And would she be good to him? Olivia thumped her pillows and turned over with unnecessary energy. Of course she wouldn't.

It was still snowing the next morning. Olivia, wrapped up in one of Mevrouw van der Eisler's hooded padded coats and wearing borrowed wellies, went into the gardens with Nel to make a snowman. It gave her the chance to inspect the house from the outside. It had a solid front, crowned with a wide gable, with neat rows of windows on either side of a vast front door and smaller windows higher up across its face. Round the back there were two narrow wings, almost enclosing what she thought might be a lawn once the snow cleared, and at one end a large conservatory. There were outbuildings too, and a brick wall, the same faded colour as the house, running away into the distance. The fields around were hardly visible, for the snow was falling steadily and was already deep underfoot. The snowman made to Nel's satisfaction, they went back indoors, through a side entrance, where they took off their outdoor things and were led by a tolerant Tober to the hall. They hurried upstairs, tidied themselves, and went down again. Olivia, for one, not sure where to go.

'In here,' called Mevrouw van der Eisler from a half-open door at the back of the hall. 'Did you have a good game? Come and sit by the fire. This is the small sitting-room—I spend a good deal of my time here and you must use it as much as you like. There is a cupboard over there—Nel knows it, don't you, my dear?—full of games. We'll have coffee and then I must go and talk to Anke. Do make yourself at home, Olivia—go anywhere you wish. Perhaps this afternoon I will show you the rest of the house, if you would like that.'

'I'd love it,' said Olivia. 'You must wish that Mr van der Eisler stays single so that you can live here forever.' She blushed to the roots of her hair. 'I beg your pardon, that was very rude of me.'

'Not a bit of it, my dear. It is to be hoped that his wife won't object to my paying a visit from time to time.' She smiled. 'Besides, he—and his wife—won't live here all the time. It might be too lonely for some-one used to big cities.'

'But you're not lonely—I wouldn't be either…' Olivia went red again. 'Sorry, I just meant that I like the country. Some people do, some don't.'

Mevrouw van der Eisler didn't appear to notice her embarrassment.

'One need never be lonely,' she observed, 'it's a state of mind, isn't it? Now, my dear, when this snow has stopped do you suppose you would both enjoy a trip to Leeuwarden? Tober shall drive us there once the roads are clear. Do you skate, Olivia? No? A pity, but Dirk will be here tomorrow and he'll enjoy teach-ing you. He taught Nel last winter. We could all go…'

So the day passed pleasantly, with the promised tour of the house after lunch, tea round the fire and then card-games with Nel while Mevrouw van der Eisler sat with her embroidery. The leisurely wander round the house had been a delight to Olivia. It might be severely plain from the outside but inside it was a pleasant mixture of dignified high-ceilinged rooms, beautifully furnished with antiques but still having the air of homeliness, and smaller rooms, dark-panelled, reached by narrow passages, steps up or steps down, with small latticed windows, and all of them in use. The kitchen was vast, with a great Aga along one wall, an old-fashioned dresser facing it, laden with plates and dishes, and a long table with wooden chairs round it. Anke was there, and another woman, cutting up vegetables at the sink. They both beamed at Olivia and shook hands before she was swept on to look at pantries, dairy and a larder.

'Of course we don't really need these rooms now that we have a refrigerator,' said Mevrouw van der Eisler, 'but the grandchildren love to play hide-and-seek down here. That door leads to the garden and that staircase in the wall leads to the attics. We don't use those either—only the children love to go there.'

Dirk arrived the next morning, shortly after breakfast. He was very like Haso—just as tall, but not as heavily built, and he laughed a lot more. He shook Olivia's hand, swung Nel in the air and declared that he would stay for several days. 'I've just taken some more exams,' he explained, 'so I'm entitled to a holiday. This snow will stop by tonight so we will get out in the car.' He smiled at Olivia. 'You're not nervous?'

'No, although as I've never been driven by you I can't be quite sure, can I?'

He gave a shout of laughter. 'I say, we're going to get on, you and I—trust old Haso to find someone as pretty as you.'

They were sitting at the table in the small sitting-room, playing Snakes and Ladders with Nel. It seemed to Olivia that they had known each other for years. He was younger than she and she felt like a big sister towards him, and he made her laugh. She threw the dice and they all laughed when she had to take her counter all the way down a snake and start again.

'I like you, Dirk,' said Nel. 'I like Uncle Haso best, of course, but you're very nice.'

He gave a mock-sigh. 'It's always the same. I wear

myself out being charming and amusing, and Haso doesn't do anything at all and everyone falls about trying to catch his attention. What did you do to catch his critical eye, Olivia?'

He had asked jokingly but when he glanced up and saw her face he said quickly, 'But of course you are so beautiful that you do not need to catch anyone's attention, is that not so, Nel?' He made a great show of throwing the dice. 'I expect Olivia has some glamorous job waiting for her—we shall see her on the front page of the ladies' magazines, all gloss and pearls.'

They all laughed and the awkward little moment was over, but much later that day, when Dirk and his mother were sitting together having a talk before going to their beds, he said, 'Mama, does Haso like Olivia?'

'Why, yes, dear.' She looked at him without surprise at his question.

'Well, I said something today—oh, teasing—and it seemed to me that Olivia...'

'Yes, dear, she is, I feel sure, and she would be so right for Haso, but he has never allowed his feelings to show, has he? And now we have this upset with Nel and Rita. To an outsider the solution is so plain— let him marry Rita, who I suspect would like that very much, and make Nel a happy child again. You see, he and Rob were such friends; Haso may feel that he should do this—that it is his duty.'

Dirk got up and prowled around the room. 'They were friends, so would Rob have wanted Haso to be unhappy for the rest of his life? He could manage Rita because he loved her, but I doubt if Haso loves her.'

He kicked a footstool out of his way. 'Olivia doesn't say much about her life. Is it a happy one?'

'From what Haso has told me, and he knows very little, I believe, she lives with her mother and a rather terrible grandmother, who gave them a home when her father died and never ceases to remind them of the fact. He told me that he had been to her home once or twice and it was obvious that her grandmother dislikes Olivia. Her mother is a small, dainty woman, very gentle and quiet, and Olivia hasn't taken after her. That has annoyed the old lady. And of course Olivia has had no training for a career of any sort.'

'I'm surprised that she isn't married.'

'She was engaged, I believe, although Haso told me nothing more than that.'

'How long is Nel to stay here?'

'Until Haso and Rita have solved the problem. Nel is quite happy to go back to school and stay with her grandmother in England, she's devoted to her, but each time she comes here to stay with her mother she becomes most unhappy. It is not my place to criticise Rita but it is a pity that she has to leave the child with someone whom Nel doesn't like. It was quick thinking on Haso's part to persuade Olivia to come here to look after Nel.'

'Is she being paid?'

His mother looked surprised. 'I have no idea. Why do you ask?'

'Her clothes are hardly this year's fashion, are they? Good, but well-worn.'

'You're right, of course. I noticed that her things were useful rather than fashionable; I thought she had brought suitable clothes for the job and the time of year.'

'I'm surprised Haso hasn't noticed…'

Haso had noticed. Indeed, he was so conscious of every aspect of Olivia that he knew to the last button what she was wearing and that it was well cared-for, out of date and had been chosen with an eye to hard-wearing qualities rather than fashion. Beyond a wish to see her dressed in the kind of clothes her beauty merited, he would have found her just as enchanting in a potato sack. He thought about her a great deal while he saw his patients, operated and did his ward-rounds, and he thought about her when he was at Rita's flat, doing his best to persuade her to give up her job and make a home for Nel.

'But the child's quite happy at that school, and what would I do while she's away?'

'Find somewhere to live in England. You don't need the money, Rita.'

'I would be bored to death—of course, if I lived in a town and had a social life…' She paused and smiled at him, and met a blank mask which told her nothing. 'Well, I have no intention of giving up my job,' she said pettishly. 'It's fun, I meet lots of interesting people and I go out a lot—I must have some fun, Haso, I'm young still and I've been told I'm pretty. You can't expect me to spend the rest of my life being a housewife, just with Nel for company.'

'You will remarry, Rita.'

She said at once, 'If that's a proposal, Haso, I will accept at once.'

He remained unperturbed. 'It wasn't. I shall be going to Tierjum this weekend. Would you like to come with me? You could spend some time with Nel.'

'Darling Haso, I'm flying to Paris to spend the weekend with friends. I can't possibly put it off at such short notice. Give Nel my love, won't you, and tell her I'll come and see her soon. Shouldn't she go back to school?'

'When you decide what is to be done, yes. Have you dismissed that woman with the wart?'

'Juffrouw Schalk? Of course not. She's a splendid housekeeper and I'd be lost without her. Nel must learn to like her. The child's spoilt.'

'Would you object if Nel were to live permanently with her grandmother in England? You could, of course, visit whenever you wished?'

'It might be a good idea. I'll think about it. Now, can we stop this disagreeable talk and go somewhere and have a drink? It's barely nine o'clock...'

'I have to go back to hospital. I'm operating tomorrow, going to Rotterdam on the following day and then to Friesland. Let me know if you change your mind, Rita.'

She reached up to kiss his cheek. 'Darling Haso, we would make a lovely pair, you know.' She spoke laughingly, watching him closely. His small, indifferent smile infuriated her.

Mr van der Eisler left directly after breakfast on the Saturday morning and drove himself through the snowy landscape to Tierjum, Achilles sitting beside him. The snow had ceased and the sky for the moment was a cold blue and pale sunlight gave an illusion of warmth. He wondered what Olivia was doing, and then dismissed her from his mind while he reflected on Nel's future. He was no nearer a solution by the time he turned the Bentley into the drive and saw the house ahead of him. He stopped on the sweep and got out, smiling at the sounds of laughter from somewhere behind it. With a warning to Achilles not to bark he walked to the side of the house, making no sound in the thick snow, and went unhurriedly along the shrub-lined path until he reached the vast lawn at the back. Covered now with snow, of course. Nel and Olivia and Dirk were there, building a snowman and making a good deal of noise about it, stopping to throw snow-balls at each other. Mr van der Eisler stood for a moment, watching them, a hand on Achilles' great head, and as he watched Nel flung a snowball at Olivia, who ducked, slipped, and would have fallen if Dirk hadn't put out an arm and caught her. They stood for a moment, his arm around her shoulders, completely at ease with one and other. It wasn't until Nel caught sight of Haso that they turned to see him.

Achilles bounded forward, barking happily, and Nel rushed to hug her uncle. Dirk started forward too, shouting a welcome. Only Olivia hung back. The glorious surprise at seeing him again had left her with a thumping heart and no breath.

Dirk said over one shoulder, 'Look who's here, Olivia—come and say hello.'

She went over to him then, and said, 'Hello, Mr van der Eisler,' but anything else she might have said died on her tongue. His, 'Hello, Olivia,' was pleasant, but he looked at her with eyes like blue ice. What had she done? she wondered in panic, searching his bland face for some sign. But it showed nothing. Only his eyes betrayed the fact that he was angry.

Five minutes later she decided that she had imagined it; he was throwing snowballs like a schoolboy, with Nel capering around him and Achilles barking his head off. It was Dirk who called to her, 'Olivia, be an angel and tell Mama that Haso's here—we'll be in presently for coffee.'

She nodded and sped away, glad to be gone. Was Haso here for the weekend? she wondered. And had anything been decided about Nel?

She found Mevrouw van der Eisler sitting placidly in her sitting-room, writing letters. She got up from her writing-desk, beaming.

'I wasn't expecting him—he usually phones. How delightful. Anke must get the coffee at once. Where is he?'

'In the garden snowballing.'

'Then fetch him in, my dear, if you will, and tell him to see that Achilles' paws are wiped.'

They were still racing around; she went and stood in the middle, ducking the snow. Her face glowed with the exercise, her bright hair almost hidden in the hood of one of Mevrouw van der Eisler's all-enveloping gardening coats. Mr van der Eisler thought that she had never looked so beautiful. It was inevitable that Dirk should fall for her; he was a young man her own age... And she had looked so happy when she had turned round, Dirk's arm around her shoulders.

They all went indoors, and when they had had coffee Olivia took Nel off on the pretext of choosing what frock she should wear that evening, since she was to be allowed to sit up for dinner for a treat.

'Such a tactful girl,' said Mevrouw van der Eisler. 'Nice, quiet manners and so kind and thoughtful. I am so surprised that she is not married.'

Haso stirred his coffee. 'She had a fiancé. He married another girl—we went to his wedding.'

'You did?' Dirk gave a chuckle. 'The pair of you? Not top hat and morning coat?'

'Indeed, yes.' Haso spoke lightly. 'We drove there in the Bentley and Olivia had a charming hat...'

'But why...?' asked his mother.

'Oh, keeping one's end up—showing the flag.' He smiled. 'I enjoyed it.' He put down his cup. 'I've seen Rita several times. She is unwilling to give up her job, in fact she refuses, and she also refuses to get rid of Juffrouw Schalk. If possible I'll bring her up here next weekend, when I think she must decide what she wants.'

'Does she plan to marry again?' asked his mother.

Dirk said quickly, 'Of course she does—she wants to marry you, Haso.'

'Yes.' Mr van der Eisler spoke calmly. 'But I have no intention of marrying her.'

His mother kept an admirable silence and flashed a warning glance at Dirk. 'Well,' she said presently, 'I'm glad to know that, Haso, for Rita is very much a career-woman. Indeed, I have wondered if Rob could have coped with her if he were still alive.'

'She seems very successful,' said Haso, noncommittally, 'It is a question as to whether Nel is more important to her than her career. We shall have to see if she and Nel can compromise.'

Nel came in then with Olivia, and he got up out of his chair. 'I must do some phoning. Let me know if I am upsetting any plans for the afternoon.'

'We haven't made any,' said Dirk when he had gone out of the room. 'But since he's here with that great car of his how about all of us piling in and doing some sightseeing?'

'In this weather?' asked his mother.

'It's just the weather to see Friesland, and Olivia may not get another chance. We could drive to Sneek and see the lakes and then go north up to the Wadden Zee. Would you like that, Nel?'

Of course Nel would like it, and so would Olivia, only she restrained her enthusiasm, merely remarking that it sounded very interesting.

'We'll take Achilles,' said Dirk, 'he can sit between us. Nel and Olivia must sit with Haso so that he can point out all the interesting sights.'

Olivia opened her mouth to protest but he stopped her. 'Haso knows every stick and stone in these parts, and you won't get another chance.'

'Perhaps another time?' suggested Olivia, anxious not to look too eager.

'No hope of that. He's bringing Rita with him next weekend and she hates Friesland—too cold and empty.'

He didn't say any more for Nel, who had gone to the other end of the room to play with Achilles, had joined them again.

Haso came back presently and they sat around, carrying on a desultory conversation over their sherry, and presently they went to lunch.

Over that meal, Dirk broached his plans for the afternoon. 'I'll drive,' he offered, 'if you're tired.'

'On the contrary, driving relaxes me. I think it is a very good idea. When do we go?'

Olivia, nervous at the idea of being with Mr van der Eisler for hours on end and at the same time overjoyed at the prospect, settled beside him in the car with a cautious air which secretly amused him. She need not have worried; the outing was a tremendous success. He took the road to Sneek, going south until they reached the little town, and then driving along narrow country roads, still covered by snow, so that she might see the lakes, frozen now, although not yet safe for skating. He joined a main road presently and, when they were almost back in Leeuwarden, turned north.

'Dokkum, I think,' he observed. 'A nice old town— we might stop there and have coffee and then take a quick look at Lauwers Meer.' He glanced at Olivia. 'You're comfortable?'

'Yes, oh, yes, thank you. It's beautiful, isn't it? So still and everything covered by snow. Is it always like this in the winter?'

'Not always, but usually we have snow during the winter.' He looked over his shoulder at Dirk. 'When did we last go skating for more than a few days?'

'Two years ago—last year the ice didn't hold. We might get a day in before these two go back. Do you skate, Olivia?'

'No—at least, roller-skating, but I don't think that's the same, is it?'

'But you can balance—it should be easy. Here's
Dokkum. We'll have coffee at de Posthoorn.'

Olivia was enchanted by the little town, with its
canal running through its centre and the old houses
leaning against each other on either side of it. The
hotel was very old and shabby, in a nice way, and
when she asked for tea instead of coffee she was
served a glass of hot water and a tea-bag. Nel, drinking
hot chocolate, thought it was very funny, chattering
away happily, the very picture of a contented small
girl.

It was cold outside and there was no one much
about; Nel walked between the two men, skipping and
jumping over the snow, and Mr van der Eisler drew
Olivia close and tucked her hand under his arm.

There wasn't much to see and it was too cold to
stand about so they went briskly back to the car, stopping on the way to buy four pokes of *potat frites* with
generous dollops of pickles on top, which they sat and
ate in the car.

Mr van der Eisler, offering Achilles the last of the
chips, said, 'It must be years since I ate these. I'd
forgotten how delicious they are.'

Olivia poised the last of the pickle on a chip and
took a bite. 'Why don't we do this in England?' she
wanted to know, and glanced at Nel with a warm
smile. The child was so happy—it was a pity she had
to go away from all this kindness and fun. It was a
pity, too, she reflected, that she had to go as well.

She wasn't going to let such thoughts sadden her,
though. Dirk was fun but Haso was a perfect companion; she could have sat for hours on end beside him

while he drove. It was strange, she thought, that she felt so at ease with him when by rights she should have been feeling awkward, spending hours in the company of a man she loved but who treated her with kindly indifference and at the same time, she had to admit, made sure of her comfort. He would do that anyway, she reminded herself, for his manners were impeccable. She had a fleeting uneasy memory of the icy stare he had given her when he had arrived that morning. She had taken care not to meet his eyes since then and she wondered if they were still as cold.

They were still going north, this time to the coast. The villages were few and far between but the road was clear of snow, although the fields on either side were white as far as her eye could see.

'What do people do here?' she asked.

'Shrimp-fishing and a big fish auction at Zoutkamp. We're going round the Wadden Meer—Zoutkamp is on the farther side. Actually we are on the border of Groningen and Friesland, but we turn to the west presently and then we are back in Friesland again. We'll take the road through Engwierum and pick up the E1O at Buitenpost.'

It was almost dark by the time they got back, to be welcomed by Mevrouw van der Eisler with piping-hot coffee in the lovely drawing-room. Nel was tired and a little excited, and wanted to stay up for dinner again, but Haso said no in the nicest possible way, which gave Olivia the chance to suggest that supper in bed might be quite fun.

'If you'll stay with me,' demanded Nel.

'If you promise to eat every scrap and go to sleep afterwards.'

'We are all going to church in the morning,' said Mr van der Eisler cheerfully, 'and after lunch we might take Achilles for a walk. You'd like that?'

The next day's plans having been made, Olivia bore Nel upstairs and, presently bathed, and, by then quite sleepy, the child sat up in her pretty room, her supper on a tray before her. A very tasty supper too—little pastry tarts filled with creamed chicken, a few *potat frites*, the merest suggestion of carrot purée and to follow this a little dish of *poffertjes*—tiny, crisp pancakes, smothered in fine sugar. The glass of warm milk which accompanied these dainties was drunk almost unnoticed and without any persuasion on Olivia's part. It only remained for her to take away the tray and tuck the little girl in, kiss her goodnight and turn on the little nightlight—a small comfort which it seemed Juffrouw Schalk had vetoed.

In her room Olivia showered and got into the one dress she had brought with her. It was a pretty shade of blue, plainly made of good material, and hopelessly out of date. 'Not that it matters,' she muttered, bundling up her hair in a ruthless fashion.

A discreet tap on the door surprised her. It was Tober with the request that she should join the professor in his study at her convenience.

'I'll come now,' said Olivia. Of course he was going to tell her when she was to go back to England with Nel—or without the child? Hadn't he said that Rita was to accompany him when he came the following weekend? So they hadn't decided about Nel yet. She slowed her steps—or they had decided, and Nel was to stay with her mother and he and she were to marry.

Her head full of muddled thoughts, she knocked on the study door.

Mr van der Eisler was sitting behind his desk with the faithful Achilles beside him. He got up as she went in.

'Come and sit here, nearer the fire,' he invited. 'You must find it colder here than in London.'

'Well, yes, but it's a nice cold, isn't it? Dry and bright.'

She sat down, her hands still in her lap, and waited for him to speak. He sat back in his chair, watching her. He thought she looked beautiful in the dull blue dress. 'You're happy here, Olivia?'

'Yes, thank you.'

'So is Nel, but of course matters cannot remain as they are, you realise that?'

'Yes.'

'Do you have any plans as to your future? A job in mind?'

She shook her head. 'No, but of course as soon as I get home I'll find something to do. Miss Cross promised me a good reference—for a similar post, you know.'

'But it is too late for such a job until the summer term, surely?'

She had hoped he wouldn't think of that. 'Well, yes, but it would be nice to be at home with my mother for a little while.'

He smiled. 'My dear girl, do you take me for a fool? I have met your grandmother and am only too aware that living with her is by no means ideal for you or for your mother.'

She said coldly, 'You have no need to bother with my affairs, Mr van der Eisler.' She met his gaze. 'I am quite able to manage my own life.'

His smile widened. 'You wouldn't consider working over here in Holland?'

She was too surprised to speak for a moment. 'Here, in Holland? What as? I haven't any skills.'

'There is plenty of work for someone like yourself.' But she only shook her head, and after a moment he said, 'I shall be bringing Nel's mother here next weekend—her future must be settled before any other matter can be considered. Once that is decided you and I can talk.'

'What about?' asked Olivia.

'Why, you and I, Olivia.' He got up. 'Shall we join the others for a drink before dinner?'

As they walked across the hall he asked idly, 'You get on well with Dirk?'

A straightforward remark she could answer. 'Oh, yes, he's a dear, isn't he? If I'd had a brother I would have liked him to be just like Dirk. He's very young still, isn't he? All those girlfriends.'

'Something all men experience when they are young.'

She stood still for a moment. 'You too?'

'Certainly. It smooths the rough edges, as it were, while waiting for the one woman in the world...'

'She might not come.'

'Oh, but she does. Make no mistake about that.'

He was looking at her very intently and she looked away. He was thinking of Rita, no doubt.

They all went to church in the morning, standing in a row in the family pew, Olivia with one arm round Nel, her other shoulder wedged against Haso's vast person. The hymns were familiar, even though the words meant nothing to her, and the *dominee* thundered his sermon from the pulpit in what she considered a very severe manner, but when she was introduced to him as they left she found him to be a mild man with a splendid knowledge of English and a friendly manner.

They ate their lunch and then got back into their outdoor things and took Nel for a walk, with Achilles racing to and fro. Haso and Dirk talked comfortably of the village and the country round them and never mentioned Rita once.

Mr van der Eisler was to leave after tea. They all went into the hall to see him off but Olivia slipped back into the drawing-room when she thought no one was looking—after all, she wasn't one of the family.

Of course Haso had seen her; he made his good-byes, kissed and hugged Nel, and went back into the drawing-room.

'Are you not going to wish me goodbye?' he wanted to know.

She had retreated to the window overlooking the garden. 'I hope you have a good drive back,' she told him soberly, 'and a successful week.'

'Certainly it will be a busy one.' He crossed the room to stand close by her. 'When I come again ev-

erything should be settled. Until then you do understand, do you not, that there is nothing I can say.'

About working in Holland? she wondered, and
raised a puzzled face to his. He stared down at her for
a long moment.

'And so much for my good resolutions,' said Mr
van der Eisler in a goaded voice, and swept her into
his arms and kissed her soundly.

Even if she had intended to demur she had no
chance. He had gone before she had got her breath
back.

CHAPTER NINE

OLIVIA stood where he had left her, her heart galloping along at a great rate. As well as surprise, happiness was welling up and threatening to choke her. Why had he kissed her, and in such a manner? And what had he meant about good resolutions?

She allowed her thoughts to become daydreams, standing there in the centre of the room until the others, returning, shook them free.

'The house always seems so empty when Haso isn't here,' said Dirk. 'A pity I shan't be here next week to see him—and Rita.'

'You will stay for another day or two?' asked his mother.

'Oh, yes. I need to be back in Leiden on Wednesday—I'm starting that new course then.'

'But you are qualified?' asked Olivia, glad of something to talk about.

'Oh, yes, but by no means finished. I can't hope to be as brilliant as Haso, but I shall do my best to uphold the family name.'

'Surgery or medicine?'

'Oh, surgery, it's in the blood, you know, generations of us.' He saw Nel's downcast face. 'Who's for a game of Ludo?'

Two days later she saw him drive away with real regret. He had been an amusing companion and delightful with Nel, and he had made her laugh, something she rarely did at her grandmother's home. She was honest enough to admit to herself that even if he had done none of these things she would have liked him because he was Haso's brother, and anything or anyone close to Haso was close to her too.

There were several days before Haso would come again and there was Nel to keep happy. Because she thought it would please him, she did her best to persuade Nel to live with her mother during her holidays. She didn't have much success, but she persevered.

The snow had ceased several days ago although it still lay thick on the ground. The sky was a cold blue and the sun shone, albeit just as cold as the sky. They wrapped themselves up and went walking, and one day Mevrouw van der Eisler took them to Leeuwarden, with Tober driving.

They had lunch at a large restaurant—Onder de Luifel—and then they went to the shops and Olivia, with woefully few coins in her purse, bought two small vases in the local pottery, wishing that she had had the money to buy some of the silverware—delicate spoons, small bon-bon dishes and silver wire brooches. Her companion admired the vases and wished that Haso had done something about paying Olivia. After all, the poor girl had been whisked over to Holland at a moment's notice, with no chance to go to a bank. Perhaps, thought Mevrouw van der Eisler, she hadn't got a bank. Haso would be vexed when he knew about it. Having more than enough money himself, he nevertheless was thoughtful of the needs of other people. Too generous, she reflected, remembering the money Rita had borrowed from him from time to time and never repaid. Even with the money Rob had left her, and her well-paid job, she never had enough to pay for all the expensive clothes she loved.

Olivia viewed the approaching weekend with some anxiety; so did his mother. True, Haso had said that he had no intention of marrying Rita, but she was a clever young woman—pretty and amusing, and charming when she wished to be. Olivia longed to see Haso again but she doubted if they would be together at all—and how was she to behave? As though he hadn't kissed her? As though she had found it an amusing episode and dismissed it as such? And would he tell her when she was to return to England? What-ever was decided, surely Nel would have to go back to school as soon as possible? And, worst of all, had Rita coerced him into marrying her?

She lay wakeful, wondering about that. If, she re-flected, I had been someone like Rita, would he have fallen in love with me and married me? She thought that he might. Given the right clothes and background she would have competed with Rita quite happily and probably won. She shook up the big square pillows and closed her eyes. Negative thinking, she told her-self sternly, gets you nowhere, my girl.

She took Nel down to the village to buy sweets on Saturday morning because to wait in the house for Haso and Rita was too nerve-racking. Far better for them to return after they had arrived when any awk-

wardness would be glossed over in the bustle of greetings. Mevrouw van der Eisler, when consulted, had
agreed. 'The child's on edge. I do hope that Rita has
agreed to Haso's proposal and that everything is arranged satisfactorily.'

Proposal, thought Olivia unhappily, but she went off
with Nel and spent a long time in the village shop
buying toffee. When they got back the Bentley was in
front of the house and at the sight of it Nel's small
fingers curled tightly around Olivia's hand.

'We'll go and say hello quickly,' said Olivia, 'and
then go and tidy ourselves. It will soon be time for
lunch.'

'It will be nice to see Uncle Haso again,' said Nel
in a very small voice.

'And Mummy. I'm sure she's excited at seeing you
again.'

Nel gave her an old-fashioned look. 'Don't be silly,'
she said.

They went round the house to one of the side doors
and got out of their wellies and outdoor things. Olivia
was of two minds as to whether to creep up the back
stairs and do something to their ruffled persons before
going to the drawing-room, but Anke had seen them
and swept them along, lecturing them sternly in her
own tongue and flinging the drawing-room door wide.

They stood on the threshold and the persons gathered there turned to look at them.

Mevrouw van der Eisler and her son spoke at the
same time. 'Good, here you are, my dears,' and
'You've been to the village to buy toffee,' said Mr

van der Eisler, and tossed a delighted Nel into the air and gave Olivia the briefest of smiles.

Rita didn't get up from her chair but held out her arms. 'Nel, how very untidy you are. I don't think Olivia can be a very good nanny. Come here and give me a kiss.'

And when the child went reluctantly she put her arms around her. 'Have you missed me?'

'Olivia is a very good nanny,' said Nel in a shaky voice, 'and she's not a nanny, she's a person. Like you or Granny or Mevrouw van der Eisler.'

Her mother said impatiently, 'Yes, yes, of course she is. Now go away and have your hair brushed and your hands washed. Why is there a bulge in your cheek? What are you eating?'

'Toffee. The village shop...'

'Yes, yes, never mind that now. It's almost time for lunch and then Uncle Haso is going to talk to you.'

All this time she had ignored Olivia who, in response to Mevrouw van der Eisler's beckoning finger, had gone to sit by her. Mr van der Eisler, in his chair again with Achilles beside him, took no part in the conversation. What his thoughts were could be anybody's guess.

Well, we will know soon enough, thought Olivia, and I for one can't get back home soon enough. She was aware that this idea had no vestige of truth in it; to go back to England never seeing Haso again wasn't to be borne and, worse, the thought of his marrying Rita made her feel sick.

The woman looked so right against the background of the lovely old house—casual tweeds, costing the earth, boots of leather as supple as silk, a cashmere jumper, hair with not a single strand out of place, perfect make-up...

She and Nel went upstairs and the child dawdled around, reluctant to go downstairs again. Olivia, ruthlessly tugging tangles out of her own hair, knew exactly how she was feeling. Mr van der Eisler's aloof air boded ill for their future.

'Uncle Haso won't make me go back to that horrid lady, will he?' Nel whispered.

Olivia put a comforting arm round her. 'Your Uncle Haso loves you; he won't let you be unhappy. Whatever he decides will be right, my pet.'

'But you'll go away...'

'Yes, and you'll go back to school, and I'll come and see you, I promise.'

'Are you sad?'

The question was unexpected. 'Sad? Me? No, dear, why should I be sad?'

'Your face looks sad.'

'I dare say that's because I'm hungry.' She would have to remember to look cheerful... 'Let's go down.'

Lunch was eaten without haste and the conversation was of the general kind so that everyone took part in it. Olivia, aware of Mr van der Eisler's sharp gaze, smiled when she wasn't actually eating. It must have looked pretty foolish but at least she didn't look sad. She replied politely when Rita spoke to her, agreed with her host that the weather had been quite pleasant during the week and tried to ignore Rita's snappy asides to Nel, whose table manners weren't quite perfect—hardly to be expected at her age.

Rita wasn't snappy with Haso. On the contrary, she was amusing and attentive to his every word, looking at him with a sweet smile which Olivia longed to wipe off her face. A man—any man—would be flattered by her obvious interest in him and the inviting looks she gave him.

Mr van der Eisler, of course, wasn't any man. He was the perfect host—attentive, carrying the talk effortlessly from one topic to another—and all the time he was aware of Olivia, sitting there saying little, avoiding his eyes, outwardly serene, inwardly, he had no doubt, seething.

'Shall we have coffee in the drawing-room? Perhaps Nel would like to go and see what Anke is doing in the kitchen? Cakes for tea, no doubt...'

Nel escaped willingly enough but when Olivia started to go with her she was asked if she would be good enough to go to the drawing-room too.

'For this concerns you, Olivia,' he told her.

Mevrouw van der Eisler was pouring the coffee when the phone on the table by his chair rang. He listened without speaking and even when he did, at some length, Olivia was none the wiser, for he spoke in Dutch, but she could see by the concern on his mother's face that it wasn't good news.

He put the phone down presently. 'This is most unfortunate; I have to return to Amsterdam at once. Even if I should operate this afternoon I shan't be able to leave my patient until tomorrow morning at the earliest. We must delay our talk until then.'

Rita pouted, but his mother said placidly, 'We quite understand, dear. I hope you will be in time.'

He was already on his feet. 'They'll keep me informed—the phone's in the car. I'll let you know how things are as soon as possible.'

He kissed his mother, said briefly, 'You'll stay, Rita?' And to Olivia, 'Don't worry, leave everything to me. Kiss Nel for me.'

'What a lot can happen in five minutes,' said Olivia.

Mevrouw van der Eisler smiled at her. 'Yes, my dear. Being married to someone in the medical profession isn't easy but you get used to it.'

'There's no need for it,' said Rita. 'If Haso *will* work for all these hospitals instead of just keeping his private patients—heaven knows, he's famous enough to do what he likes.'

'I don't think it has anything to do with fame,' said Olivia, forgetting to whom she was talking. 'It's something he does because he wants to do it. I don't suppose he notices if it's a VIP or someone without a farthing to their name; they're patients and he knows how to help them...'

'What sentimental nonsense,' said Rita. 'Though if I heard aright this patient is a VIP.'

'Yes,' agreed Mevrouw van der Eisler, 'but if it had been a beggar off the street Haso would have gone just the same.'

'Oh, I'm sorry,' cried Rita. 'You must think me a heartless creature. I know how good Haso is—better than most people, I believe, for he has taken such care of me.' She smiled sweetly, 'And now we cannot tell you our plans until he returns.'

She became all at once a changed person, listening with interest to what her hostess had to say, talking about Nel's school, asking Olivia if she had enjoyed working there. Olivia didn't trust her an inch.

Nel came in presently. 'Tober says that you are going to the church to do the flowers, Mevrouw. May I go with you? Please? I'll be very good, and Tober said perhaps you'll let me sit in front with him.'

'The flowers—I had quite forgotten.' Mevrouw van der Eisler looked at Rita. 'Perhaps you would like to come with us? It will pass the time.'

'If I may,' gushed Rita, 'I'll stay here. If I might use your desk? I have so many letters to write; this is a chance to do them in peace.'

'And you, Olivia?'

'I shall need to sort out Nel's clothes before we go back—I'd be glad of an hour or two to do that.'

'Run along, then, darling.' Rita was the loving mother. 'I'm sure Olivia will help you with your things…'

'Why not, since we are both going upstairs,' observed Olivia airily.

She sent Nel downstairs again presently, suitably dressed, and followed after a minute or two to stand at the door and wave goodbye as Tober drove away with Nel, as pleased as Punch, sitting beside him.

She went back to Nel's room, for there was little point in joining Rita, who wouldn't expect it anyway. She had just finished making neat little piles of clothes and putting them on the bed ready to pack when she looked up to see Rita at the door.

'Olivia, I must talk to you.' She came into the room and sat down on the chair by the bed.

She looked serious, even worried, and Olivia asked, 'Is something the matter? Don't you feel well?'

Rita had her hands clenched in her lap. 'I know you don't like me.' She gave a rueful smile. 'Well, I suppose I don't like you, but all the same I can't see you humiliated…'

Olivia folded a small nightgown. 'Why should I feel humiliated?' she wanted to know. 'If it's something to do with going back to England, I knew I'd be going as soon as everything was settled between you and Mr van der Eisler.'

Rita said slowly, 'We are to be married—quite soon—before Nel has her Easter holidays. But you must have guessed that. It's something…I'm not sure how to tell you, and probably you won't believe me, but I beg you to take my word.'

Olivia sat down on the bed. 'I'm quite in the dark. Could you explain?' She was pleased to hear how steady her voice was, and although her insides were turning somersaults she looked, she hoped, normal.

'You're in love with Haso, aren't you?' Rita spoke quietly. 'He didn't realise that at first. He thinks you are a very nice young woman and so reliable, and you have been such a help to him—to both of us. Now he is anxious to spare your feelings, he intended to say goodbye to you and give you your tickets so that you could leave as soon as you wished.' She paused. 'I don't expect you believe me, but I should like to help.'

'Why?'

'Because I am happy and you are not, and to meet Haso again, knowing that he pities you… He would never throw your love back in your face, he is too kind, but you will see the pity…'

Olivia studied Rita's face and had to admit that she looked and sounded sincere. 'And how would you help me?'

'Haso won't be here until tomorrow morning at the earliest—he is always near his patient after that special operation he does, until he feels that he can leave him or her to his registrar. Would you like to go back to-day? He has your ticket, unfortunately, but I have money with me. You could get the boat train to the Hoek and get the night ferry.' She paused. 'No, perhaps you would rather stay and see him before you go; you will want to say goodbye.'

Olivia didn't see the sly look. And look up into that loved face and see the pity and concern there? Olivia shuddered at the thought. 'I'd like to go today. I can pack in a few minutes and if you will lend me the money I'll go home. What am I to say to Mevrouw van der Eisler?'

Rita frowned in thought. 'You could say that you weren't well—no, that would sound very silly.' She sat up in her chair. 'Of course—could you not say that you have had a phone call from home? That you are needed there? Someone is ill, perhaps?' She frowned. 'And Nel—she will be unhappy, but of course if she thought you were going home to look after some-one…'

Olivia was suddenly weary of the whole thing. 'Yes, all right. How am I to get to the train?'

'Mevrouw van der Eisler will send you to Leeuwarden in the car and, when Haso does come, she will explain. If you would like it, I will ask him to write to you.'

'No, no, thank you.' Olivia got up. 'I'll just finish seeing to Nel's things—is she to go back to school?'

'We shall take her in a few days and go to see Lady Brennon.'

Olivia nodded. 'I'll pack my things,' she said, and Rita got up and went to the door.

'I'll get the money,' she said, and added soberly, 'I am so sorry, Olivia.'

When she had gone Olivia sat down on the bed again. After all it was only what she had expected. Well, not quite, she thought. She hadn't expected Haso to discuss her with Rita, although that would be natural enough since they were to marry. At least Nel would have a loving stepfather and perhaps Rita would turn into a loving mother. Perhaps she had misjudged her. She swallowed the threatening tears and began to pack Nel's clothes and, that done, she packed her own. When Rita came back presently she took the money she was offered, thanked her politely, and asked her where she should send it once she was in England.

'Well, Haso had your ticket, and money for expenses, so you don't owe anyone anything. Does he owe you any wages?'

'They haven't been mentioned. So, no, he doesn't.'

'You have been here for several weeks. You can't work for nothing. Poor dear, he has so much on his mind—I'll remind him. I'm sure he'll send you whatever is owing.'

'No,' said Olivia, 'I don't want any money. I would

prefer not to…' She smiled. 'A clean break is the expression.'

When Mevrouw van der Eisler came home she had her story ready and, looking at her stony face, that lady believed her, and so did Nel, although she was tearful at the idea of Olivia going away so suddenly.

After that it was easy—Tober was warned to have the car ready, there was tea to be drunk, farewells to be said to the staff, and finally all the right things to be said to her hostess. 'I've written to Mr van der Eisler,' said Olivia, 'and put it in his study.'

She shook hands with Rita, kissed and hugged Nel, and got into the car beside Tober. She didn't look back as he drove out of the grounds and into the narrow road.

'That was very unexpected,' observed Mevrouw van der Eisler. 'I had no idea Olivia's mother was ill. She did have a phone call?'

'Oh, yes. She was here with me, asking me about Nel's clothes, when she took the message. It was a shock for her. I believe she is very fond of her mother.'

'You will, of course, stay here until Haso comes?'

'Oh, yes, of course. Nel must go back to school as soon as possible now that we have everything settled.'

Mevrouw van der Eisler didn't ask what had been settled. She picked up her embroidery and stitched in silence.

Everyone was in bed and the house was quiet when Rita stole downstairs and took Olivia's letter from Haso's desk. Later she would read it. For the moment it was safe enough in her handbag.

*   *   *

Mevrouw van der Eisler was at breakfast when Haso walked in. He was his usual elegant self but his face was grey with fatigue. As he bent to kiss her cheek in reply to her delighted greeting he observed, 'Coffee— good,' and sat down opposite her.

'Where is everyone?' he wanted to know.

'Nel's in the kitchen, helping Anke make vol-au-vents for lunch. Rita is in bed—she prefers her breakfast there.'

'And Olivia?'

His mother buttered a piece of toast. 'At her home in London, dear.'

Mr van der Eisler, about to take a drink of coffee, put the cup down again. His face was as impassive as usual but his eyes were suddenly bright and alert. 'Oh? This is sudden. What has happened?'

'I phoned you at the hospital, Haso, but you were in Theatre and I decided that a message might distract you.'

'As indeed it would have done,' he agreed, although they both knew that nothing distracted him from his work—even the sudden departure of the girl he loved.

'There was a reason?'

'She had a phone call while Nel and I were down at the church. Someone—I don't quite know who— was ill and she was needed at home. When we got home she was already packed, for Rita had advised her that she would be able to get the boat train from Leeuwarden and cross over with the night ferry from the Hoek. I suggested that she phone home again to find out just what was wrong and then tell you, for you could have arranged everything for her, but she had made up her mind.'

'Was she upset?' He spoke very quietly.

'Not crying, just stony-faced and very anxious to be gone.' She poured more coffee. 'She told me that she had left a letter for you in your study.'

'Ah...' He went off at once to fetch it, and came back empty-handed.

'You're sure of that, my dear?'

'Positive. Rita was there, she must have heard her telling me.'

Mr van der Eisler buttered a roll and took a bite. He was no longer hungry, but performing small, everyday acts would help damp down his rising rage.

He glanced at his watch. 'She won't be home for another two hours at least. I believe that Rita and I must have a talk.'

His mother said regretfully, 'I'm sorry I couldn't stop her, Haso.'

His smile was kind. 'Dearest Mama, I'm sure you did your best. I had already arranged to take Nel back tomorrow and stay in England for a couple of days...'

'With Rita?'

He smiled slowly. 'With Olivia,' he corrected her. He might have said more but Rita came into the room, showing all the signs of having dressed hurriedly. She tripped across the room, wreathed in smiles.

'Haso, what a lovely surprise—we didn't expect you so soon. I got up and dressed the moment I heard you were here.'

He had got to his feet, and something in his face stopped her halfway across the room. She said quickly,

'Isn't it a shame that Olivia had to go home so suddenly? I did all I could to help her…'

'Perhaps you will tell me exactly what happened,' suggested Haso softly.

His mother, taking a look at his face and seeing the bottled-up rage behind its blandness, said quickly, 'I'd better go and see Anke about lunch,' and went quickly from the room. She had no doubt that Rita had been at the bottom of Olivia's departure and her vague dislike of her became something stronger. All the same, she had it in her heart to be sorry for Rita—Haso in a cold fury was hard to face.

Rita sat down. She said chattily, 'So fortunate that I was here—Olivia had no money, you know. I gave her enough to get home.'

He ignored this. 'You were here when she had the message?'

She opened her eyes wide. 'Yes, she was so shocked. She had no idea how to get herself back to England—so lucky that I was here to advise her. By the time your mother was back everything was seen to.'

Mr van der Eisler, impassive in his chair, spoke pleasantly. 'You have a letter of Olivia's, addressed to me, have you not? Give it to me, please.'

Rita went red and then white. 'A letter? I don't know what you're talking about—and why should I take it? I haven't got it.'

He got up and went to the table by her chair, where she had put her handbag. He picked it up, opened it, and turned it upside-down so that its contents rolled from the table to the floor. The letter he took, and walked over to the window to read it, taking no notice of her indignant cries. 'My lipsticks, my powder compact—it's smashed—and my money's spilled over the floor.'

He gave her a look of utter contempt and opened the envelope.

Olivia hadn't written much and her usually neat handwriting showed signs of the writer's strong feelings. He read it quickly and then a second time, before folding it and putting it in a pocket.

He sat down again and Achilles settled beside him. 'And now, if you please, you will tell me exactly what you have said to Olivia. There was no phone message. That was a tale to tell my mother, presumably.'

Rita said sulkily, 'What are you going to do?' She squeezed out a tear.

'Drive you back to Amsterdam as soon as you have packed. You have decided to let Nel stay at school in England and spend her holidays with her grandmother so that you may lead your own life. That decision rests. Why did you do this, Rita?' He sighed. 'And let us have the truth this time.'

'That great girl,' said Rita nastily, 'and such a fool too. I only had to tell her that you found it tiresome that she was in love with you for her to agree to leave at once. Didn't want to spoil your happiness.' She laughed. 'It was such a chance to get rid of her. Such a pity you had to find out. I'd rather set my heart on marrying you, Haso.'

She shrugged her shoulders. 'Well, there are plenty of fish in the sea—you see, what I want is a rich husband, you understand, who won't interfere with my career.'

'What did you tell Olivia?'

'Why, that we were going to be married, of course, that you loved me and found her an embarrassment.' She glanced at him. 'Don't look at me like that, Haso. You can't blame me for trying.'

He said very evenly, 'Go and pack your things, Rita, we will leave in half an hour.'

When she had gone he took Olivia's letter from his pocket and read it again, and this time he was smiling.

The following day, with Nel beside him, he drove over to England.

Sylvester Crescent looked unwelcoming. It was drizzling with rain, the ferry had got in late, and so of course the boat train up to London was late too. Olivia was tired and hungry and unhappy, and the sight of the prim, net-curtained houses depressed her still further. She got off the bus at the corner, carried her case to her grandmother's flat and knocked on its door.

Her mother opened it. 'Darling, what a lovely surprise. And how sudden.' She looked at Olivia's tired face. 'Come on in. We'll have a cup of tea and then you shall go and have a nap. You can tell me all about it later.'

'Granny?'

'She has gone to that old Mrs Field for lunch. We'll have something in the kitchen. Sit down while I make the tea, then you can have a hot bath while I get something to eat.'

The best part of an hour later, sitting at the kitchen

table with her mother, supping soup, and warm from her bath, Olivia felt decidedly better. It wasn't the end of the world. She would find another job and start again. Forgetting Haso wasn't going to be easy, but nothing had been easy for the last year or two.

Her mother hadn't asked any questions while they ate, but over another pot of tea Olivia told her what had happened. She told it without trimmings and in a steady voice, and when she had finished her mother said, 'I'm sorry, my dear. But you have nothing to reproach yourself with. You've done the right thing, although I think that Rita should have left it for Mr van der Eisler to say goodbye to you. I said before that he was a good, kind man, and I still think that. He wouldn't knowingly hurt you or anyone else.'

'It's better this way, Mother. I feel such a fool— Rita made me feel like a silly, lovesick teenager. I'm sure she didn't mean it like that, but that's how it sounded to me.'

Mrs Harding kept her thoughts to herself. 'Well, love, you're home now. Go to bed for an hour or two and I'll break the news to Granny when she gets back.'

'Poor Granny—lumbered with me again. But I'll get a job just as soon as I can.'

Sooner than she expected! Going to Mr Patel's shop for extra groceries, which her grandmother had proclaimed would be necessary now that there was another mouth to feed, her ears still ringing with the old lady's pithy comments about great healthy girls idling their time away at home, she found Mr Patel darting around his shop in an agitated manner, muttering to himself and wringing his hands.

'What's the trouble?' she asked sympathetically.

'Miss, my wife is ill in bed and my daughter is by the side of her husband, whose mother is being buried today. I have no help—I am in a state…'

'Will I do?' asked Olivia. 'I don't suppose I can serve, but I can fetch and carry and arrange things on the shelves.'

His gentle brown eyes widened. 'You would do that, miss? Help me in the shop? It will be only for a day or two—perhaps for one day only. I shall pay you.'

'Just let me take this stuff to my grandmother's and I'll be back.'

He lent her an apron, showed her how the till worked, and handed her a broom. 'I have no time,' he said apologetically, 'and I cannot keep the customers waiting.'

She swept the floor round the feet of the customers, smiling at the astonished faces of the ladies who lived near enough to her grandmother's to know her by sight. That done, she stacked tins of food, pots of jam, packets of biscuits and then, since there were any number of customers now, went behind the counter and did her best. She was quite worn out by the end of the day and thankfully too tired to think. She sat at supper with her mother and grandmother, listening to the latter lady's comments on suitable work for young ladies and not hearing a word of it. After supper she went back again to the shop, to help Mr Patel arrange his stock for the morning. By the time she got into bed nothing was important any more, only going to sleep as quickly as possible. Which she did.

Mr Patel opened his shop at eight o'clock. It was a chilly, dark morning and spitting with rain, but he was his cheerful self again. His daughter had phoned—she would be back in the evening—his wife was feeling better and he had willing help. Together they handed over bottles of milk, bags of crisps and Mars bars to the steady flow of customers on their way to work. There was just time for a cup of coffee before the housewives came and the day's work really got going.

There was no closing for lunch at Mr Patel's; they took it in turns to eat a sandwich and drink more coffee in the little cubbyhole at the back of the shop before facing more housewives and presently the children, coming home from school wanting their tins of Coke and crisps.

Olivia, pausing for a cup of tea, reflected that Mr Patel would be a millionaire before he was fifty, if he didn't die of exhaustion first. There was a lull from the shoppers; she went outside and began to pile oranges from a crate on to the bench where the fruit and vegetables were displayed. Since it was the end of the day she hardly looked her best—her bright hair coming loose from its pins, an elderly cardigan over the outsize pinny Mr Patel had been kind enough to lend her.

Mr van der Eisler, driving fast round the corner in the Bentley, let out a great sigh when he saw her, swept the car across the road and stopped in the shop's small forecourt.

The passing traffic had masked any sound he might have made; he was inches from her when he spoke.

At the sound of her name Olivia shot round, dropping oranges in all directions. She said, 'Oh, it's you,' in a hollow voice and backed away. Not far, though, for he put out an arm and drew her gently towards him.

'My darling love…'

'No, I'm not,' said Olivia, and blinked back her tears.

'None of it was true,' he told her gently. 'Not a single word. When we came on Sunday, Rita and I, it was to tell you that she had decided to go on with her career, that Nel was to go back to school and stay with Lady Brennon and that I would drive you and Nel back here. I was going to ask you to marry me too…'

'Then why didn't you?' snapped Olivia crossly. 'You never said a word…'

'My darling, I was afraid that you would turn me down…'

'Turn you down? But I love you….'

He smiled. 'Yes, I know that now.' He put his other arm around her. 'Tell me, why are you here, tossing oranges about?'

'I'm helping Mr Patel until this evening—his wife's ill and his daughter is away for the day.' She gave a wriggle without much success. 'You can't park the car here…'

She felt his great chest shake with laughter. 'Dear heart, stop being cross and keep quiet while I propose to you. This is hardly the place I should have chosen for such a romantic occasion, but it is a matter which needs to be dealt with at once. Will you marry me, Olivia? I find that my life has no meaning without you.

I suppose that I have been in love with you since we first met and now I cannot endure being without you.'

'Oh, yes, I will,' said Olivia, 'but I must know about Rita and Nel, and what—'

'Time enough for that,' said Mr van der Eisler, and bent his head to kiss her, an unhurried exercise which held Mr Patel's admiration from where he stood in the shop doorway watching them. It was a good thing that there were no customers, for Mr van der Eisler was obviously intent on making the most of the opportunity. Mr Patel, a sentimental man, watched with ready tears in his eyes as Mr van der Eisler reached up and took the pins from Olivia's hair and it tumbled down in a tawny cloud.

'Love,' said Mr Patel, and started to pick up the oranges.